SLEEP IN
HEAVENLY PIZZA

SLEEP IN
HEAVENLY PIZZA

MINDY QUIGLEY

St. Martin's Paperbacks

This is a work of fiction. All of the characters, organizations, and events portrayed in this novel are either products of the author's imagination or are used fictitiously.

First published in the United States by St. Martin's Paperbacks, an imprint of St. Martin's Publishing Group.

SLEEP IN HEAVENLY PIZZA

Copyright © 2024 by Mindy Quigley.

All rights reserved.

For information, address St. Martin's Publishing Group, 120 Broadway, New York, NY 10271.

www.stmartins.com

ISBN: 978-1-250-32628-7

Our books may be purchased in bulk for promotional, educational, or business use. Please contact your local bookseller or the Macmillan Corporate and Premium Sales Department at 1-800-221-7945, ext. 5442, or by email at MacmillanSpecialMarkets@macmillan.com.

Printed in the United States of America

St. Martin's Paperbacks edition / November 2024

10 9 8 7 6 5 4 3 2 1

ACKNOWLEDGMENTS

Rabbi Ilene Schneider did me a mitzvah by serving as a sensitivity reader and adviser on Judaism and Hanukkah celebrations. Plus, she shared her latke recipe! If you're in the mood for another Hannukah mystery, check out hers—*Chanukah Guilt*. Danna Agmon, bestie and beta reader royale, once again came in clutch with essential insights on Judaism, romance, and hot beverage preparation.

I owe thanks to Kelly Kennington for suggesting a great character name (Hadley Hoffman) and to Cassie Wagner for coming up with a "killer" tagline. I didn't get to use it this time, but "O Come, All Ye Slayful" will be in my back pocket for the next holiday murder mystery. Thanks also to *USA Today* bestselling writer Nancy Naigle, who told the incredible true story of the mystery-meat mobile at the Suffolk Authors' Festival a few years ago. Sending gratitude to Neyda Yejo, who shared her warm childhood memories of celebrating *parrandas* in Puerto Rico.

Deepest gratitude to the members of the New River Writers Group, especially H. Scott Butler, Elisabeth Chavez, Tracee De Hahn, Tom McGohey, Piper Durrell,

Charlie Katz, and Carolyn Matthews, for sticking with me since pizza cat was a mere pizza kitten.

Thanks to Dr. Kevin Lahmers for imparting his extensive and disturbing knowledge of dead and dying creatures. I'm now convinced that the only people who have weirder interior lives than murder mystery writers are pathologists.

Tanya Boughtflower, you are my most treasured beta reader, but there is nothing beta about you. You are my Alpha Reader and my Omega Reader.

Thanks to Anna Zeide and Sonya Steckler for help nailing down which of the many spellings of Hanukkah I should use and for being wonderful friends.

The support of my family and friends has been essential. Writing isn't always easy, but with y'all, even the hard bits are fun. I feel so supported by my extended network of peeps—former high school teachers, old friends and colleagues, fellow writers, cousins, Unitarian Universalists, etc. I hope you know how thankful I am every time you post about my books on social media or recommend them to a friend or review them online or ask your local library to purchase copies.

My editor, Hannah O'Grady, is a paragon of bookish wisdom. You rock! Many thanks to my agent, John Talbot, for your guidance. To the fabulous team at Minotaur Books-St. Martin's Press—thank you with extra cheese on top. Sara LaCotti and Sara Beth Haring have worked tirelessly to help readers discover this series. John Simko and John Rounds do an amazing job keeping the books looking spiffy and error-free. Danielle Christopher and Mary Ann Lasher once again killed the cover design. Maddie Alsup has kept everything humming along smoothly, plus she's good at character names—what a great addition to the team.

The supremely talented audiobook narrator Holly Adams has been with me from the very beginning, and has done an amazing job bringing these characters to life.

To the many readers groups, booksellers, reviewers, influencers, and librarians who have championed this series, I hope you know how much you mean to me. My local bookstore, Blacksburg Books, is the spiritual home of this series and has done so much to support my success. Thank you all. I'm so glad to be on this ride with you.

CHAPTER 1

Melody Schacht bounced into the kitchen, her springy blond curls accentuated by an enormous reindeer antler headband. The perennially cheery hostess at Delilah & Son, my upscale pizzeria, straightened her headgear as she deposited an armload of used plates into a waiting bus tub. "Everybody *loves* the food," she said.

The plates she'd brought in from the main party room were practically licked clean. I was too tense to be pleased, though. "What's with the antlers?" I asked.

"Oh, cripes." Melody's hand flew to the headband and plucked it off. "They have a photo backdrop with props. One of the girls asked me to be in a picture 'cuz they needed another reindeer to even the numbers, and then everybody started talking about how much they loved the food, and then I started clearing up the dishes, and I forgot I was still wearing antlers . . ." She spoke at her usual rapid-fire pace, the blush in her cheeks forming matching circles on her porcelain-doll complexion.

"Keep your eye on the ball, okay? Don't get distracted." I lifted a basket of cheese curds from the vat of the deep fryer, setting the sizzling golden nuggets on a wire grate to drain.

Melody hung her head. "Sorry, chef."

"Lay off her, Dee," Sonya Perlman-Dokter, my best friend and sous chef, said, moving next to me to plate the freshly fried cheese. She added ramekins of cranberry-orange dipping sauce to the platter. "It's a *party*. People are having fun. That's a good thing."

"Delilah and Son isn't some kind of street-corner, dollar-a-slice pie joint," I countered. "Even with off-site catering, we have standards."

Part of me knew that my mini-sermon was unneces-sary. Sonya and Melody had been with the restaurant since the beginning. Sonya, in fact, was the namesake "Son" of Delilah & Son, and Melody had been the one to come up with the restaurant's name in the first place. But I couldn't keep my edginess from bubbling over.

We'd been hired to furnish the nosh at a glitzy late-December Chrismukkah house party, providing a menu that would cater both to guests who were here celebrat-ing the first night of Hanukkah and those who'd be gathering around their Christmas trees the following week. The buffet menu was an eclectic mash-up of the traditional offerings of Hanukkah and standard Christmassy fare, jazzed up with my usual emphasis on high-quality, locally sourced ingredients. In addition to unctuous cheese curds with citrusy-sharp cranberry ketchup, the spread included smoked salmon dip with homemade bagel chips, a tear-and-share Christmas tree–shaped pizza bread, and jelly-filled Hanukkah do-nuts, called sufganiyot. And, of course, my restaurant's signature menu item: deep-dish pizza.

I'd sworn to steer clear of off-site catering gigs after our previous foray ended with me and my entire crew trapped in a mansion with a murderer. But when I got an email telling me I could practically name my price, my misgivings evaporated. With the winter dead season coming, I had no qualms about cashing a check so fat I could practically fry donuts in it.

"I don't want anything to go wrong," I said.

"Nothing's going to go wrong," Melody replied, balancing platters of food on her arms to carry out to the waiting party guests. "I'm telling you, chef, this party is a hundred percent perfect."

Sonya winced and simulated spitting three times over her shoulder—a superstition for warding off evil. "Don't say stuff like that. After what happened the last time we catered a fancy party, are you trying to jinx us? We've still got almost an hour to go."

"That was nuts for sure, but it's not going to happen again," Melody said.

I hoped she was right. "Have the hosts said anything about the food?"

"Um, which ones are the hosts?" Melody asked.

"Daffi and Adrian Hoffman. Tall, well-groomed, expensive clothes . . ." I began.

Sonya turned to me with a wry arch in her perfectly shaped eyebrow. "We're catering a holiday party at the most expensive property at the most luxurious resort in Geneva Bay. They're *all* tall and well-groomed and well-dressed."

She had a point. Geneva Bay, Wisconsin, was a posh vacation destination with no shortage of good-looking bigwigs. The glamour was further concentrated at tonight's party location—the Grand Bay Resort. The huge property boasted two golf courses, a man-made ski slope, and a massive Frank Lloyd Wright–inspired lodge. Communities of owner-occupied villas and townhouses dotted the resort's grounds, and the four-thousand-square-foot home whose kitchen we were working out of tonight was among the largest and best-located of the resort's private residences.

Melody reached across the counter and picked up a stray cheese curd. She dipped it in the cranberry ketchup and popped it into her mouth. "*Mmm*. I wish Lutherans had a holiday that revolved around fried food. Hanukkah is awesome."

"We live in Wisconsin. There's not exactly a shortage of opportunities to eat fried cheese," Sonya pointed out.

"Yeah, but it's not, like, a religious obligation," Melody said.

"Cheesiness is next to godliness." Sonya picked up a curd of her own and bit into it. "I'm pretty sure that's written somewhere in the Books of the Maccabees, and if it's not, it should be."

I waved them away, rearranged the ramekins of sauce, and garnished the plate with parsley sprigs. "Stay focused, ladies."

As Melody opened the kitchen door to leave, Robert "Rabbit" Blakemore, our dishwasher, back-waiter, and all-around kitchen minion, hurried in carrying an empty buffet pan.

"Everything okay out there?" I asked.

Usually, Rabbit and Melody were a yin-yang dynamic duo, with Melody working the front of house and Rabbit in the back. Rabbit, recently paroled after spending the better part of the previous decade in prison, wasn't much of a people person, while farm-girl Melody could carry on a two-way conversation with a Pet Rock. Although their personalities and life experiences were in many ways opposite, they both had internal remote controls that were stuck on fast-forward. Tonight, Rabbit was taking that to the extreme, exhibiting a quick-twitch jumpiness that would make an actual rabbit look sluggish.

"Yeah, good. You sure you don't need me in here, though, chef?" His eyes darted toward the door he'd just come through as he shifted his weight from one foot to the other.

The first strains of "Winter Wonderland" emanated from the sound system, along with the noise of happily chattering guests and clinking dishware. I didn't want to jinx it, but it really did sound like a perfect holiday party.

For home-based catering gigs, we typically packed out everything we brought, dirty dishes and all, leaving the host with little-to-no clean-up, and Rabbit with little to do on-site. "It's a well-oiled machine back here," I said.

Sonya raised a freshly fried latke, a look of delight on her face. "Well-*oiled*! Get it?"

Rabbit, typically one of the few living beings who appreciated Sonya's dad jokes, couldn't muster even the slightest hint of a smile.

I shook my head and groaned. Turning back to Rabbit, I said, "What I meant is we're going to do one more round of the fried stuff so it stays fresh, but we're starting to wind down. Why don't you take some gear out to the van?" I suggested. "The snow's coming down pretty heavy, and it'll be harder to load if it gets much worse." Rabbit hopped to, seeming grateful for the chance to escape.

Once he was out of earshot, I turned to Sonya.

"Something's off with him. Do you think he's upset that I put him out front? I know he doesn't like being in crowds."

"I'm not sure it's that," Sonya said. "He doesn't love being front-of-house, but he's never seemed so on edge about it before. Maybe the holidays are upsetting for him. It's a hard time of year for a lot of people."

"True," I agreed, readying another batch of mulled-spiced sweet potato latkes for the fryer.

"For my family, Hanukkah is a pretty low-stakes holiday—light some candles, eat some latkes, and boom." Sonya mimed dusting off her hands. "Bob's your uncle. Well, Avi, or Morrie or Lev's *my* uncle, but you get the picture."

"I've resigned myself to crummy Christmases." I sighed.

"I take it your sister declined your invitation again?" she asked.

"Yeah, they're busy. As usual," I said. My only sister, Shea, and her family always seemed to have unbreakable commitments that kept them from traveling for the holidays.

"Do you think it's because Shea's husband is Jewish?" Sonya spooned jelly into a squeeze bottle to pipe into a batch of sufganiyot. "You know me, if it's a party, I'm there. I have a special outfit just for Festivus parties, and Festivus isn't even real. But Christmas and Hanukkah don't have a lot in common, other than the time of year and the lights. Some Jews prefer to steer clear of all the Christmas hoopla."

"I don't think that's it," I said. "Jonathan's not all that observant. They served bacon-wrapped shrimp at their wedding reception. Plus, I've offered to host a

Hanukkah celebration instead, or any combination of Christmas and Hanukkah. Hell, I'd cook a five-course pagan-themed winter solstice banquet and dance naked around a fire circle if it would get them here. Shea just doesn't want to make the effort."

My voice wobbled a little, betraying more emotion than I'd intended. I turned my back to Sonya and pretended to check the oven.

At nearly thirty-six years old, I was staring down the barrel of middle age. I wasn't sure if I'd ever have kids of my own, and I longed for the chance to spend time with my sister's children. Ten years ago, Shea had married Jonathan, taking an active role in the upbringing of Piper, Jonathan's daughter from his previous marriage. Then, three years ago, they'd adopted Caleb, when he was a newborn. They were both great kids. Since my mother died when I was twelve, I'd had more than my share of lousy Christmases, and I wanted so badly to make some better family memories.

"The worst part," I continued, "is that it really hurts Aunt Biz. Besides me, Shea and Shea's kids are her only living family. The one time Shea deigned to let us host them, Biz went all out. She cooked for days and decorated every inch of her house."

"How could I forget?" Sonya asked. "It looked like Liberace was staging *The Nutcracker* in there."

"Exactly. That was five years ago, before Shea's youngest was even born. I'm still finding tinsel under her couch cushions," I said. My octogenarian great-aunt and her tinselly couch had recently moved in with me, as had Melody, who, in addition to being my restaurant's hostess, also served as Biz's live-in helper.

"Biz is a totally different person during the holidays," Sonya observed. "Honestly, knowing her, you'd think she'd be a little Scroogy, but she's freaking Tiny Tim."

It was true—the holidays transformed Biz from her usual cagey, curmudgeonly self into someone effusive, overtly loving, and cheerful. But only if everything went according to plan. She needed everyone around her to play their parts, and it seemed that Shea and her family were refusing to even show up for the performance.

"At least this year it'll be more than just me and Biz," I said. "Daniel's mom is visiting from Puerto Rico, and they're going to come over for Christmas dinner."

Sonya let out a knowing chuckle. "Well, if Daniel's going to be there, there's a decent chance that Melody will show up, too."

"She *did* mention something about sticking around 'in case Biz needed her help,'" I replied, adding air quotes. Melody had been pining after Daniel, Delilah & Son's suave bartender, since the moment she laid eyes on him and rarely missed a chance to bask in his radiance. I had little doubt she'd find her way to the table around dinnertime on Christmas day.

Sonya wiped her hands on her apron and looked around. "Hey, where are Melody and Rabbit? These donuts are ready to go out. Melody said the ones on the buffet are almost gone."

"I'll go outside and find Rabbit," I said. "He should've been back by now."

I loaded my arms with empty Rubbermaid containers and made my way out the side door. As soon as I opened it, I was hit with a shivery blast of air that contrasted sharply with the cozy warmth of the kitchen.

The snow fell around me in large, feathery flakes. I'd lived in the Midwest long enough to know that the slow, zigzagging descent of this kind of snow belied how quickly it could accumulate. It had only kicked off an hour or so earlier, but already our rented catering van was frosted with an inch-thick layer of the stuff.

I slid the containers into the back of the van and then scanned the surroundings. The night had the otherworldly, pinkish brightness of snowy skies. Further illumination came in the form of the elongated, yellow rectangles of the house's windows. Sound spilled out as well. I could just make out the tinkly strains of Mariah Carey's "All I Want for Christmas" over the guests' chatter and laughter. But Rabbit was nowhere to be seen. He was a smoker, and given how on edge he'd been all night, I wondered if he'd ducked into a corner to sooth his nerves with nicotine. But in this weather, in the middle of service, surely he would've raced through his cigarette double-quick and hurried back inside?

I was casting my eye over the house for the likeliest hideaway when something stopped me in my tracks. Namely, *somebody else's* tracks—two sets printed into the snow. One set originated from the kitchen door. The feet had scuffed the snow around the van—clearly made by Rabbit's Crocs. The practical, water-resistant clogs were a favorite of professional dishwashers, and Rabbit was no exception. Not the warmest choice for a snowy December day, but Rabbit was a Wisconsin native, and for him, real winter didn't set in until the lakes were frozen enough for ice fishing.

The other set of footprints, though, had me mystified. These came from around the side of the house and intersected with Rabbit's. Someone had come out, encountered Rabbit, and then the two had headed off together. I looked more closely. A delicately tapering triangular sole, with a little needlepoint of a heel. Who was traipsing through the snow in stilettos, and why would Rabbit go with them?

As I followed the tracks to the back of the large house, away from the noise of the party, the muffled crunch of my own footprints gradually became the only sound. No doubt there was a simple explanation for Rabbit going off with a random high-heeled partygoer. The possibility of a tryst flickered across my mind. I adored Rabbit, but had a hard time imagining which stiletto-wearing millionaire's taste ran to wiry, weathered ex-cons who lived with their mothers and washed dishes for a living. Maybe a drunk guest had wandered out into the snow and Rabbit was guiding her back inside? But then why not go through the front door, which was no more than twenty feet from where the van was parked? Or, if discretion was required for some reason, why not enter via the kitchen door, directly next to the van? If the guest needed help, wouldn't Rabbit have come inside and alerted me and Sonya?

The trail ended at the house's rear door—not the large glass French doors that opened from the patio into the party room, but another, more utilitarian entrance, shielded by a small phalanx of evergreens. An exterior light was on, spotlighting the falling snow. I looked side to side. Even though I had every right to be in the house, as I entered and then closed the door behind me, I felt like a burglar. This part of the house was dim and quiet, the sounds of the party audible only as the subdued thumping of music through the walls. I found myself at the base of a back staircase. Wet footprints marked the way up. I thought briefly of turning back. Rabbit was entitled to his private life. But a person would have to be almost pathologically incurious not to want to find out what was going on. Besides, I told myself, when my employees were on the clock, their business was, quite literally, my business.

I reached the second floor. Ahead of me was a short hallway, where a single door on one side stood ajar. I peeked inside to find a large storage closet stacked with cleaning and household supplies. Straight ahead was another door, this one closed. The footprints had become less obvious, but I could still make out the damp shapes of feet leading that way.

I opened the door cautiously. Another longer and wider hallway opened before me, with two closed doors on each side. Beyond was a walkway, open to the room underneath. From here, the light and sound of the party surrounded me in full effect. As I came into the hallway, I almost ran smack into a young woman who stood next to the nearest door. She faced away, leaning in so that the mass of coppery curls on her head grazed the wooden doorframe. *Eavesdropping?*

Startled by my presence, she spun toward me. She wore a low-cut white dress, only a shade or two lighter than her pale complexion. A mottled blotch of livid pink crept from the top of her cleavage to her neck, melding with her abundant freckles. Her dark eyes, fiery with anger, met mine, and for a brief, strange moment, I thought she was going to punch me. Clutching a plate of half-eaten hors d'oeuvres, she pushed past me, not bothering to cover her anger with pleasantries. Her steps didn't skip a beat as she marched down the hall I'd come from, not even when she threw her plate against the wall and sent the shrapnel of my carefully crafted menu flying in every direction, smashing it all to kingdom come.

CHAPTER 2

I instinctively hurried over to clean up the food and the broken plate. Twenty years in restaurants had ingrained quick reflexes for tidying up messes. Luckily, the storage closet of cleaning supplies stood directly adjacent to the red-haired woman's destroyed plate. As I emerged from the closet holding a dustpan and broom, a striking middle-aged woman met me, having come from the room where the younger woman had been eavesdropping. I looked past her to see if anyone else would emerge, but the door stayed closed.

"What on earth was that racket?" the woman asked, her hand rising to her chest. She had stunning black hair, cut through with an even more striking streak of pure white. I glanced down to see that she wore teetery-tall heels. Even without them, she probably matched my own five-foot-ten height, and between her heels and her voluminous hair, she towered over me. I stole another glance at her feet. *Could this be the woman Rabbit had come up here with? Or had that been the angry, younger woman?* She, too, wore spiky shoes.

"Looks like someone dropped a plate," I said. "I heard a crash."

I left it at that, hoping she wouldn't question how I'd

gotten upstairs so quickly. There was no way to explain my presence that didn't make me seem like I was being a colossal busybody. Mostly because I *was* being a colossal busybody.

The woman recovered quickly from her agitation. "Well, it wouldn't be a party without broken dishes." She patted an out-of-place lock back into her updo. "You must be with the catering staff," she said, gesturing to my uniform. "I'm Natasha La Cotti, a friend of the Hoffmans." She extended her hand in greeting. "Did you happen to see who broke the plate?" Her wide, expressive mouth sunk briefly into a frown as her eyes scanned the empty hall behind me.

"Umm . . ." I was weighing how to dodge the question when an approaching stranger created the distraction I needed to save myself from potential perjury. The middle-aged man lumbered through the same door that Natasha La Cotti had come out of. He was broad-shouldered and stocky, with deep-set eyes and hair the color of peach flesh.

"Did you break that?" he demanded, his voice booming over the volume of the party downstairs.

"No, I was cleaning it up. I'm the chef." I gestured to my white jacket. "Delilah O'Leary, of Delilah and Son. You're Mr. Hoffman, right? I've been dealing with your wife, but I saw you when we arrived."

"Adrian Hoffman," he grunted.

Even as we shook hands, he eyed me with a wariness I couldn't quite understand. Most people expressed at least passing interest when they learned of my line of work. This man, though, looked at me as if I'd introduced myself as a rogue arms dealer with a side hustle clubbing baby seals. And although he appeared to be solidly built, his grip was as spongy as a lump of unrisen pizza dough.

Footsteps sounded on the stairs behind me. Before I could turn around to see who was coming, I recognized a familiar voice. "We have a serious problem with Hadley." The tone expressed irritation and concern in equal measure.

I spun around. "Jonathan?!"

"Delilah?!"

My brother-in-law stood before me, looking like a kid who'd been caught shoplifting. In my shock, I nearly dropped the dustpan and broom I still held. Jonathan Savage had been a professional tennis player before becoming a private coach, and he looked the part. Sun-kissed dark blond hair, taut physique, and mocha-colored eyes. Typically, his conversational style bore the same easy, confident grace he'd displayed on the tennis court. Now, however, he gaped like a freshly caught trout. His eyes ping-ponged from me to Adrian to Natasha.

He and I stood awkwardly mired in place as Natasha walked to his side and strafed his cheek with air kisses. I could see her whisper something, but I couldn't make out the words. His gaze darted to the broken shards of crockery on the floor and his face darkened.

Natasha, by contrast, painted a broad smile on her face as she took the broom and dustpan from me and set them against the wall. "The cleaners can take care of that in the morning," she said lightly. She caught me and Jonathan under the elbows and herded us, plus Adrian, along the hallway away from the mess.

We made our way past the closed doors, presumably bedrooms, and through the indoor balcony area that overlooked the party. On our left, an expanse of glass loomed. It contained large sliding doors that gave way to an outdoor balcony, populated with covered patio furniture. Snow blanketed everything and gave the landscape the look of an old-time, static-filled TV broadcast. Through the white haze, I could make out the lights of the man-made ski slopes and the main resort lodge beyond it.

Inside the house, dozens of guests milled around in the softly lit party room, dolled up in glittering holiday finery. Daniel manned the bar, and Melody zipped past with a tray, gathering empty glasses. But where was Rabbit? In the flurry of surprise encounters, I'd forgotten the footprints that had led me upstairs in the first place. Was he in one of the closed upstairs rooms? And who was his mysterious high-heeled companion? The young, red-headed woman who'd stormed past me? Or the tall, glamorous Natasha La Cotti? I eyed her shoes. Certainly a possibility, but I hadn't observed the prints closely enough. That mystery would have to take a back seat to the conundrum before me—what on God's green earth was my brother-in-law doing here? And why hadn't anyone told me he would be in town?

"You two know each other?" Natasha prompted Jonathan and me as she led us toward the main staircase—a sleek, curved piece of architecture with a glass balustrade.

I was the first to recover my power of speech. "Yes. Jonathan's married to my older sister, Shea." I scanned the crowd of party guests as we descended the stairs. "Is she here?"

"No, she and Caleb stayed in Pasadena," Jonathan answered, referring to their younger child. "Shea had to work."

Shea had been an officer in the U.S. Navy, after which she got a job in the autonomous systems division at the government's Jet Propulsion Lab in California. That's right, my sister was a literal rocket scientist.

I was surprised to find that, rather than feeling disappointment at Shea's absence, I felt relief. I'd been in awe of Shea for as long as I could remember—her beauty, her skill, the ease with which she breezed through school, dominating everything from quadratic equations to dodgeball. When I stood alongside the spotlight dazzle of her, I dimmed. Every time I saw her, I fell into my old pattern of trying to please her, wanting her to turn my way, to shine a little of that bright light on me. No matter how hard I tried, though, I'd find myself shunted back into the role of the perpetual little sister—tongue-tied, awkward, inept. Weird as it was to admit, I was a little afraid. Not of her. Not exactly. I was afraid of the me I became in her presence.

If my sister was an emotional laser maze, Jonathan was a human Easy Button. Friendly, laidback, and eager to be liked. He was a devoted partner to Shea and a great dad to my niece and nephew. As with many grown-up jocks, he'd never quite achieved the greatness his early tennis career had promised, which stained him with an insecurity that his outward confidence couldn't always paint over. Still, I'd gladly take his occasional overcompensating mansplanations and humblebrags over my sister's emotional landmines.

Jonathan winced as his foot landed on the top step.

"You okay?" I asked.

"Trick knee," he said. He flashed a smile that looked like a close cousin of a grimace. "The price of thirty-plus years on the tennis court." He grasped the handrail and continued down, more gingerly this time. "Piper and I flew in for a long weekend. She was invited to go skiing at the resort here with one of her friends from Palisades," he said, referencing the college where my niece was enrolled. "Adrian and Daffi Hoffman's daughter, in fact." Jonathan's eyes shot to the large, pale man who was barreling down the stairs a few paces in front of us. "I had some business in town, and Daffi was kind enough to extend the party invitation to me. We're heading back on Tuesday."

"Piper's here?"

I hadn't spent much time with my niece in years, and I hadn't seen her at all since Shea's family came to town for my father's funeral more than a year prior. It was hard to believe Piper was now a freshman at Palisades, one of the most prestigious colleges on the West Coast—not only because I still thought of her as a kid with a mouth full of braces and a crush on Harry Styles, but also because she'd never seemed particularly focused on her studies.

Ambitiousness was one of my sister's core traits, though, and I imagined her ambitions probably encompassed her stepdaughter's choice of college. For Shea, lack of achievement was a character flaw. Two decades had passed since I told her I was going to enroll in a culinary program instead of college, and I could still feel the sting of her words: "*That's* what you're doing with your life? Chopping onions and stirring pots?" Based on my experience, I had little doubt Shea had pushed Piper to buckle down and aim high.

"Piper's around here somewhere . . ." Jonathan said, waving vaguely into the crowd.

"Why didn't you let me know you were in town?" I tried to keep my voice even to conceal my seesawing emotions. It was bad enough that my sister and her family refused to come to Geneva Bay for the holidays. Now, it turned out that half of them actually *had* come, and hadn't bothered to tell me.

As I alighted the bottom step, a swirl of sand-colored hair in an electric blue minidress appeared and folded me into an embrace. "Oh my god, Aunt Dee!" Only once Piper pulled away did I realize who she was. My niece bore a strong resemblance to her father—the same athletic figure; long, slightly equine face; large teeth; and lively brown eyes. While this mix of features lent a haughty cast to Jonathan's face, Piper's natural expression was more open, as if she was always on the verge of breaking into laughter.

She turned to her father, eyebrows creased. "Wait, did you and Shea fly her here as a Hanukkah present?" My niece's speaking voice also mirrored her father's, with a husky radio DJ quality.

I held up my hands. "Nope, not a present. I'm here working." Piper's look of confusion deepened, so I elaborated. "I'm catering this party."

"Huh?"

"I remember Shea saying you'd moved out of Chicago last spring and were opening a new restaurant," Jonathan said. "I didn't make the connection."

Recognition broke over Piper's face. "Oh, yeah, I think she said something about that to me, too."

The knowledge that my niece and brother-in-law had given barely a second thought to my whereabouts pricked my heart. But what did I expect? I'd sent holiday gifts to the kids and called them on their birthdays, but the gifts often went unacknowledged and the calls usually went to voice mail. My only connection to Jonathan was through Shea. And Piper, especially, had a life of her own. She'd always lived mostly at her mother's, and now she was a young adult, with her own concerns.

"So you're heading back on Tuesday?" I smiled, hoping to mask the sting I felt.

"That's right, day after tomorrow," Jonathan said. "Just a quick trip."

Natasha, who'd dropped out of sight momentarily, reappeared. "Jonathan, there are some people I want you to meet." She hooked her arm through his. Turning to us, she said, "Okay if I steal him for a minute?"

Jonathan was a natural schmoozer—the type of person who had "a guy" for everything: a guy who could find tickets to sold-out concerts, a guy who could get a table for two at an exclusive restaurant—and he networked like a pro. I'd grown up a working-class gal from South Chicago, and that sort of bro-style glad-handing often left me feeling slime-coated. But Jonathan had a certain puppyish exuberance that made him hard not to like.

I watched as Natasha and Jonathan evaporated into the crowd, as had, it seemed, Adrian Hoffman.

"Your dad said you're here skiing?"

"Yeah, my Big invited me," Piper said. "It's not exactly Aspen, but the snow's been awesome today. We were out all morning."

"Your big?" I asked, repeating the unfamiliar term.

She laughed. "Sorority lingo for my big sister at Nu Delta Nu. I'm her Little because she's a year ahead of me; she's my Big." She looked behind me and waved someone over. "Oh, there she is now. Hey, Hadley, come and meet my aunt!"

Hadley sidled over, and we both did a double take, realizing that we'd already met upstairs a few moments before. As she shook my hand, I got a better look at the plate-thrower. She had a curvy figure and rust-colored hair that fell in loose curls around her face. Her apple-round cheeks were spangled with freckles. The furious expression I'd witnessed earlier had been replaced by an unfocused, alcohol-induced detachment.

Hadley flashed a lopsided smile. "Very nice to meet you." She seemed determined to pretend our earlier encounter hadn't happened.

"It's great to meet a friend of Piper's," I replied.

An awkward silence fell.

I decided to address the elephant in the room. "Is everything okay, Hadley? You seemed pretty upset earlier," I said, probing delicately to see if I could uncover the reason for her outburst.

"Yeah, I'm fine." The corners of her mouth curled into a bitter smirk. "There's nothing quite like the holidays with the fam, right? And to think, we still have seven whole nights of candles to light. I'm just so god-damn excited." She burped softly and then shoved past me into the crowd. "I gotta go."

"Sorry," Piper mouthed over her departing friend's shoulder, miming drinking from a bottle.

It seemed like an inadequate explanation to me. I'd seen plenty of drunk people in my years of restaurant work, but alcohol alone didn't usually cause people to start throwing dishes. It also worried me. I trusted that Daniel checked to make sure Hadley was of legal drinking age, but he should know better than to overserve a young person, even at a private party. If Hadley was drunk enough for others to notice, Daniel should've cut her off or watered down her drinks.

I glanced over at him. He chatted with an elderly female partygoer as he mixed her drink. As usual, he

had his sleeves rolled up, the better to show off the
definition in his muscular forearms as he jiggled his
cocktail shaker. He said something and winked at his
patron, causing her to throw her head back in delight.
The man knew how to earn a tip.

"You and Auntie Biz throw the *best* holiday parties,"
Piper was saying. "Do you remember the Chrismukkah
thing we did a few years ago? That was a blast."

"It *was* fun, wasn't it?" I agreed, pivoting to happier
thoughts. "Caleb has yet to receive the full O'Leary
holiday treatment."

"I know, right?" Piper said. "I mean, Shea's always
saying how much she hates the cold weather here and
how you and Biz are too *extra*, with all the presents and
decorations and food and whatnot, but I think Caleb
would love it."

"Shea thinks we're 'extra'?" I knew my sister well
enough to pick up on a subtle dig.

Piper waved away my offense. "She's always so
moody around the holidays. That's why I usually go to
my mom's. Less stressful."

"Yeah, she's always been that way," I agreed. "People
think I'm a type-A personality—until they meet Shea.
If my standards are high, Shea's are . . ." I searched for
an appropriate metaphor.

"Higher than Snoop Dogg riding a hot air balloon?"
Piper let out a throaty laugh at her own joke. There was,
however, a rough edge to her voice that revealed the unpleasant truth of a family trait me, my sister, and Biz
all shared—we seemed to harbor a particularly viru-
lent and chronic strain of perfectionism.

"Hey, would you and your dad have time to come by
my restaurant for brunch tomorrow? The restaurant's

closed on Mondays, so it'll just be us. I'd love to cook
for you and show you the place."

"That'd be great!" she replied. "Can you bring Butterball? Or isn't he allowed to come to the restaurant?"

I smiled, remembering how Piper had immediately
hit it off with my orange tabby when they'd met after
my father's funeral. Butterball had always been a kid
magnet, and I knew he'd be as jazzed to see Piper as
she was to see him.

"As a matter of fact, he comes to work with me every
day now. I've been stashing him in the apartment upstairs. We're having handrails and a walk-in bath put
in Biz's bathroom. I'm keeping him out of the way
while the work's going on."

"Awesome. I love that cat."

Before we could firm up the plans, I heard an al-
mighty crash from across the room. A scream rang
out, shrill and pained. So much for our one hundred
percent perfect night.

CHAPTER 3

The crowd parted and the source of the ruckus became clear. Rabbit stood trembling, surrounded by the carnage of broken glasses scattered across the floor. He'd obviously made his way back downstairs at some point and resumed his duties. It appeared that he'd been clearing empties and dropped the tray. Rabbit, however, didn't even look at the jagged shrapnel. Instead, he stared in horror at Hadley, who was bent double, clutching her leg. I pushed my way toward them.

"Are you okay?" I asked, rushing to Hadley.

She stood up, displaying her hand, slick with blood. She wiped it clumsily on her white dress, leaving a claret smear. "He bumped into me," she sniveled, flinging an accusatory arm toward Rabbit. "Some glass cut my leg."

Rabbit looked horrified, as if he'd been ordered to burn at the stake.

Daniel, with reflexes honed by six years in the Army Reserve, sprang from behind the bar and was at my side in a flash. Since no one else was forthcoming, the two of us bent down to examine the girl's leg. A small, razor-fine cut, about an inch long, marked her shin. Although an ooze of blood seeped out, I was relieved to see that the injury didn't seem serious. Daniel produced a clean bar towel and gently tended to Hadley's cut. Her sniffles quickly escalated to full-blown sobs, a reaction that seemed entirely out of proportion with her injury.

"Don't worry," Daniel soothed. "My name is Daniel. I'm trained in first aid. What's your name?"

"Hadley," the girl answered, heaving in a shaking breath.

"That was a bad surprise, Hadley, but you'll be okay now." His tone was hypnotic, the kind of cadence that could calm a frightened bird.

Instead of being soothed, though, the girl shouted, "I will *not* be okay!"

Adrian Hoffman pushed his way through the crowd and stood in front of his daughter, his hands on his hips. "For god's sake, Hadley. It's a scratch. And I saw what happened. *You* staggered into that waiter. Pull yourself together."

I felt someone else come alongside us. "Adrian, please, she's hurt."

I turned and found myself face-to-face with Daffi Hoffman. I'd met her briefly the previous week when she stopped by to go over the menus, but I hadn't paid much attention to her appearance. She and Hadley were clearly related, but Daffi was shorter, with a full figure softened by middle age. Her auburn hair swung around her face, flashing in the soft light like a new penny.

Adrian hadn't taken his eyes off his daughter. "How much have you had to drink tonight?" he demanded.

"Don't pretend to care," Hadley spat back. Daffi tried to guide the girl to the edge of the room, but Hadley slapped her mother's hands away. "Don't you *dare* touch me," she seethed.

Adrian threw his hands up and stormed out of the room.

The chatter of the party died down completely as the remaining guests gawked at the scene before them. Smashed glass, a stunned waiter, a sozzled coed, and Daffi, whose efforts to smooth things over were going nowhere. Perry Como's version of "Silver Bells" drifted out of the surround-sound speakers like a dreary dirge. Daniel and I made eye contact, realizing it would be up to us to end the uncomfortable standoff.

"Do you have a first aid kit?" I asked Daffi.

She nodded. "Master bathroom, upstairs."

"We should wash out the cut," Daniel said. "It's not bleeding much, but you may want to get it looked at in the morning. Small pieces of glass could be embedded in the wound."

He laid a gentle hand on Hadley's back, and she seemed to really notice him for the first time. A flush flowed upward from her décolletage to her cheeks as she took in Daniel's smoldering good looks—inky black eyes, lashes a drag queen would envy, and a movie-idol jawline. He smiled at her, revealing his single dimple, which Sonya aptly referred to as "the dimple that launched a thousand ships." As he guided Hadley up the stairs, she leaned on him, more than seemed strictly necessary given the minor scratch.

"I'm sorry about this," Daffi said, turning to me and Rabbit. "You look like you've seen the Ghost of Christmas Past." She put a steadying hand on Rabbit's still-trembling arm. He shied away from her like a frightened dog.

"Why don't you take five?" I suggested.

"Or better yet, call it quits for the night if Delilah

can spare you," Daffi said, with a worried glance at me. "The party's wrapping up anyway."

Guests had indeed started to gather their coats and make for the door. Apparently, nothing stops a party in its tracks quite like the hosts' daughter causing a drunken bloody scene.

By now, Melody had come over to help clean up the broken glass. Piper had also stepped through the small ring of onlookers. Melody cast a worried frown toward Rabbit, who'd stopped shaking but, more worryingly, was now stock-still.

"You okay?" Melody asked.

Rabbit rocked nervously on his heels. "Sorry."

"It wasn't your fault," Melody assured him. "I saw what happened."

"No, it was me," Rabbit said miserably, looking from me to Daffi. "I was distracted or I would've seen her. I hope I didn't mess this up for you, chef. I know how you like everything to go perfect."

Looking at his downcast face, guilt stirred inside me. First, I'd jumped on Melody about the antler head-band, and now I'd upset Rabbit. It was true that I was mortified that a member of my staff had inadvertently injured a party guest, but I hated that the suffocating miasma of my perfectionism was causing such distress.

"I'm just glad everyone's okay," I said, hoping he knew I was sincere.

"That's right," Daffi said. "Don't give it a second thought."

"Is it all right if I go early, like Mrs. Hoffman said? I think I gotta get to a meeting at Saint Benedict's," Rabbit said.

"Of course," I said.

"I'll walk you out," Daffi said.

He beat a hasty retreat, with Daffi speaking to him in soothing tones. She flashed a chagrined smile at me over her shoulder as she moved away. It struck me that she was being unusually solicitous toward the man who'd just injured her daughter, and I wondered briefly at the chances that the wealthy hostess could be the mystery woman Rabbit had followed through the snow.

Piper turned to me. "Your employee has an urgent church meeting at nine o'clock at night? Totally normal. I have no follow-up questions."

I smiled, realizing how shady it must sound. "Rabbit's in recovery," I explained. "The parish runs a late-night AA meeting."

Rabbit had always been open about his past—he'd struggled with alcohol addiction for most of his life, and bore the burdens that sometimes went along with it: spotty employment history, fractured relationships, a substantial criminal record.

"Ah, that explains it," my niece replied.

Melody began sweeping the broken glass into a dustpan.

"Hey," Piper said, turning to her, "thanks for being a good sport earlier when Hadley dragged you into being a reindeer."

"It's okay," Melody said.

"Hadley can be *a lot* sometimes," Piper added.

"So I gathered," I said.

"Tonight wasn't normal," Piper said. "She's usually *a lot* in a fun way. Tonight was *a lot* in a back-of-the-squad-car kind of way. School's been really hard for her lately and she's kind of dreading talking to her folks about how she's bombing her classes." She frowned, looking up the stairs. "Anyway, it sucks about what happened with the guy who works for you. Rabbit? He looked really shaken up."

"I wonder if he's extra upset because his mom is moving to Texas after the holidays," Melody said.

"I didn't realize," I said. "That must be rough. I know Rabbit and his mom are close."

Melody nodded. "Yeah, she has a long-distance boy-friend out there she wants to be closer to, but Rab-bit has no choice but to stay in Geneva Bay because of his parole. Well, and Everleigh," Melody explained. "There's no way her mom would move to Texas."

Rabbit's behavior suddenly made a lot more sense. His mother had been steadfast in her support of him, bringing Everleigh, his young daughter, for visits when he was incarcerated and helping him get back on his feet when he got out. Rabbit had only recently regained visitation rights with Everleigh and he was determined not to do anything to jeopardize that. His mom had sacrificed a lot for her wayward son over the years. Now that he was on a more even keel, it seemed she was ready to do something for herself. Fair enough, but still, I wished she wasn't leaving Rabbit to his own devices. He'd made great strides toward independence and restoring his self-worth, even in the half year I'd known him. But if tonight had proved anything, it was that his recovery was as fragile as glass.

The aftermath of a catering gig typically gives me the same kind of warm-glow buzz I imagine theater per-formers get after a successful show. Tonight though, even cleaning—an activity I loved—failed to boost my gloomy mood. The party had ended with a whimper, clearing out within minutes of what I'd already started to think of as "the incident."

"It's okay, Dee," Sonya assured me, pausing as she readied the last load of gear for the van. She laid her head on one of my slumped shoulders.

"Yeah," Melody agreed. "The food was great."

"Not sure anyone will remember that part of the night," I sighed.

"*I* will," said a voice from the door. I looked up to find Daffi Hoffman leaning against the doorframe. "It was phenomenal, really. Filling the donuts with eggnog cream?" She smacked her lips. "You have a way of layering flavors that's really magical."

Sonya gave me a "damn girl" look. "See? Good food matters to people."

"She's right," Daffi agreed. "I order takeout from Delilah and Son whenever we're in town. That's how I got the idea of you catering for us," she continued, grabbing a sponge to wipe down the sink. "Adrian travels quite a bit for work, and I help him with his business when I can. It doesn't leave much time for cooking."

"What line of work is he in?" I asked.

"Real estate, property development, that sort of thing."

The sound of footsteps interrupted us. "What are you doing?" Adrian Hoffman glared at his wife.

Daffi dropped the sponge as if it had caught fire in her hand. "Just chatting."

"Well, there's no reason for you to be cleaning. The caterers can take care of it, and anything they miss, the cleaners will get in the morning," he said. "I need to speak with you. Now."

She smiled apologetically. "Thanks, everyone, for your work tonight. I'll have to come to the restaurant sometime so you can show me around." She let out a tipsy giggle and her husband shot her a look that made me think the proposed visit was unlikely.

Sonya and I watched them depart, and she turned to me, muttering, "I don't like that guy. He seems like someone whose car sports a bunch of bumper stickers I disagree with."

"I think that brand-new Range Rover in the driveway is his," Melody said. "Probably too high class to put any bumper stickers on it."

Sonya pursed her lips. "I also disagree with the idea of a car that's too fancy for bumper stickers."

Daniel came into the kitchen with Piper in tow. "Well, *jefa*," he said, "the bar is packed up, the snow has stopped, and everyone's gone."

"Everyone except me," Piper clarified. "My dad left early, after the whole Hadley thing."

"How's she doing?" I asked.

"We put her to bed," Daniel said.

Melody's mouth fell open, aghast. "You were in her *bedroom*?"

Daniel shrugged. "Seemed the best place for her."

"He's basically the hero of the night," Piper said. "I bet Hadley would take a glass cut any day if Daniel would patch it up for her."

Daniel shot Piper a good-natured smile, but then his face darkened. "Hadley seemed really drunk, which is strange because she only had Coke."

"Let me guess," Piper said, "you probably served Daffi a bunch of Jack and Cokes, right?"

Daniel nodded.

"Well, there you go." Piper held out her hands, regarding us as if we were doing a particularly bad job guessing at charades. "Come on. Half of those were for Hadley. Her dad doesn't let her drink, but her mom gives her whatever she wants. She was probably slipping her drinks. They do it all the time."

Sonya gave voice to my thoughts. "That's messed up."

"Yeah, well, their family dynamic is a whole deal . . . but whose isn't?" Piper observed with a philosophical shrug. "Hadley's really nice, though, once you get to know her."

"She seemed kind of bratty to me," Melody said. Usually deferential, Melody was showing no such restraint. Her arms were crossed over her chest, and her jaw was set firmly, yielding nothing. "I didn't like how she acted with"—she eyed Daniel, but changed course mid-sentence—"Rabbit." *Uh-oh*. They say jealousy is a green-eyed monster, but just then, it looked a whole lot like a blue-eyed Wisconsin farm girl.

"She's going through some stuff," Piper said. "She's really stressed about school. Palisades is *so* hard. Way harder than I thought it would be, and I'm a comms major. But she's usually really fun."

"Is it still okay if I skate, even with Rabbit gone?" Daniel asked, using the restaurant lingo for leaving without helping with the scut work.

Usually after a catering gig, both men would've come back to Delilah & Son to help unload the van. Tonight though, Daniel had driven separately so he could leave straight from the party and pick up his mother for a nightcap.

"If you're driving back now," Piper cut in, "could you give me a ride? I was supposed to spend the night here, but Hadley isn't really up for company. My dad and I have a room in the main lodge. I called him for a ride, but he's not picking up his phone. I know it's only a few minutes' walk from here, but it's freezing and I'm not exactly in the right clothes." She gestured to her skimpy dress and high heels.

Daniel dipped into a chivalrous bow. "For Delilah O'Leary's niece, I would drive to the moon. Assuming *la jefa* is okay with it?" he asked, turning to me.

"Of course. We can handle the unloading."

"I'll go and get my car," Daniel said to Piper. "Meet you out front."

Piper popped out to the hallway to grab her things and returned a moment later, wearing a stylish puffer coat. A second, longer coat was draped over her arm. "It looks like that tall lady left her coat here. Natasha, I think her name was? She caught the shuttle over from the main lodge with me and my dad. He introduced us. He knows her from somewhere."

I walked over to examine the garment, a chic camel-colored shearling number in a single-digit size. It exhibited the kind of sublime tailoring that no doubt cost a pretty penny.

Sonya came alongside me. "That's weird," she said. "I can't imagine who would leave their coat behind on a night like tonight."

I looked out the window at the wintry landscape, my eyes tracing the path that skirted the eighteenth green and the back of the ski slope. The lights of the main lodge twinkled in the distance.

"You're sure Natasha's not still here somewhere?" I asked.

"Not unless she's hiding in a closet," Piper answered. "When I was upstairs saying goodnight to Hadley and her parents, they were the only ones here."

"And you're sure the coat is hers? Could it be Hadley's or Daffi's?"

"Nope, it's definitely hers," Piper said. She shrugged.

"Maybe she hitched a lift back to the hotel. I can leave it at the front desk."

Piper's explanation was logical. Natasha had probably been offered a ride back to the hotel in somebody's warm Audi or Benz, and simply forgotten her coat. Maybe she, like Hadley, had over-imbibed. Yet somehow, I couldn't stop picturing Natasha La Cotti, coatless, in her stilt-like heels, staggering down the snow-covered path into the frigid darkness.

CHAPTER 4

When I came downstairs just after seven the next morning, my great-aunt Elizabeth "Biz" O'Leary, usually a late sleeper, was already dressed in a freshly ironed white blouse and red cardigan, her snowy hair set and sprayed into tight curler furrows. She paced near the front door like an anxious puppy. She'd practically danced on air when I arrived home after the Hoffmans' party last night and told her we'd be hosting Piper and Jonathan for brunch at the restaurant. Of course, I'd glossed over the details of how the plan came about—instead of admitting that it arose from a painful near-snubbing, I spun it as a planned surprise.

"You're not ready? We have a lot to do," she said.

I held up my hands, warding off her impatience. "Piper and Jonathan aren't coming until ten. Let me get a cup of coffee before I try to herd Butterball into his cat carrier."

"I put a to-go mug on the kitchen counter for you," she said. "I'll get Mr. Butterbutt into *his* to-go container while you grab it." On cue, my ample-figured feline sashayed into the hall and smooshed his face into my ankles. I moved to scoop him up, but my octogenarian aunt shot across to collect him. "Come here," she said, gathering his ample bulk into her arms. "We've got to get you into your carrier, don't we? Your cousin Piper's in town!"

My eyebrows shot up. Although I suspected Biz secretly adored my cat, she rarely showed it, much less offered to do any cat-related tasks, *much less* baby-talked to him. I hadn't seen her this happy since, well, since five years ago, when Shea's family came for the holidays.

"I thought I saw your sister the other day," Biz said.

I'd taken a few steps toward the kitchen, but stopped. "You did?"

"Melody took me to the Woodman's in Janesville, you know how I like their deli section, and I saw a woman I thought was Shea." I stared at her, unsure what to make of it. Biz wasn't known for flights of fancy. "Oh, it wasn't her," she said, waving her hand. "I know she's not coming. But there was a resemblance."

I couldn't quite force my smile to reach my eyes. What Biz said made me feel uneasy. Last Christmas had been our first since my father's passing. I was still living in Chicago and had made the drive up to Geneva Bay with my ex-fiancé to pass the holiday with Biz. The three of us had gone through the motions: opening presents, cooking, eating, raising a toast to my parents, flopping on the couch to watch the Bears get clobbered by the Packers. But it had been exhausting, each of us working to meet the others' unspoken expectations of what Christmas should be. I wanted so badly to be able to fill the empty spaces for Auntie Biz, break myself into enough pieces to plug the gaping holes where the rest of my family should be. But I couldn't. Which meant that just below the surface, there was an ever-present, throat-constricting emptiness, a feeling that I wasn't enough. My mother died when I was young, a freak collision on an icy road. Then my father died of cancer the year before last. Maybe one person wasn't enough to fill all that space.

Truth be told, I wished it was different, too. Neither of my parents had siblings. I'd always fantasized about waking up on Christmas morning to a house stuffed with relatives, gathering around a table brimming with food, but that had never been our reality. Even when my parents were still living, our holiday gatherings had been small. Now Biz seemed to be conjuring up visions of my absent sister, a sister so distant she might as well be a ghost. I just prayed that having a brief visit from Piper and Jonathan would be enough to see her through the season.

Biz and I had stayed up into the wee hours the previous night planning the menu and we continued to discuss it on the drive to the restaurant. Delilah & Son's parking lot had been plowed, but little diamond flurries still twirled in the breeze as the late-rising winter sun glinted off the lake. Ice had formed along the shoreline and in the shallows. The remaining water had grown slow, flat, and heavy—despite the wind, barely a ripple creased the surface. I reckoned the lake would be iced over completely before the new year.

With Delilah & Son closed for the day, we intended to take full advantage of the free time and the restaurant's kitchen to craft a knock-your-socks-off brunch. Biz, a top-notch home cook, helped in the restaurant most days, and she quickly settled into a high-backed stool we'd dubbed "Biz's perch" to get the meal underway.

Although our too-similar personalities often clashed, in the kitchen we worked with perfect synchronicity.

Before long, we'd created two deep-dish breakfast pizzas with hash brown crusts, loaded up with eggs, pepper jack cheese, and sausage. We'd top them with fresh pico de gallo right before serving. Homemade waffles were staying warm in a low oven. These would be served à la s'mores with a buttery Nutella drizzle and blowtorch-toasted marshmallows on top. As I juiced pomegranates for non-alcoholic mimosas, Biz scooped little spheres of honeydew and casaba into a bowl for a melon ball salad. She hummed along with the music on the "Seasoning the Season" playlist Son and I used during prep. Holiday cheer practically gushed out of her. Generally speaking, my aunt wasn't a gusher. Unless a person could be effusively curmudgeonly. Or could gush stubbornness. *That*, I'd seen.

"We should set the table," Biz said, counting out plates and cutlery. "Is Sonya coming?"

"Yep, she'll be here any minute," I answered.

"Melody?"

"Nope, she had errands to run," I replied.

"Daniel?"

"Busy hanging out with his mother."

"Rabbit?"

"Haven't heard from him." I'd sent a text when we got back to the restaurant last night, asking if he was okay. I made a mental note to check in with him again later. It wasn't like him not to reply, and I was especially concerned given last night's drama.

"What about Calvin?" she asked, referring to Calvin Capone, the hunky police detective who I'd first met when things got a little . . . *murdery* at my restaurant's grand opening. The two of us had been dating—or at least trying to date—for the past few months.

"He can't come over until later," I replied. "I'd love for him to meet Piper and Jonathan, but he has work to finish at the station before he and his family leave for their cruise tomorrow."

"I'm all for industriousness, but that man is too busy. We see less of him now than we did before you allegedly started going together," Biz observed.

"Tell me about it."

Capone and I each worked insane hours, and our relationship had had a stuttering start. My gig involved an endless succession of punishing fourteen- and fifteen-hour days, and given the small size of the Geneva Bay PD, Capone was practically always on call if a major crime cropped up. We were also each juggling caregiving responsibilities, with me often shuttling Biz to appointments and social engagements and Capone pitching in to look after his two-year-old granddaughter. Capone's family had a complicated history. First, there was his notorious mobster forebearer, i.e., his great-grandfather Al Capone, whose grandson sired *my* Capone, who then became a grandfather before he turned forty. Our worlds were so hectic that in two-plus months of dating, we'd rarely finished an entire date without one of us being summoned to deal with some kind of emergency, either at work or on the home front. Every time our romance heated up, a wave of responsibility rolled in to quench it.

I followed Biz out to the dining room, where we laid a table for the brunch. Dazzling winter sun streamed in the huge picture window that overlooked the restaurant's outdoor patio and the lake just beyond. Nestled in the windowsill, Butterball resembled a warm loaf of bread. Under normal circumstances, he was firmly banned from being anywhere in the kitchen or dining room. I'd made a one-time exception today, though, so he could visit with Piper.

"It's a shame Calvin and his family can't come for Christmas dinner," Biz said, placing red carnations and sprigs of holly into a vase. "It's been a long time since we had a full table."

"Uh-huh."

I turned my back to Biz and began to fiddle with the handheld blowtorch. It had been acting up, and I didn't want to singe anybody's eyebrows when I toasted the waffles' marshmallow topping tableside. Truth be told, I also didn't want Biz to see how disappointed I was that Capone hadn't broached the subject of our spending any part of the holidays together. He and his family had a long-standing plan to take a week-long Caribbean cruise over Christmas. It's not that I expected an invite after such a short time dating, but I expected . . . *something*.

To set the stage for romance, I'd organized an idyllic seasonal outing for later that day. Capone and I would get hot cocoa and walk around Geneva Bay's downtown park, where preparations had begun for the annual snow sculpting contest. Watching the sculptors at work was one of the highlights of the town calendar, making the Wisconsin winter's excess of snow and frigid weather something to look forward to. Gigantic, room-sized mounds of snow would already have been trucked in and dropped at each competitors' station, waiting to be transformed into sea monsters, jungle animals, or whatever other whimsical creations the artists could conjure from their frosty raw materials. If all of that didn't get Capone caught up in the magic of the holidays, I was out of ideas.

Biz sprinkled chopped mint on the melon salad in time with the beat of "Let It Snow! Let It Snow! Let It Snow!" As the melody came in, Biz, with an ear honed through fifty years singing alto in the Saint Francis de Sales choir, chimed in with a low harmony.

Just then Sonya burst in the front door, pausing to stomp the snow off her fur-lined boots. She, like Biz, had an ear for music, and she joined in the chorus of the song without missing a beat. Biz went over to Sonya, helping her doff her winter gear item by item and hang everything on a coat rack. Sonya, as usual, was dressed to the nines. She wore a belted wool coat with a faux-fur collar. Underneath that, she sported a white-and-gold plaid fifties-style flare dress with a wide gold belt. Her makeup, too, was pin-up perfection—matte red lips and cat-eye black liner.

The door opened once again, and Piper and Jonathan stepped through. Sonya and Biz were so caught up in their performance that they didn't immediately notice the new arrivals. My niece and brother-in-law watched with amusement as Sonya and Biz held Sonya's scarf between them, swaying back and forth as they belted the last "let it snow!" along with Frank Sinatra.

As the note died down, Sonya let out a contented sigh. "What a banger. Written by Sammy Cahn, aka Samuel Cohen."

"I know, right? Some of the best Christmas songs were written by Jews," Piper said with a wink.

Biz rushed over to Piper and Jonathan. "How wonderful of you to make a surprise visit!"

Catching their confused expressions, I realized I hadn't brought them up to speed on Biz's belief that this had been a planned visit. I mouthed *Go with it*, hoping they'd understand.

Jonathan, thankfully, caught on. "Surprise!"

For the holidays, I mouthed.

"For the holidays!" Piper chimed in.

"Shea and Caleb really wanted to come, but they just couldn't get away," Jonathan added.

The next song started up and Jonathan took Biz in his arms, waltzing her around the restaurant. "Normal Biz" would've slapped him away, protesting such foolishness. "Holiday Biz" glided along, giggling when he lowered her into a dip.

"Dad, your knees," Piper called, laughing at them.

Jonathan and Biz took another turn around the dance floor as Piper caught sight of Butterball basking in the windowsill. "B-Man!" she squealed, running toward him.

Meanwhile, I turned down the music and introduced Jonathan to Sonya. The group spent a few minutes exchanging pleasantries, but with little common ground, conversation stayed at the surface level. Once we'd covered "Do you like college?" and "How about this cold weather?" I felt like I was talking to strangers. I knew only sparse details about Jonathan and Piper's lives, and they knew next to nothing about mine or Biz's.

"How's Hadley?" I asked. "She seemed pretty shaken up."

Piper frowned. "I haven't talked to her. She's probably still sleeping off last night's party."

"I think you should put some distance between yourself and that girl," Jonathan cautioned. "I know you want to be a good friend, but she's unbalanced. She was saying a lot of crazy things last night."

"Like what?" I asked. I remembered how he'd come up the stairs shortly after Hadley smashed the plate.

Maybe he'd elaborate on what he meant when he told Natasha and Adrian that they had "a serious problem with Hadley."

He waved his hand. "Weird stuff about her parents. I couldn't make sense of it, but it seemed like she was spiraling, just making things up. That's why I came upstairs to find Adrian during the party. I was worried about her."

On the surface, he'd provided an explanation for what I witnessed during the party. But if it was as simple as that, why did I feel like he was deliberately feeding me kernels of information? Whenever I'd seen him, Jonathan was relaxed and spontaneous, a study in contrasts with my carefully calibrated sister. Yet he'd delivered the account of his interaction with Hadley as stiffly as a third-rate community theater player.

Sonya didn't seem to pick up on the whiff of subterfuge. Instead, as usual, her heart was hemorrhaging sympathy. "What a hard situation."

"Yeah, it's sad," Piper agreed. "Hadley's a great person, but she's been super stressed lately. She's tried tutors and everything, but she's still not passing her classes."

"Palisades is a top-tier school," Biz said. "I'm sure it's challenging. In all my years of teaching, only a handful of my students got in."

"It's tough, but I keep telling her she was smart enough to get in, so she can handle it," Piper said. "She's really freaking out about school, which makes her anxiety worse, which makes it harder to concentrate, which tanks her grades, which makes her freak out even more . . ."

Jonathan turned to his daughter, his voice uncharacteristically stern. "I know you're a grown woman, but you've got to look out for yourself. You can't let Hadley pull you into her drama."

Piper lifted Butterball and used him like a ventriloquist's dummy, making gestures with his paws and raising her voice an octave. "If Piper unfriended everyone who got wasted and fought with their parents, there wouldn't be anybody left to hang out with."

"Piper . . ." Jonathan began.

Biz held up her hand. "This isn't a suitable topic of conversation for a holiday brunch. We're so rarely together, let's enjoy it."

"But Auntie Biz . . ." I protested. It was true that we were rarely together. And for once, we were talking about something real. I felt like I was getting to know my niece and brother-in-law, seeing a new complexity in Piper and a rough layer underneath Jonathan's smooth veneer I'd never noticed before.

Biz tut-tutted. "Let's talk about happier things."

"Biz is right," Jonathan agreed. In an instant, the wattage of his smile was dialed up to its usual brilliance. The happy-go-lucky mask was firmly back on his face. "How about we talk about this *food*? Everything looks incredible."

We sat down and dug into the meal, but I felt off-balance. I found myself popping up from the table like a demented jack-in-the-box—refill the coffee, reheat the syrup, arrange and rearrange things on platters. Even as I tried to keep Butterball, agent of chaos that he was, from jumping on the table, I felt a strange, conflicting impulse to let him run amok. Almost as if I *wanted* him to wreck everything. Instead, I smiled tightly as everyone gushed about the delicious meal. "These waffles! How do you get them to be fluffy on the inside but crispy on the outside?" "What kind of cheese did you use on the breakfast pizza?" Through it all, I felt anesthetized, like a wall of fog had risen up around me.

As I walked back out of the kitchen for the tenth time, I realized with startling clarity that after Biz changed the subject, we hadn't talked about anything of substance. We'd fallen into a picture-perfect pantomime. A whirl of confusion raged inside me. I wanted everything to run smoothly, didn't I? For everyone to be happy holiday campers? Perfectionism was my MO. But another feeling tickled the edges of my consciousness. A longing to be close, even if that came with messiness. We'd replicated the pattern of all the holidays since my mother died—me and Biz occupied with cleaning, decorating, and food prep, creating all the trappings, with none of the heart.

After the meal, me, Sonya, Biz, and Butterball waved Piper and Jonathan out of the parking lot, not knowing when we'd see one another again.

Biz sighed, a contented smile forming the creases on her face into an unaccustomed arrangement. "Wasn't that just perfect?"

"Yes," I lied.

CHAPTER 5

I was still wrestling with my muddled feelings an hour later when I walked up to the front desk of the Geneva Bay Police Department. *This is the happiest time of the year. You got to spend the morning with your best friend and your family, enjoying a delicious meal. There is no cause for inner turmoil. But . . .*

I shoved my emotions back in their cave and flashed a smile at the officer who manned the desk. He was on the phone, but he recognized me—and the stack of Delilah & Son take-out containers balanced in my arms—and buzzed me through to the back offices.

I deposited most of the leftover brunch bounty in the breakroom and made my way to Capone's office, carrying boxes laden with two s'mores waffles and a thick slab of breakfast pizza.

Capone sat alone, hunched over his computer keyboard in the modest office shared by the department's criminal investigative team. I'd seen him at work plenty of times, and each time I was struck by just how incongruous his large, muscular physique looked behind a desk, hunt-and-peck typing, with gold-rimmed reading glasses perched on his nose. He'd told me he actually enjoyed research and the administrative side of detective work, but I couldn't help thinking that Capone behind a desk was some sort of Clark Kent–style fiction. I knew he'd been working long hours, but he looked pin-neat—tawny brown face clean-shaven, curly black hair cut into a tight fade. His dress shirt was rolled up at the sleeves, but crisp and white as a winter morning.

I rested the food boxes on a corner of the desk.

He looked up and smiled, leaning back in his desk chair to stretch. Watching him take his glasses off sent a little thrill up my spine. Sexy librarian vibes for sure.

"What are you working on?" I asked.

"We brought a guy in this morning for selling unlabeled meat out of the back of a van," he said.

I scrunched up my face as I took the visitor's chair opposite him. "Ew."

"Believe it or not, 'the sketchy steak van' is a fairly common scam this time of year."

"Wow, all this romantic talk. You really know how to put a gal in the mood for a date," I teased.

He came around and perched on the edge of the desk directly in front of me. "Do you want to know how they do it?" he asked, lowering his already-deep voice to a sensual purr. "They use a grocery store or wholesale contact to get ahold of expensive roasts and filets that are out of date"—he took my hands in his—"remove them from their original packaging"—he kissed the inside of one of my wrists—"rewrap them"—he kissed the other—"and resell them for the holidays to people who are trying to stretch their budgets and willing to roll the dice on questionable meat. Was that romantic enough for you?"

I smiled as he leaned in to kiss me. "I thought you handled major crimes," I said, threading my arms around his neck for another kiss. I still couldn't believe I had unfettered access to those lips. "What are you doing filling out paperwork on the *E. coli*-mobile?"

"With so many people off around the holidays, it's catch-as-catch-can. I'm covering for some folks this week so they'll cover for me next week while I'm away." He pulled the container of breakfast pizza close and dug in with the fork I'd packed. He let out a moan of pleasure. "This is incredible."

"Thanks. I'm surprised you're hungry when you've just spent the morning on a case about dodgy meat."

"If I had a weak stomach in this line of work"—he twirled his finger around to take in the entirety of the police station—"I'd starve to death."

There was a single knock at the door and a ruddy, round face peeked around the corner.

"Sorry to interrupt. Just wanted to say those marshmallow waffles are outta this world." Officer Lee Stanhope patted his ample midsection. He was a balding, cheerful man, who told anyone who'd listen about the plans he and his wife had to buy an RV "and travel the lower forty-eight" when he retired. "I ate three. Gotta prepare myself, so I'll be ready for Rhonda's Christmas dinner." He walked over and placed a piece of paper on Capone's desk. "Here's that case report you asked for."

"Thanks, Lee."

Stanhope peeked into the to-go container I'd brought. Capone swatted him away. "Hands off."

"Come on. Rettberg's mad at me 'cuz I didn't leave any chocolate sauce for her waffle," he said. "You got any extra?"

I had, indeed, packed extra condiment cups of Nutella drizzle for Capone, and I handed one of them to Stanhope.

"We've all been telling him he can never break up with you," Stanhope said to me. "The whole department would starve without you feeding us all the time."

Capone cast a skeptical eye at the straining buttons on Stanhope's uniform shirt. "Doesn't seem like you're in imminent danger."

Stanhope reached out to give Capone a playful chuck on the arm, apparently forgetting that he was holding the container of chocolate hazelnut sauce. When his balled hand made contact with Capone, the container burst open, splattering sauce on the floor, the desk, and Capone's bright white shirt.

"Jeez o' Pete, sorry about that," Stanhope said. "Lemme get some paper towels."

Capone shook his head and gave a weary sigh. "It's okay. I've got a spare shirt in the locker room."

The two of them departed, leaving me alone. I swiped a drip of sauce that had landed on the report Stanhope brought in, and licked it off my finger, idly scanning the page.

It appeared to be an old arrest report for a man named Travis Staggs. Under "Nature of Complaint" the arresting officer had written "passing worthless checks" and "receiving stolen goods." Nothing terribly salacious, and not enough detail to hold my attention. Just as I began to move back to my chair, though, my eyes caught on another name—Robert Blakemore.

Capone came through the door, pulling a dark green fleece zip-up over his white undershirt. "Not sure that chocolate stain's going to come out," he said.

"Use a stain stick, leave it overnight, pre-soak in bleach solution, and then wash it with OxiClean," I said quickly. I was something of an expert on the matter, having removed stains from chef's jackets more times than I could count. "What are you doing with this guy's rap sheet?"

He looked startled at the sudden conversational pivot. "You shouldn't be looking at that."

Undeterred, I continued, "Why do you care if a guy named Travis Staggs was passing bad checks eight years ago?"

"It's not important." Capone stuffed the report into a folder.

"The name *Robert Blakemore* is listed as a known associate. There can't be that many Robert Blakemores associating with criminals in Geneva Bay. That's Rabbit, isn't it?"

Capone's face registered surprise. He removed the paper from the folder where he'd just placed it and scanned the page. "Huh."

"Huh, what?" I rose and looked over his shoulder. He pulled away from me. Capone was too much of a professional to cough up info about a case easily. Plus, he was stubborn. If it came to a battle of wills, though, he had nothing on me.

I snatched the report, stuffed it down the front of my V-neck sweater, and crossed my arms over my chest. "You might as well tell me."

"Maybe I'll go in there after it," he said.

I cocked my head. "Maybe you should try."

He was quiet for a long moment, trying to work out whether my statement was an invitation or a threat. For the record, it was both.

Finally, he sighed. "Fine, but only because you knowing won't harm my case, and I don't want this hanging over our date today."

"*Today?* If you don't tell me what's going on, I'll

harp on it for a year at least." I cracked a smile, but we both knew I wasn't entirely joking.

"I had no idea Rabbit's name would show up on that report," he explained. "Travis Staggs is the purveyor of questionable meat that I told you about. One of the pages that had been scanned into his criminal record got pixelated. I asked Stanhope to find the original and make me a copy. Staggs has a long record, and I want to make sure we give the prosecutor's office the full story about him so they can charge him appropriately. The meat truck alone may not net him a lot of time, but with a guy like Staggs, they want to look at the whole picture. See if he's trying to walk the straight and narrow, or just making the same old mistakes."

"So you're not looking into Rabbit?" I asked.

"No." He peered into my face. "Should I be?"

"No." I paused. "No."

"You sure?"

"I'm just a little worried about him. He's been acting strange for the last couple days, and he hasn't replied to my texts."

"Strange how?"

"Jumpy. Skittish." I frowned. "Maybe even scared?"

"Could he be on a bender?"

I inhaled sharply. The thought had been in the back of my mind all day, but hearing it vocalized still hit me like a sucker punch. Of course it was possible that Rabbit had started drinking again. I'd worked in the restaurant biz for years, and I wasn't born yesterday. Restaurant work, with its late nights, punishing hours, and physical demands was a breeding ground for bad habits of all kinds. Combine that with ready access to booze, and you have a recipe for danger.

I took out my phone and started typing out a text. "I need to check in on him. He lives with his mother. I'll ask Son to find her home address. I've got it in a file somewhere back at the restaurant."

"Why is Sonya at the restaurant? I thought you were closed today?" he asked.

"She's watching TV in the apartment upstairs with Butterball."

His forehead creased in confusion.

"Her cable is on the fritz," I explained, "and she and Melody have plans to make caramel corn and watch cheesy Christmas movies this afternoon."

"I thought Sonya was Jewish."

"She claims that watching corny romance is a mitzvah."

"I see," he said, with a wry lift of his eyebrow. "And Butterball is invited . . . why?"

"He's hanging out there today so he won't harass the contractors who are working on Biz's bathroom."

"I've seen you use that apartment as the restaurant's office, Daniel's locker room, Sonya's overflow makeup and wardrobe storage—everything except an actual apartment."

I shrugged. "Small price to pay for custody of Butterball."

My ex-fiancé owned both the building that housed Delilah & Son and the lakefront mansion Biz, Melody, Butterball, and I lived in. Although Sam and I weren't right for each other, I couldn't deny that he was a great guy. When we split, I'd been staying in the one-bedroom apartment over the restaurant. Around the same time, an unexpected foreclosure left Biz and Melody suddenly homeless. I hadn't had the space to house them, nor the money to pay for alternative accommodations. Since Sam knew all three of us needed a place to live, and that I was too proud to agree to live rent-free in his mansion, he used Butterball as bait. He put the mansion into a trust for our fur-baby and allowed me to take full custody of the cat—as long as I lived in "Butterball's" house. To ensure that I kept up my part of the bargain, I had to sign a contract saying that I couldn't live in the restaurant apartment anymore, nor could I rent it to Biz or Melody. It was a sweetheart deal, but it had left the space in a no-man's-land limbo.

"Well, I'm pretty much done here," Capone said. "Just need to finish off the Staggs paperwork, and then we can head out. But first"—he held out his hand—"I'm going to need that report you stuffed down your shirt."

I tilted my head coyly to one side. "If you come and get it, the date could start right now . . ."

Early afternoon found Capone and me strolling around the town's lakefront park, watching as the snow sculpting contest got underway. The air held a damp chill, and a leaden sky, threatening more snow, hung overhead. Still, the atmosphere felt festive. In the wee hours of the morning, trucked-in snow had been packed into huge wooden molds, which were then removed to reveal perfect, white cylinders. The place looked as if a giant had built a dozen sandcastles using a ten-foot-tall bucket.

Over the next two days, teams from all over the country would transform their chilly raw materials into works of art using only hand tools. They were allowed to plan their creations in advance, so each team brought a scale model that they'd size up to fit the massive proportions of the snow blocks. Some teams were already furiously hacking the excess material away, but most sculptors were still in the planning stages, marking their snow cylinders with spray paint to guide their planned carvings.

Capone let out a long whistle. "How do they even know where to begin?"

"There's a system to it, very mathematical. I took a basic sculpting class when I was in culinary school," I explained. "It helps with visualizing how a finished dish will look on the plate. I'm no Rembrandt, but I can carve a very respectable fruit salad swan."

"Impressive. What else can you do?"

"I'm well-known for my salami and prosciutto rose bouquets. I've been told that my true artistry shines through when I handle meat."

His mouth fell open.

My innuendo hadn't been deliberate, but I allowed it to hang in the air. This was a date, after all.

"*Jefa!*" a cheery voice called out.

I turned to find Daniel striding toward us holding an insulated cup. "Hey, man," he said, sticking out his free hand for Capone to shake.

"Did everything go okay after I left last night?" he asked me.

"Unremarkable, especially compared to how the party ended," I replied. "Dropping off Piper went smoothly, I take it?"

"Yes." He paused. "Something strange happened after I left her, though."

I raised my eyebrows expectantly.

"On the way out of the complex, I had to drive back past the Hoffmans' house," he explained. "There was a man walking along the road, coming from their house."

"In that weather?"

"I pulled over to see if he needed help," Daniel said. "It was one of the guests from the party."

"Which guest?" I asked.

"I'm not sure, but I recognized him," he said. "White guy. Tall, good-looking." I smiled, remembering Sonya's observation about Geneva Bay's well-to-do doyennes. "Anyway," Daniel continued, "he said he was fine, so I left him to walk."

"And he was definitely coming from the Hoffmans' house?" I asked.

Daniel nodded. "He came out of their driveway. Maybe he forgot something at the party."

"There *was* a coat left behind," I said. "Piper found it, when you went out to warm up the car. But it was a woman's coat. Piper was sure it was Natasha La Cotti's."

A flicker of recognition passed over Daniel's face at the mention of Natasha's name.

"You know her?" I asked.

"Not well. Anyway," he said, hurrying to change the subject, "that was the only excitement to my night. My mom was tired after her flight, so we watched TV and went to bed."

We fell quiet for a moment, watching the sculptors whittle away at the snow.

"Remarkable, huh?" Capone said, nodding toward the mounds.

Daniel nodded. "My mom was amazed. She never gets to see snow."

"Where is she anyway?" I asked. "I'd love to meet her."

"She was just here," Daniel said. "I went to get her some cocoa to warm up with." He lifted the cup he held. "Well, I better see if I can find her before this gets cold. Good to see you."

Capone rubbed his gloved hands together. "A hot drink sounds like a good idea."

He wrapped his arm around my waist and we moseyed toward the food kiosks, where vendors sold a variety of warming treats, including cocoa, mulled wine, and apple fritters. Clusters of people were gathered in front of each stall. As he and I stood debating whether it was too early in the day for mulled wine, a commotion nearby drew our attention.

An attractive woman of about seventy was poking a leather-gloved finger into Adrian Hoffman's chest. Her lips were painted a deep burgundy and her dark eyes flashed with rage. A white ski hat was perched above her strong-featured face, the bobble on top of it flailing as she gesticulated. Her heavy New York accent conjured bustling city streets and rush-hour subway cars. Ensconced in a bright red, knee-length winter coat, she had the air of a packaged firecracker—ready to go off the second the fuse was lit. I could picture the woman on a Brooklyn corner, using a three-fingered whistle to hail a yellow cab. The driver would stop. He'd be scared not to.

"How dare you show your face in public?" the woman yelled. Her breath formed little clouds in the glacial air, making the anger emanating from her almost tangible.

"Don't touch me," Adrian hissed. "I'll call the police."

"*You'll* call the cops?! That's rich, coming from you," the woman scoffed. "You're a parasite. You should be behind bars, or better yet, six feet underground." She pushed her finger forcefully into Adrian's chest. Adrian, though, was twice her weight and didn't budge.

Daffi Hoffman stormed out from behind one of the kiosks, her face a picture of outrage. "Don't touch my husband," she hissed, stepping between Adrian and the woman. "I don't know who you are, but if you don't leave, we'll file an assault charge."

By now, the small knots of people who'd been waiting in line for food and drink had given up any pretense of ignoring the conflict. No amount of Midwestern politeness could paper over this. Still, while a Chicago or New York City crowd might've started catcalling or placing bets on who'd win the throwdown, the Wisconsinites rubbernecked quietly, confining themselves to whispers and disapproving looks.

Capone's body tensed. He began to jostle through the onlookers toward the quarrelling trio. I followed in his wake. He could flip on his cop switch in a millisecond, but he wasn't a kick-down-the-doors-and-barge-in type of police officer. I could picture his mind working, sizing things up, weighing whether identifying himself as law enforcement would calm or inflame the situation.

The woman in the red coat pivoted toward Daffi, placing her face inches away. "This is your husband? Well, you're married to a monster. You know that, right?" She stepped back, eyeing Daffi as if she were a bug stuck on her shoe. "Look at you, with your Burberry bag and your two-hundred-dollar haircut. What else did he buy for you with *my money*?" She spat on the ground in front of the Hoffmans. "Your husband is the worst kind of lowlife. I hope God judges you both . . . *soon*."

Capone, with me trailing behind, reached them, but before he could do anything, another commotion broke out behind us in the snow sculpting area. A scream cut through the frigid air—a man's voice, pitched high and ragged with fear. Further shouts rang out, and the heads of the bystanders whipped toward the sound. Daffi, Adrian, and the woman ceased hostilities and craned to see what was happening. Rather than subsiding, the chorus of frightened shouts rose in volume. This time, Capone moved swiftly and without hesitation. Something was seriously wrong, and it trumped the argument we'd just witnessed.

Although we took off at the same time, Capone was the faster runner and he reached the snow mounds before I did. I slowed my pace as I approached the mound that appeared to be the epicenter of whatever calamity was occurring. On the far side of the snow block from where I stood, one of the sculptors sat on the frosty ground, his knees drawn to his chest. The two other members of his team crouched next to him, murmuring in low voices and rubbing his back. The man appeared insensible to their efforts. His pop-eyed stare was fixed on the mound of snow before him. About half the spectators stared in the same direction, while the other half were in various states of backpedaling away from whatever they saw.

As I rounded to the front of the mound and turned to behold the scene, I tried to gulp down the lump of dread that had solidified in my throat. At first, I could see nothing amiss. The block of snow was mostly intact at the base—a pristine wall of white. The sculptors had set up a scaffolding platform alongside it, allowing them to access the topmost section, where they'd begun to clear away the excess material. That's where I saw the source of the trouble. A person's feet and ankles, frozen stiff, stuck out at a perpendicular angle to the smooth surface of the snow.

The link between my eyes and brain spent a few seconds in a sputtering short circuit of incomprehension. *Human feet? Sticking out of the snow?* The bare feet had a mottled blue-gray color, a spine-chilling mirror image of the frozen-over appearance of the lake just beyond. The feet hung suspended at least eight feet off the ground, near the top of the snow cylinder. *Was I really seeing this?* I could imagine the sculptors' shock as they exhumed this macabre spectacle, their confusion turning to disbelief and then horror as more of the puzzling object was uncovered.

Capone had stepped slightly away from the scene, clenching his cell phone. As he spoke into it, his amber eyes were almost expressionless, betraying no hint of what he was thinking. Many of our previous dates had ended prematurely, but none had ended quite this dramatically. I wanted to run to him, have him wrap his arms around me and tell me not to be scared, that I was okay. I wanted the giddy warmth I'd felt not ten minutes earlier when he'd threaded his arm around my waist. But he was on another planet—Cop World. I wasn't close enough to hear what he was saying into the phone, but by now I knew him well enough to understand that the worse the situation, the more unreadable his emotions became. And just then Capone's face was blank as a wall of tightly packed snow.

CHAPTER 6

"Jeez-o," Melody said, shortening the mild Wisconsinese oath. "So all you could see was the person's feet?"

I nodded. "I'm assuming there was a body attached to them, but I didn't stick around to find out."

"Yeesh, sounds like the Wicked Witch of the East when she got smushed by Dorothy's house," she said.

Following the gruesome discovery at the snow sculpting competition, I'd hurried back along the shore path to the restaurant. I found Melody, Sonya, and Butterball in the upstairs apartment, curled on the couch, watching a straight-up schmaltz bomb called *Christmas Wishes & Mistletoe Kisses*.

Sonya had changed out of her glam-wear into comfy pajamas for the movie fest, and she pulled the hood of her onesie pjs over her ears. "I don't want to hear any details. Some of us have delicate constitutions and have recently eaten a metric ton of caramel corn."

I stripped off my coat and hat and threw them on a side chair while Sonya and Melody made room between them on the couch. Butterball, deploying his "needy human" sensor, was in my arms before I fully sat down. I buried my face in his fur. Sonya handed me the bowl of caramel corn. I shoveled a fistful into my mouth, happy to find that they'd used my recipe for nutty, buttery homemade Cracker Jack.

"Do you want hot cocoa or a hot toddy?" Melody asked, pointing to the two thermos flasks on the coffee table in front of us.

"I can't believe that's even a question," Sonya chided. "This woman needs alcohol, stat."

"My bad." Melody got a clear mug from a kitchen cupboard and popped a lemon slice into it before filling it to the brim with amber liquid.

I sat quietly for a moment, breathing in the scent of whiskey, honey, and lemon. The apartment had changed quite a bit since Butterball and I lived there with Sam. It was a compact one-bedroom with an open-plan kitchen/dining/living room and a single bathroom. Both the bedroom and the main room had sliding glass doors that opened onto a balcony over-looking the lake.

My neat-freakery had always kept the place spick-and-span when I lived there, but since it slipped into communal ownership, standards had tanked. Sonya, who was renting a small guesthouse tucked behind one of Geneva Bay's historic mansions, had taken full advantage of the unoccupied space—she'd stuffed the closets and half of the bedroom with the overspill of her vast wardrobe and set up an informal makeup studio in one corner where she could do touch-ups during the workday. Daniel was using the space formerly occupied by a king bed as off-season storage for his kayak. The bathroom was chockablock with his grooming products, since he often showered there after hitting the gym. Even Biz had contributed to the scruffiness, having set up a shelf near the sliding door to overwinter her begonias. She claimed the light here was better for them than at our house.

I hadn't gone away to college, but I strongly suspected this was what dorm living was like. Even though it sent my OCD into overdrive, I had to admit that there was a certain coziness to the lived-in look. Butterball certainly seemed right at home sprawled on a comfy blanket between the pajama-clad Sonya and the Slanket-clad Melody, tongue-bathing his nether regions. The curtains were closed to facilitate TV watching, and I was glad. I couldn't purge the image of the frozen feet from my mind, and seeing the freezing lake, with its murky blue hue, would only further cement the memory.

"Has anybody heard from Rabbit?" I asked, taking a generous glug of my hot toddy.

Melody and Sonya shared a glance.

"He called off for the rest of the week," Sonya said.

"Off for a *week*?"

"Well, it's really only two-and-a-half days, since we're closed anyway from the twenty-fifth through the twenty-seventh," Melody pointed out.

"Still, that's going to leave us in the lurch. That's not like him." I frowned. Rabbit was one of the most dependable employees I'd ever had. He hadn't taken more than a smoke break in the six months he'd been working for me, and now he was calling off with zero notice after fleeing the catering gig the previous night.

"He didn't explain," Sonya said. "It was a text." She pulled her phone from the pouch in the front of her onesie and held it up for me to see. "That's it—that he'll be off the rest of the week." She tucked the phone away. "Maybe he's sick and needs to quarantine."

"And maybe I'll sprout wings and fly to Jupiter," I muttered.

Something felt off. Rabbit had been increasingly on edge for weeks, culminating in last night's debacle. And now he was going AWOL when he knew we were already short-staffed. I found it especially interesting that he texted nice, understanding Sonya instead of his more cynical boss. That seemed like a classic dodge.

Jarka, our usual server, was on vacation this week. She and her boyfriend Harold, the sweetly irritating head of Geneva Bay's Chamber of Commerce, were traveling to her home country of Bulgaria to see her elderly father. I'd granted the request, but the timing of her trip was far from ideal. The run-up to Christmas was often busy, usually the last big tourist hurrah before the winter doldrums set in. But I hadn't wanted to stand in the way of their meet-the-parents moment. Jarka and Harold's romance had turned more serious recently, and from the lovey-dovey way they looked at each other, it seemed like a Christmastime marriage proposal might be in the offing. We were all pitching in to cover for her, which meant Rabbit handling extra front-of-house tasks. Now, we'd have to shuffle Melody to the server position and get either Sonya or Auntie Biz to back her up. Even if we limited new bookings, we'd barely manage our existing reservations with that kind of skeleton crew.

"Something fishy's going on with Rabbit. I'm worried," Melody said.

She wasn't a suspicious person and was somewhat naïve about the ways of the world, so if this was setting off an alarm bell for her, I had a whole carillon clanging in my head. I didn't like being played. I could feel my blood beginning to simmer.

"I'm going over to his mom's house to get to the bottom of this," I resolved. "I'll bring him some soup."

"That's nice of you," Sonya said.

"Nice, schmice. I'll be bringing Trojan Horse chicken soup, to get me through the door so I can suss out what's really going on. I've vouched for him to his parole officer and to the judge in his custody case. I'm not going to let him mess up his life." I knew that lying was part and parcel of the disease of addiction, but that didn't mean I had to be okay with it. "If he's falling off the wagon," I continued, "I'm going to get him back on board even if I have to hogtie him and chuck him back on myself."

I pushed the literal cold case I'd witnessed earlier that afternoon out of my mind as I pulled my Jeep Wrangler in front of the house Rabbit shared with his mother. It was a modest one-story rectangle of a place, about ten miles south of town, with a two-car garage and aluminum siding the color of a manila envelope. A string of Christmas lights ran in a neat row along the gutters, and some kind of inflatable decoration slumped in the yard, waiting for its nightly revivification. Evergreen bushes, whittled into exacting little cubes, lined the front walk. While southern Wisconsin contained a few chichi enclaves like Geneva Bay, modest, quasi-rural hamlets like this were much more the norm. The neighborhood felt like a bastion of Midwestern solidity.

As I stepped out of my Jeep and walked toward the door, the frigid air twanged my lungs with a burning, menthol chill. Characterizing Wisconsin winter weather as especially cold was akin to saying certain types of hellfire were especially toasty. Still, this level of knife-blade frostiness was unusual for December.

I'd imagined that the snow sculpting competition had been put (figuratively) on ice after the discovery of the dead body, and I couldn't help wondering if the participants might feel some relief at the postponement. I wasn't sure how they'd keep their fingers from going numb in this cold.

I rang the doorbell and pasted on a smile, holding the soup before me like a bouquet of flowers. A short, barrel-chested woman of about seventy opened the door. She took a step forward and propped the storm door open with her hip.

"Can I help you?"

"I'm here to see Rabbit. Is he home?"

As she scanned me up and down, her dark green eyes formed penetrating little crescents, feathered at the sides by crow's feet. A strong jaw and weathered features told the story of a life of long hours and not enough rest. Although the resemblance to Rabbit in her facial features left little doubt that they were kin, her figure was altogether different from his. While he looked like a collection of wires packed loosely into skin, she was solid as a cinder block and appeared just as immovable. Even the fuzzy fleece zip-up jacket she wore did little to soften her. It's not often I'm intimidated by senior citizens who are a foot shorter than me, but if I ever squared off with Rabbit's mom in a bar fight, I didn't like my chances.

A blond girl of about six edged up behind the woman and peeked around her hip. She looked up at me, blue eyes wide as a Kewpie doll's. She shared the same fireplug sturdiness as her grandmother, but any further resemblance was tempered by her angel's face and her small, dimpled hands shyly clasped in front of her body.

I smiled at her and turned to the older woman. "I'm Delilah O'Leary, Rabbit, I mean Robert's, boss."

Hearing my name, the woman unstiffened by a degree. "Maureen Blakemore," she said, giving my hand a firm shake. "Robert's mother."

"And you must be Everleigh," I said to the little girl. "I've seen a million pictures of you on your dad's phone." I stuck out my hand to greet her.

The girl reached for my proffered hand, dainty as a princess waiting for her ring to be kissed. "Nice to meet you, Daddy's boss," she lisped. The reason for the hiss on her *s*'s was revealed when she flashed a cautious smile—a space gaped from the place her front teeth should've occupied.

"Ah," I said, "'All I Want for Christmas Is My Two Front Teeth' must be on repeat in your house this year."

Everleigh shook her head determinedly. "Nope. I want a purple sparkly Batman unicorn bed with curtains and a slide. These"—she pointed to her tooth gap—"were only worth two bucks according to the Tooth Fairy, so I can just buy new ones from my allowance if I need them. But Daddy says a real Batman unicorn bed costs a lot, so that's what I want Santa to bring me. Santa's got probably millions of dollars."

I laughed as her grandmother laid an affectionate hand on the girl's head. "Your little wheels are always turning, aren't they?" she said.

"Is Rabbit home?" I asked again. "I brought him some soup."

Maureen turned to her granddaughter. "Everleigh, honey, me and Miss O'Leary need to talk. Can you set that soup in the kitchen for me, and then go on to your room and finish up that friendship bracelet you were working on for Daddy's Christmas present?"

Everleigh gasped. "Nana! It's a *surprise*."

"I won't breathe a word," I said.

"Double pinky swear? It's the strongest kind of swear," Everleigh said.

I handed the soup to Maureen, took off my gloves, and enacted the inviolable ritual oath. "I double pinky swear."

Satisfied, Everleigh skipped off into the house, clutching the soup container.

Once the girl was out of range, Maureen turned back to face me. Instead of inviting me inside, she let the storm door fall shut and stepped onto the front stoop.

"Robert isn't here," she said. The creases on her face, which had arranged themselves into kindly furrows in her granddaughter's presence, morphed into a frown. "I hoped he was at the restaurant, doing an extra shift or something, but since you're here looking for him, I guess not."

I shook my head. "So you don't know where he is?"

"Nope. It's not like him to miss a minute of his time with Everleigh," she continued, "but he skipped out this morning without saying where he was headed."

"I'm worried about Rabbit. I thought he might be sick."

She looked at me quizzically. "What made you think he was sick?"

"He texted our sous chef to say he'd be out for the rest of the week."

Maureen Blakemore's frown deepened. She wrapped her arms around herself, but I got the impression it wasn't the chilly air that gave her the shivers.

"Are you worried about him?" I asked.

"Of course I'm worried about him. I've been worrying about that boy his whole life."

"But more so lately?" I asked.

"Yeah." She patted her pockets and then looked up at me. "Times like this, I wish I still smoked."

"Any idea what's going on with him?" I asked. "Do you think he's drinking again?"

"Maybe. But if I had to guess, I'd say it was something else."

"What kind of something else?" I asked.

"I can't say for sure. After I went to bed last night, I got up to use the restroom and heard him on the phone. Thought maybe he's seeing someone. When I saw you pull up, I thought you might be his mystery woman." Her gaze was intense, burning with suspicion. "Are you?"

"No," I assured her.

"So there's nothing between you and him? You brought him soup because . . . ?" She rolled her wrist, urging me to fill in the blanks. "I mean it's nice and all, but above and beyond the call of duty for a boss."

I decided to be straight with her. The bleak winter darkness was gathering around us, and Maureen Blakemore didn't strike me as someone who spent a lot of time beating around the bush. "I brought him soup because I feel like something shady is going on, and I wanted to check it out for myself."

She gave a single grave nod of her head. "Well, he was definitely on the phone to someone last night, and he definitely didn't want anyone to hear what he was saying. By how he was talking, struck me that it was a woman. He's always a little nervous talking to women, and that's how he sounded."

"You think Rabbit's involved with someone?" The thought that he could be tangled up in a love affair with whomever had left the high-heeled tracks in the snow occurred to me on the night of the party, but only fleetingly. Now I wondered if I'd been too hasty to dismiss it.

"I know you'll think it's nosy for me to listen in," she said, apparently taking my astonishment at the suggestion of Rabbit having a secret lover for surprise at her eavesdropping. "You deal with alcoholics long as I have, you're gonna learn that privacy is for suckers. Robert's dad drank his way through a liver before he was fifty. He couldn't get on the transplant list because he couldn't stay sober long enough to prove he wouldn't drink his way through another one. Died at fifty-two."

"I'm sorry," I said.

She swatted away my sympathy. "It is what it is. God deals the hands, and we got to play 'em. Anyways, I didn't hear what Robert and the other person were talking about, but I heard him say something about money."

"Money," I repeated.

My thoughts flew back to the confrontation I'd witnessed that morning at the snow sculpting competition. That had been about money, too. The older woman accused Adrian Hoffman of buying things with funds he'd swindled or stolen from her. But surely the two things weren't related?

"Could he be dealing?" I asked. Years ago, Rabbit had been involved in a scheme to steal and resell prescription medications.

She shrugged. "Nothing in this world surprises me. Robert's a hard worker, but he's been tempted by easy money before. I know better than to think that this time'll be different."

Pity tugged at my heart. Bitter experience was hard

baked into her words, but the tenderness in her eyes betrayed her. She might talk as if she didn't have faith that Rabbit could really change, but it seemed obvious that her rigid façade was a coping mechanism—her way to avoid tempting the gods. If she didn't give voice to her hopes, maybe misfortune would pass her by this time.

A muffler-less pickup rolled down the street, the percussive cough of its exhaust causing us to fall silent until it passed.

"I heard that you're moving away soon," I said.

Maureen's eyes fixed on me. I hadn't meant the question to sound judgmental, although as soon as it was out of my mouth I realized that it could seem like I was attributing Rabbit's swerve off the rails to her imminent departure. She was having none of it.

"Yeah, Rabbit's moving into his own place. It's about time he stood on his own two feet."

"Does he have somewhere lined up?" I asked. "The housing market around here is tight."

"Look," she said, "I know Robert thinks highly of you and I'm grateful to you for giving him a job, but if he's fallen back into his old ways, that's on him. I love my son. I've devoted the better part of the last two decades to rescuing that boy from his demons. When he was locked up, I wore a groove in the roads between here and the penitentiary. And before that, I tried my best with his father, for all the good it did." She took a deep breath of the cold air, responding with a phlegmy cough when it walloped her lungs.

When she recovered, she continued, "I smoked for fortysomething years. You can hear for yourself what it did to my chest. I got a boyfriend, Pedro, down in Galveston. He's a mailman. He can't call it quits for two or three more years or he'll miss out on a pension. We've been together long-distance for five years, but we only get to see each other a few weeks every year. I drove a school bus for twenty-seven years, got up at four thirty every morning. Now that I'm retired, I'm ready to have a life of my own, and take things a little easier. Pedro's condo is only two miles from the ocean. The ocean air is good for me. Pedro's good for me. I deserve something good."

"You do," I agreed.

She looked back toward the house. "'Course I'll miss that little girl like crazy. Luckily, Everleigh's mom's got a good head on her shoulders. She comes from a good family, and they're around to help. They managed for years when Robert was locked up. Everleigh's mom is going to do whatever it takes to keep her safe, even if that means cutting Robert off."

She reached for the handle of the storm door, making it clear with her body language that the subject was closed. "I made a vow to myself," she said. "No matter what, I'm not going to stick around here just to try to pull him out of whatever mess he's gotten himself tangled up in this time." She took a step toward the door, but stopped and leveled a hard gaze at me. "You shouldn't either. 'Cuz one of these days, he's gonna pull somebody down with him."

CHAPTER 7

I was awakened early the next morning, as usual, by the naggingly insistent paws of a sixteen-pound tabby.

Pat. Pat. Pat. Rreoww. Pat. Pat. Pat. Rreoww! Roughly translated: *Mom, I'm starving. If you don't feed me right* MEOW *I might actually* die *of hunger.*

"Okay, Butterbutt," I groaned. "Give me a minute."

This time of year, when the sky stayed pitch black until well past seven a.m., it was hard to muster the willpower to extract myself from the cozy cocoon of my down comforter. I rolled over and picked up my phone. I was surprised to see a message from Capone. He was supposed to have driven to O'Hare early this morning to rendezvous with his mother, son, and granddaughter for their holiday cruise.

Can you come down to the station? We need to take your witness statement.

I rubbed my bleary eyes. *Huh? Witness statement?* Surely a dozen people had seen exactly what I'd seen at the snow sculpting competition. Other than the heated argument Capone and I witnessed, I couldn't say I remembered anything remarkable about the events prior to seeing the dead person's feet. As I threw off the covers, it dawned on me that if Capone hadn't left by now, he'd almost certainly be missing his flight and therefore his cruise. I remembered what he'd said about the department being shorthanded. While the cause and manner of the snow-bound person's death probably hadn't been established yet, it seemed unlikely that he or she accidentally fell inside a packed mound of snow. Capone, who'd spent more than a decade with the Chicago PD, was one of the few officers with significant experience leading suspicious death investigations. Given the very public nature of the body's discovery, the department would be under pressure to solve the mystery. No doubt he'd felt unable to leave in the midst of this.

I felt a pang of remorse. A hundred times, I'd wished that he and I could pass a cozy Christmas together. I sent a silent curse to whatever evil fairy had granted my heart's desire in this twisted way.

An hour later, I found myself back at the Geneva Bay Police Department. The mood had shifted sharply from the previous day, when the major concerns had been peddling iffy roasts and pilfering chocolate waffle topping.

Officer Stanhope, manning the front desk, looked haggard, the usual rosy glow of his complexion replaced by a washed-out pallor.

I held up a quart container of the Trojan Horse soup I'd made the previous night. I'd cooked up a whole stockpot full, intending to bank the surplus in the deep freezer. But, as Stanhope had observed the previous day, I rarely came to the PD empty-handed. Food was my love language, my gratitude language, my sympathy language, my "thank you for your service" language. Really my everything language. I spoke food better than I spoke English.

"You look like you could use this," I said.

"You ain't lying."

He took the container and quickly filled me in. Capone was indeed missing his family's holiday cruise. Since he was leading the investigation, the *SS Capone Family Christmas* would have to set sail without him. But even though he was going to be around this week, I had little hope of actually seeing him.

"Why did this have to happen three days before Christmas?" Stanhope grumbled. "Now I'm probably not gonna be home for Christmas dinner. It's gonna be all-hands-on-deck 'til we get this homicide solved."

"Homicide?" I said, surprised to hear him use the word so definitively. Typically, cops were careful about using a term like that before all the information was known.

"You know why you're here, right? Capone told you?"

I shook my head. "All the text said was that I should come in and make a statement. But I don't know anything more about the death than what everybody else saw."

"Well, for starters, you may have been one of the last people to see the victim alive."

"I don't know what you mean," I said. "Whoever owned those feet was definitely dead when I saw them."

Stanhope waved me around to his side of the large desk and pulled up a rolling stool for me to sit on. "Take a look at this."

He entered a password, then clicked through a few nested folders until he reached what he wanted to show me. If Capone was notably conscientious about keeping evidence close to his chest, Stanhope had the opposite reputation. His loose lips could sink a whole fleet.

He clicked again and a black-and-white video popped up on his monitor. A single angle, taken from high up, showed a wide swath of gently rolling land. The backs of half a dozen large homes could be seen in the distance. Everything was still, save for the swirling eddies of snow the wind kicked up every few seconds.

"This is security camera footage from one of the golf courses at the Grand Bay. Taken the night before last," Stanhope explained. He double-clicked on a portion of the image to zoom in on one of the houses.

"Is that . . . ?"

"Yeah, that place is owned by Adrian and Daffi Hoffman. You catered their party the night this was taken. The Grand Bay's got real good-quality security cameras. They don't do things by halves over at that place, that's for dang sure."

I leaned closer and peered at the video. A figure was visible on the home's second-story balcony, standing against the railing. Although I agreed that the footage was surprisingly good quality considering that it was taken on a snowy night, it was still impossible to make out any distinguishing features. The night vision image made the person look spectral, a fuzzy, white, person-shaped blur. If I had to guess, I'd say whoever it was faced away from the railing, toward the house. The only thing I could say with certainty is that, based on where the railing hit, the person appeared to be tall.

"Who is that?" I asked.

"Keep watching," Stanhope said. "And brace yourself."

The person on the balcony stood almost motionless for a few more moments. At first, he or she appeared to be alone, but then another figure dipped into the frame. The two appeared to be facing each other, presumably having a conversation. Again, it was impossible to see if the new character in this little TV drama was a man or a woman. They appeared to be shorter than the other person, but even that could've been a function of the camera angle. Then, without warning, the smaller person shoved the taller one, causing him or her to fly violently backward, over the railing. As the figure plummeted two stories from the balcony to the ground, they completed most of a full rotation in the air and landed in a belly-flop position. The other figure ran to the railing and leaned over, but then drew back into the shadow cast by the house, out of the camera's view.

I gasped. Looking at the video's timestamp, this would've taken place just after the party ended. Sonya, Melody, and I were still downstairs, and maybe Piper and Daniel, too. I hadn't noticed exactly what time they'd left. And Daffi's family was certainly there, on the same floor as the balcony, only a few doors down. Given how quickly the push happened, it was possible, likely even, that the victim hadn't had the chance to cry out. But how had none of us noticed a body plummeting past the large windows and lying in the backyard?

My answer came in the following seconds of the video. The ground where the body fell sloped steeply down toward the golf course, the incline only somewhat lessened by the mounded snow that had been cleared from the rear patio and path and placed there. When the body hit the ground, it slid down the icy slope, moving so incrementally that I had to check that the video wasn't playing in slow-motion. The body slid at least twenty feet downhill before passing beyond the field of view of the camera. With the body traveling so far, the person wouldn't have been easily visible to anyone in the Hoffman house or the other homes nearby.

"Oh, that's awful." I cringed away from the monitor. "You're sure it's the same person whose body ended up at the snow sculpting contest downtown?"

"Capone's over at the resort, trying to confirm that very thing, I suppose. He must think there's a connection, though, since he requested this footage from resort security. Must've been one of the guests from that party you catered." He used his stout index finger to click the computer mouse, closing the video.

"But how did whoever was pushed off the balcony get from Daffi and Adrian's backyard to the inside of a snow sculpture?" I asked.

"That kind of speculation is above my pay grade," he said with a shrug. "What a way to go, though, eh? Becoming a human snowman."

As he'd been speaking, the rational part of my mind had kicked into gear, pushing aside my shock at the horrific event the camera captured. Understanding finally took hold.

A tall figure. A guest from the party. A forgotten coat.

And just like that, I knew. Those frozen feet belonged to Natasha La Cotti.

CHAPTER 8

Natasha La Cotti. It had to be. The person who'd fallen from the balcony was unusually tall, like Natasha. If she'd exited the party in the fashion I saw on that video, that would go a long way toward explaining why she left on a frigid night without her coat on.

Capone was off conducting whatever sleuthing needed to be done on-site, so Stanhope took my statement. I shared my suspicions with him, and he wrote Natasha's name in block capitals on a Post-it note, which he dutifully affixed to Capone's desk. I had my doubts about that mechanism of conveying important investigatory information, so I also texted my theory about the body's identity directly to Capone and waited for his reply.

And waited.

Nothing, not even a thumbs-up emoji.

It wasn't unusual for him to go dark when in the midst of an investigation, but it was nonetheless frustrating. Capone's resemblance to Clark Kent went further than just his reading glasses—I was starting to get an inkling of how Lois Lane must feel when her man suddenly needed to make an urgent visit to a phone booth halfway through every date. I tried to push it out of my mind. Even if my hunch was proven right, Capone couldn't be that far behind me in putting two and two together. He'd requested the footage from the resort, so he must already have suspected there was a connection. Besides, that very official Post-it from Officer Stanhope awaited him whenever he got back to the station.

Still, instead of heading home after my visit to the police station, I found my Jeep taking the turnoff toward the Grand Bay Resort and Spa. I knew from bitter personal experience how meticulous Capone was about going over a crime scene to gather evidence, and I had a strong inkling that he'd still be at the Hoffmans' place. Much as I wanted to leave Capone alone to his work, my control-freak tendencies were too deeply ingrained to leave open the possibility that he hadn't gotten the info about Natasha La Cotti. What if he hadn't seen my text? What if he was out here flying blind, without that crucial piece of intel?

My hunch about his whereabouts proved correct. When I pulled up in front of the Hoffman house a few minutes later, I found one of Geneva Bay's crime scene investigation vans parked in the driveway beside Capone's unmarked black Dodge Charger. The van's rear doors were open, and a technician stood there, loading equipment. I recognized him from my many food drop-off forays to the station. Darrin Jankowski had short black hair, a thin-lipped mouth filled with perfect teeth, and the kind of prim, meticulous appearance you might expect from a person who spent their days putting individual strands of hair into tiny evidence bags and measuring tire treads down to the millimeter. Geneva Bay was blessedly short of violent crime, so his remit tended to be heavy on vacation home break-ins and insurance fires and light on dead bodies. Still, his large luminous eyes, fixed in a perpetually wary expression, seemed set to seek out threats.

I climbed out of my Jeep and walked toward him, calling out a hello.

He raised a gloved hand to hail me and walked over. His cheeks and nose were kissed by the cold, bright as cherries. "Did you come to see Capone?"

"Yeah," I said, flashing a sheepish smile.

Now that I was here, I felt as out of place as a chaperone at prom. Although I'd often brought food to the station when Capone was working long hours, a girlfriend turning up at an active crime scene wasn't the done thing, even for a department as low-key as Geneva Bay's.

"He's in the yard," Jankowski said, his large eyes slightly quizzical. "I'll walk you back there."

"Are you about finished with your search?" I asked.

"Yeah, we've been at it since the crack of dawn. Me and Capone are the last ones here. Thank god, too, because it's colder than hell's frozen backside." He rubbed his hands briskly together.

We tromped along an already well-trodden path of compressed snow around the side of the house, following dozens of sets of footprints. "I hate outdoor crime scenes," he grumbled. "Cold is better than heat in terms of preserving evidence, but with wind and snow like we've had the past couple of days, you just know the evidence is going to be jacked up ten ways to Sunday. Not to mention that we only found out after the fact that this *was* the crime scene."

As we rounded the corner of the house, a blast of arctic wind walloped us. Rather than dying down, the gusts kept on buffeting us as we made our way forward.

Noting the lack of crime scene tape, I remarked, "Don't you need to close the area off?"

"There's no way we'd be able to mark and maintain a perimeter in winds like this. Tape would be blown all over kingdom come. Anyway, there's not too much foot traffic on a day like today," he replied. "We had a couple of uniforms come out to keep any nosy civilians away, but there wasn't much for them to do. It's freezing out here, so today's kind of dead."

I grimaced, but the unfortunate pun was carried away on the gusts along with the frosty clouds of our exhalations. We walked a little farther and he pointed down the slope, where a solitary figure in a black parka stood in the middle of a snow-covered fairway.

"There's your guy."

In the summertime, the view would've taken in a lush green golf course, dotted with trees, sand traps, and percolating water fountains. Now, though, the trees were stripped of leaves, the water frozen solid, and the links looked as bleak as the Siberian tundra. Even the sky overhead was forbidding. The sun perched low, a faint dot of white, alternately concealed and revealed by the banks of ragged gray clouds that raced across the dull backdrop. Snow crystals eddied around the open ground in angry vortexes. With each wind gust, they formed, then collapsed, and then formed again.

I looked toward the Hoffmans' patio, noting the mound of frozen snow where the video had shown Natasha's body impacting the ground. Some irrational part of my brain expected to see her there, splayed out where she landed. I cast a glance up to the second-story balcony. I'd barely noticed it the night of the party, only vaguely registering that it would be a nice place for a pre-dinner drink in the summertime. Now, though, it seemed to loom over me, forming a menacing protrusion from the window-filled back wall.

"Do I need to be careful where I step?" I asked Jankowski.

"In terms of disturbing evidence, no. We've already been over this whole area. If there was a scrap of evidence here, we either collected it or it was blown halfway to Lake Michigan over the past few days. But you *do* want to watch your step going down the slope. It's a sheet of ice. Torvald fell on his ass and slid all the way to the bottom. Rettberg got it on video." He let out a low guffaw, but quickly straightened his features into their usual sober expression. "I might actually enter the video into evidence, since it'll show how the body got from there"—he pointed up to the balcony—"to there." He pointed to the bottom of the hill, where Capone was. "But first I'm going to put it on a loop on the monitor in the conference room at the station," he added with a sly smile.

We picked our way carefully down the slope and rendezvoused with Capone. He somehow managed to look handsome and polished despite being bundled up like a polar explorer. By contrast, my winter gear made me look as if a fourth grader had tried to create a life-sized statue of the Michelin man using Gore-Tex and yarn.

"Delilah." Capone said my name slowly, dismay and confusion forming a groove between his eyebrows.

Not the warm welcome I'd hoped for, but probably what I should've expected. It was one thing for me to rock up at his office with a tray of lasagna on a random Thursday when he was busy preparing to give evidence in a robbery case. Showing up at an active crime scene—involving a murder that I'd been summoned to give evidence about that very morning, no less—was a dicier proposition. When things got serious, Capone tended to push aside all distractions, and judging by the past, *I* definitely fell into that category. Being shut out didn't feel good, but I understood. If a boyfriend of mine casually strolled into my kitchen in the middle of a slammed dinner service, he'd get far worse than the perturbed frown that Capone directed at me.

"Uh, hi." I gave him a wave.

Seeming to sense the awkwardness between us, Jankowski said, "Well, I better get back and start processing everything."

Capone, ever the professional, said, "Thanks for your work out here this morning, Darrin. I know these conditions are challenging."

Capone and I watched as Jankowski picked his way back up the slope and disappeared around the house. The sound of the whipping wind blessedly covered the uncomfortable silence.

Finally, Capone turned toward me. "To what do I owe this pleasure?" His tone was polite but frosty.

"I think the dead woman is Natasha La Cotti," I blurted.

"I know."

"Oh," I said.

For a long moment, neither of us spoke.

"Well, I guess I'll get going," I said. "I just wanted to make sure you got my text or the message from Stanhope."

"I got your text, but I didn't have time to reply," he said. "I was planning to call you later to find out what your line of reasoning was."

"Natasha's coat wasn't claimed at the end of the party. It seemed bizarre that she'd have left that night without it. But if she was already dead by then, it makes sense. Plus, she was very tall. From the security camera video, it looked like whoever got pushed over the balcony was unusually tall. I think the railing would've prevented an average-sized person from going over. For a smaller person, it would hit them lower and their center of gravity would've been below the railing's height. But Natasha was taller than me and she was wearing heels. With enough force, it's easy to imagine how she'd topple right over."

"Stanhope showed you, a witness and potential suspect, video evidence of the incident?" He took in a deep inhale and shut his eyes briefly. When he opened them again, his demeanor had shifted from broodingly intense to deeply irritated. "And, no, he didn't relay your message."

I grimaced. "It's basically what I just told you. He wrote 'Natasha La Cotti' on a Post-it on your desk."

I'd been hoping for an "attagirl!" for revealing the victim's identity, but instead I'd unintentionally narc'd on Capone's sweetly incompetent colleague.

When Capone remained silent, I decided that was my cue to leave. "Well, since you seem to have things under control," I said, "I'll head home."

I took a step toward the house, but then stopped. "Wait, how did *you* figure out it was Natasha La Cotti? You must've connected the dead body in the snow sculpture to the Hoffmans' party pretty quickly if you asked the resort to pull the footage. How did you come to realize the two things were tied together?"

He hesitated for a moment, and I could almost hear his internal struggle. Sure, I was his girlfriend and I was asking a perfectly reasonable question. But I was also a potential witness in a murder investigation. I'd seen Capone question his own mother, for heaven's sake.

"Look," I said. "Stanhope already took my statement. You're not going to be able to do much with my witness testimony anyway, unless you're really desperate. Even if you do find the killer, the girlfriend of the lead detective isn't going to be the prosecutor's first choice for a star witness. I'm tainted goods. There's no point in keeping me at arm's length. I'm more useful to you as a sounding board." I moved a little closer to him. "And you've got to admit that I'm not half-bad at murder investigations."

"You're too quick to put yourself in danger."

"And you're too slow to realize that you can't stop a grown woman from making her own choices," I countered.

He looked to the sky for help, and finding none forthcoming, he relented. "Fine. I followed the snow. Early on the morning after the party, before sunrise, dump trucks and front loaders rolled into the lakefront park to fill up the cylinder molds with snow, ready for the contest," he explained. "Do you remember the weather that night?"

I nodded and looked toward the house, recalling how I followed Rabbit's footprints and some high-heeled tracks through the falling snow. "Yeah," I said. "We were supposed to get only a dusting, but it ended up being pretty heavy on and off. We probably got over six inches in all."

"The storm was at its worst in the early morning hours," he said. "The snowfall was so heavy at that point that the crew doing the work could hardly see. They were blindly scooping snow from the dump trucks with an excavator and tipping it into the molds.

After every few shovel loads, one of them would climb on top and tamp down the surface so it would be evenly packed."

"I can't believe no one noticed that one of the shovel loads contained a body," I said. "Surely someone would've seen it fall into the mold or the person tamping down the snow would've noticed something was off?"

"The visibility was terrible, and they were in a hurry to get it done."

A shiver ran up my spine, no doubt caused by the fact that the longer I stood still, the more my feet turned into blocks of ice. But underneath that external trigger, there was a deeper source to the chill—the thought of Natasha La Cotti's lifeless body being trucked around like a pile of dirt by workers using heavy equipment and then carelessly packed into a frigid sarcophagus.

Wrapping my arms around myself, I said, "I still don't see how that connects to the party."

He pointed beyond the fairway where we stood toward the ski slopes. He unzipped his coat a few inches and pulled a pair of binoculars from an inner pocket. Handing them to me, he pointed again. "You see those machines?"

I raised the binoculars to my eyes and dialed the distant view into focus. The chairlift was making its perpetual round from the bottom of the hill to the top. Skiers in brightly colored gear swished down the slope, heedless of the fact that a murder investigation was going on so close by. I panned to the left of the ski hill, where the low profile of the lodge was just visible. I remembered looking out from the windows on the night of the party, seeing the lights from the ski area and the lodge twinkling in the darkness.

"What am I looking at?" I asked.

He tipped my face to the right and indicated an area beside the ski slope where three large devices stood.

"The things that look like jet engines?" I asked.

"Yeah," he replied. "Those are the Grand Bay's snow machines. The resort uses them to make snow for the ski slopes, obviously, but also to supply the snow for the contest. All the snow that filled those molds came from right over there. Using the machines makes sure the snow they get is fresh, easily packable, and a uniform consistency. They ran the machines and mounded up the snow so the excavator could easily pile it into the dump trucks."

"So you figured if this is where the snow came from, the body had to come from here, too," I said. As soon as I said it, though, another possibility occurred to me. "But how could you be sure the body wasn't added later? Couldn't someone have come in the hours between the snow delivery and the opening of the contest, shoveled out a space in one of the cylinders, dropped Natasha's body in, and then covered her back over?"

"The contest organizers had a guard stationed out there all night to make sure no one tampered with the snow. He would've noticed."

"If the weather made it hard to see, though, maybe someone snuck in without the guard clocking him," I suggested.

He shook his head. "It crossed my mind, too, but you saw how high those cylinders were. Natasha wasn't a small person. I don't think even someone my size could heft her body up a ladder. You'd need to set up a pulley or use a crane or I don't even know what. Then you'd have to dig out a good-sized space to put the body in, then repack the snow on top. It couldn't be done quickly enough or discreetly enough not to be noticed by the guard. Even Stanhope wouldn't have let something like that slip past him." He paused. "Well, maybe Stanhope could manage it."

Despite the initial standoffishness Capone had displayed when I showed up, as we slipped into our familiar back-and-forth theorizing, his attitude gradually softened. If I looked hard enough, I could see glimmers of the familiar Capone shining through the brick wall exterior he erected whenever he got caught up in a case.

"So you backtracked to the place the snow came from and hoped you'd find out who your Jane Doe was," I said.

"Exactly," he replied. "Once I found out there were functioning cameras around the property, I asked the Grand Bay's security people to send the footage over. I wasn't sure they'd yield anything, though. The cameras don't move. They're trained on the structures, not on the open spaces, so none of the angles show the snow-making machines or the snow mounds. We weren't going to be able to see the moment when the body ended up there. A few of us spent last night scrolling through the videos, hoping to see the victim or the killer pass across one of the screens. Fortunately, I happened upon the footage showing the moment Natasha was pushed. From there, it was pretty straightforward to get a definitive ID. You mentioned the missing coat when you and Daniel were talking yesterday. I interviewed Daffi, Adrian, and their daughter to see if any of the party guests were AWOL. A housekeeper at the hotel confirmed that Natasha's bed hasn't been slept in since the day of the party."

"That still leaves a big question," I pointed out. "I

saw on the video how the body hit the ground there"—I indicated the spot just under the balcony—"and then slid down the icy embankment. She would've come to rest just beneath where we're standing, right?"

Below us, there was a gully of sorts. On the far side, the ground sloped down from the house. Then there was a small depression before the ground rose gradually toward the fairway where we stood. The fairway ran parallel to the line of houses and the gully ran all alongside it. Where we stood, on the fairway itself, the topography flattened out for a few hundred feet before rising again as it neared the ski slope. There was no amount of momentum that could've carried a dead body any farther than the gully. I turned around to face the snow machines and the ski slope, which had to be a good couple hundred yards from us.

"So how did she end up in a mound of snow all the way over there?" I asked.

A frown tugged down the corners of his mouth. "There aren't any cameras that cover the space between the house and the bottom of the ski slope. It's a black hole, a gap in our knowledge. As best as I can figure it, the killer carried her there. Jankowski found a few partial shoeprints in the snow between the place the body fell and the ski slope, but no drag marks."

"*Carried?*" I repeated. I understood the reason for his deepening frown. Capone himself had pointed out that Natasha was a large person. She'd been thinner than me, but even if her bones were made of feathers, I could hardly imagine who would have the strength to hoist a six-foot-tall corpse over their shoulder, cut across the fairway, and dump it near the ski slope. I looked again at the expanse of ground between us and the snow machines. "Well, that narrows your list

of suspects considerably," I said. "It was either the Incredible Hulk or Dwayne 'The Rock' Johnson."

He chuckled unhappily. "It makes no sense," he conceded. "Maybe Jankowski can get more information
once he analyzes the shoeprints, a size or shoe type,
something. It's hard to believe anyone could've carried the body that far, but like I said, we didn't find
any drag marks or other sets of prints to indicate that
someone else helped. Mind you, the scene had been
snowed on and windblown for two days before we
realized what we were dealing with. The footprints
could be anybody's. They weren't well-defined enough
for Jankowski to make a full impression."

"Could you collect the shoes everyone at the party
was wearing and try to match them against the prints?"
I asked.

"Even if it was one of the party guests, there's been
plenty of time between that night and now for the killer
to dispose of a pair of shoes."

We were silent for a moment, each scanning back
and forth from the house to the ski slope like meerkats
on the lookout for danger. Another brutal gust of wind
kicked up, slicing through my coat and setting my teeth
on edge.

When it died down, I said, "I've got a proposition for
you."

His eyebrows arched up, his interest piqued.

"I've only been out here for a few minutes and I'm
a popsicle. You've been out here for hours. You must
be freezing. I bet you haven't eaten anything, either."

A small nod of his head granted the point.

"Me either." Despite the grim backdrop, my empty
stomach had been pinging me with alerts that no food
had passed my lips since the previous night's dinner.

"And if you made this much progress, I bet you've been up all night, too."

"Yeah, we were already late in starting since we didn't know about the death until yesterday. We're playing catch-up."

"Well, you're not going to catch a killer if you faint from hunger. You promised me a hot chocolate at the snow sculpting competition," I continued. "I'm holding you to that. The restaurant at the Grand Bay makes a mean cocoa."

"Delilah, I'm in the middle of an investigation . . ." he began.

"Standing out here isn't getting you any closer to solving this. Jankowski told me you'd been all over the scene already."

"I have work to do . . ."

"I know," I said, taking him by the arm and pulling him back toward our cars. "This isn't a date, at least not my idea of one." Looking back toward the balcony from which Natasha La Cotti had plunged to her death, I added, "And I sure as hell hope it's not your idea of a date, either."

CHAPTER 9

Capone and I ordered a late breakfast and drinks—cocoa for me, coffee for him—and settled into a private corner booth at the hotel's main restaurant. Capone, as usual, chose the seat that faced the restaurant. It was part of a habitual pattern that I gradually came to notice over the months we'd been together—he never completely let his guard down. His posture never totally slackened. The wheels in his mind spun from the moment he awakened until lights out, and probably while he dreamt. Even when he was off duty, he noticed names, scanned faces, kept careful check of the time, as if he might, at any moment, be called to give evidence. If there was a crowd of people, he never turned his back to it, as if even a cozy hotel restaurant decked out with garlands and twinkling lights could suddenly explode into an orgy of violence.

Even I felt distinctly on edge. From the safety of the restaurant's warm interior, the landscape looked positively inviting. The swirling snow, so biting when we were standing in the midst of it, glinted like diamond dust when caught in the sporadic bursts of sunlight. The beauty and festive feel of the room were so sharply at odds with the mystery that weighed on our minds, I had the odd urge to stand up and scream out a warning to the clusters of holidaymakers who surrounded us. I suppressed the impulse and settled in to continue the grim conversation with Capone as we waited for our food and drinks to arrive.

"Has the medical examiner given you any other leads to go on?" I asked. "The video made it look like Natasha was pushed, but is that all there was to it? If she was hit with something, that object might have fingerprints, right?"

He pressed his lips together. "The initial autopsy report won't come back for a few days at least. From what I saw, though, the body was unscathed. No obvious wounds. But whoever killed her might've come back, maybe when they moved her."

"What makes you think that?"

"She was only partially clothed. She had no shoes on and she was wearing only underwear. Witnesses at the party had her wearing high heels, a silk blouse, and trousers. All of those items had been removed from her body."

"Could she have taken them off herself before she was pushed?" I asked. "The video wasn't clear enough to tell if she had clothes on. Maybe she was in the middle of changing when she fell. Or . . ."

He leaned forward, waiting for me to continue.

"Well, when I met her, she came from inside one of the upstairs bedrooms. Hadley Hoffman had been listening outside the door, so I assume Natasha was in there with someone, probably Adrian, since he came from that same room shortly afterward. What if they were having an affair?"

Our server, a bright-faced teenager, came over and laid our drinks and food on the table with cheerful efficiency. I forced a smile, but Capone's expression had darkened. He could manage only the briefest nod as she set his cup before him on its perfect little saucer.

I lowered my voice, even though she'd quickly moved out of earshot. "That would explain why Hadley was so upset—if she overheard some hanky-panky between her father and Natasha."

He gave the idea some consideration. "But your brother-in-law was upstairs, too, right?"

"He came up from the back stairs, not out of the bedroom. Besides, he's totally in love with my sister. No way he'd stray." I was surprised at the vehemence of my defense, but it was true. I couldn't imagine Jonathan cheating on Shea. He doted on her.

"I haven't read your witness statement yet," Capone said. He pulled his plate of eggs Benedict and brussels sprout hash closer. "Tell me what you remember from the party."

I quickly recounted what I'd relayed during my police interview. First there was Hadley's anger upon overhearing the closed-door conversation/assignation and the seeming tension between Natasha, Jonathan, and Adrian that followed. But I didn't have a whole lot more I could elaborate on. Was the encounter odd? Yes. Did it provide someone with a motive for murder? Impossible to say. I couldn't even say for sure what happened to Natasha after she, Adrian, Jonathan, and I came down the stairs. Had Natasha gone back up, continued whatever she was doing before, and met her doom at the hands of whoever she was speaking to? Was Hadley's anger directed toward her—and was it strong enough to cause her to murder the woman?

"Interesting," Capone said, taking a meditative sip of his coffee. "None of them mentioned that incident.

The Hoffmans also said they didn't find any of the missing clothing or shoes in their house, and we didn't see it in our search either."

A knot of unease clenched in my chest. "Are you suggesting the killer removed her clothes and shoes *after* she died?" I swallowed. "Was she assaulted?"

"There weren't any obvious signs of that," he said. "However, if the killer did come back to move her body after the fact, it's possible they undressed her."

"That would explain where her clothes went," I pointed out. "But judging by the look on your face, that's not what you think."

"It's too early to say, but right now I'm not seeing a motive for the killer to move her body or to undress her." He angled his body slightly so he could point out the windows that formed the restaurant's back wall. "The golf course backs up to the row of houses, and that fairway is in full view of all of them." He tipped his chin toward the cluster of homes. Up close, they were impressive in a McMansion-y way, but from this distance they formed a dreary procession. "Even though most of those houses were empty and the visibility was poor that night, why risk moving the body?" He let the rhetorical question hang in the air. "In order for the workers not to have seen her right away, I'm guessing her body must've been covered pretty well by the snow the machines made. But the killer could've just as easily buried her right where she fell. There was plenty of snow right in the Hoffmans' backyard."

"Could the killer have wanted her to end up in the snow sculpture?" I asked.

"Not likely. It wasn't common knowledge that the snow for the contest comes from there. And it was too much of a long shot to assume she wouldn't be discovered when the workers were moving the snow. It was a freak coincidence that the visibility was so poor right then. If anything, the body was more likely to be found over by the ski slopes since that area is more heavily trafficked. And why peel the clothes off a freezing corpse?"

"True," I said. "If there was evidence in her pockets or something like that, it could've been removed without taking her clothes off."

"Of course you do get weirdos who do things like that for kicks, but this doesn't have any of the hallmarks you'd usually see with that kind of thing."

With the possibility of necrophilia seemingly off the table for now, my appetite gradually returned. I sank my teeth into the sweet flakiness of an almond croissant. I'd ordered a Denver omelet, but asked the server to swap out the toast for the delectable pastry. On a day like today, plain bread wasn't going to cut it. The familiar ritual of chewing and swallowing grounded me. If there was an emotional problem that couldn't be solved with food, I had yet to meet it. I licked a bit of powdered sugar from my thumb. "So how do you explain it?"

Capone took another sip of his coffee, and then, realizing it had cooled to an acceptable temperature, knocked it back. He must've been famished. He'd already polished off the savory bacon and brussels sprout hash, and when he dug into his eggs Benedict, I half expected him to unhinge his jaw like a python and swallow it whole. Clearly I wasn't wrong when I'd surmised that the man needed refreshment. I signaled the server to bring another croissant.

"In terms of moving the body," he said, "I can't think of a good motive. The mechanics of it don't seem to make a lot of sense." I pushed the other half of my croissant toward him, and he bit into it before continuing. "There are a lot of theories I haven't even begun to explore. Firstly, she had frostbitten fingers and toes. Frostbite only happens to living tissue. The ME reckons, based on the temperature that night, that it would've taken about an hour for her to get frostbite. That means either that she was already frostbitten before she was pushed, or that she survived the initial fall."

I groaned in dismay. "I saw her toward the end of the party, and her hands weren't frostbitten. So she must've survived the fall. What an awful thought. If one of us had seen her lying there, we might've saved her."

"Too early to say. And for all we know, her injuries may not have been survivable, even with hospital treatment. This is all just guesswork until we have at least preliminary autopsy findings."

"Even if that shows when and how she died, we're still in the dark about the motive," I pointed out.

He nodded. "It's interesting to me that the day the body was found, you and I overheard a woman make threatening statements to Adrian Hoffman, wishing that both he and Daffi would meet their judgment soon."

"Yeah," I agreed. "I have more of a temper than the average person and even for me it's not common to publicly call for someone's death."

He tilted his head thoughtfully, his eyes lighting up with a flicker of amusement. I got the impression he was actively refraining from passing comment.

"*Publicly*," I emphasized.

I brought a forkful of omelet to my lips, enjoying the silky heft of it on my tongue, the sweetness of the diced pepper harmonizing perfectly with the salty smoke of the ham. The satisfying combination of textures helped take some of the chill out of the gruesome topic.

"As far as the missing clothes," he said, pivoting back to the matter at hand, "the simplest explanation is that they were already off her body when she was pushed off that balcony. From what you just told me," he continued, "Hadley could've been angry enough to kill her. Or, if there was some sort of affair going on, Hadley might've told her mother, who caught Natasha and Adrian in the act after the party and pushed her rival over the balcony. Or Natasha and Adrian could've had a lover's quarrel."

He popped the rest of the almond croissant into his mouth just at our server brought me another pastry to replace the one I'd given him.

"Sex seems an obvious reason for taking your clothes off," he said, once she stepped away. "But there are others. Anyone at the party could've had a grudge against her."

The seriousness in his tone sent a little flutter of worry zipping around my mind. The party guests included me, my crew, my niece, and my brother-in-law. Capone's mantra was "keep an open mind," which often translated to "suspect everyone." I realized now that I hadn't looked at my phone in hours, hadn't been in touch with any of them today. Surely, if I'd been called in to give a witness statement, they all had been as well.

"The motive is definitely a question mark," he said, "but what if we focus on who had the means and the opportunity?"

"There was the mystery man," I said. "The party guest that Daniel saw coming out of the house that night after the party. The timing of that lines up with the time of the murder. Maybe if you can show Daniel pictures of the guests, he can pick the guy out of a photo lineup. Did he give you a description?"

"I left a message for him, but he hasn't responded yet. There were only fifty guests, less than half of them men. Daffi sent over the guest list this morning, so we can get started narrowing it down. The description Daniel gave at the snow sculpting competition was pretty broad—good-looking white guy." He paused. "Could be your brother-in-law."

In my shock, I inhaled a puff of powdered sugar from the top of my croissant. I coughed for a moment and then sputtered, "What?"

"The picture on the mantlepiece at your house of your sister's family. Good-looking white guy. Tall. Sounds like the guy Daniel described."

Although his tone was speculative, even nonchalant, I strongly suspected the thought hadn't come to him in that moment. I'd come to admire the man's intellect. When it came to policework, he had a game of three-dimensional chess playing in his mind at all times. But I didn't like finding my family and friends cast in the role of pawns.

I crossed my arms and leaned back in my chair. "Sounds like half the men in Geneva Bay," I countered.

"But half the men in Geneva Bay weren't at that party. Your brother-in-law was. He's an athlete, right? And that's what we're looking for, someone strong enough to carry a body."

I swallowed down a gulp of my cocoa along with my rising sense of anxiety. A memory flashed up in my mind—Jonathan at the brunch, warning his daughter to stay away from Hadley, seemingly trying to discredit anything the girl said on the night of the party, making sure that both Piper and I heard his version of events. His manner had been off, his recitation stilted. I purged the doubt from my mind. "I'm sure it wasn't him. He has bad knees. Besides, he left before the end of the party."

"To go where?"

"Back to the hotel." *Then why didn't he answer his phone when Piper called him for a ride?* I pushed the thought aside, instead saying, "Anyway, he's not the type to commit murder."

The server had replenished Capone's coffee, and he sipped it with slow, deliberate movements. "Anyone can be the type, given the right circumstances."

I sat up straight in my chair and cupped my own mug in my suddenly frigid hands. "Not him. Anyway, Jonathan and Piper are heading back to California today."

"Are they?"

I nodded. "I'm sure they can answer any questions you have over the phone."

Capone took another meditative sip and said, "Right. Well, I have Rettberg looking into everyone's backgrounds and whereabouts, but that will take time. Meanwhile, we can look at one of the obvious suspects." He paused and folded his hands on the table. "Who else was upstairs, for inexplicable reasons, the evening Natasha La Cotti was killed? Who did *you* say acted strange all night and then left the party in a hurry? Who else was likely the only person in that house with a long criminal history?"

He waited for me to fill in the blank, but I couldn't bring myself to say Rabbit's name.

"He wasn't even there when Natasha was pushed," I said. "She died after the party ended. He left early."

"Like your brother-in-law," Capone observed. "Any possibility he circled back?"

I made my voice firm. "No."

"Because he's not the type?" Capone offered. When I didn't reply, he continued, "Like I said, we're running down alibis."

Capone suspected Rabbit, *my* Rabbit. My natural instinct was to jump to his defense. The man had been nothing but reliable. *At least until this week.* He was trying so hard to turn his life around. *Unless he wasn't.* The more I thought about it, the less I could fault Capone for his suspicions. I hadn't even told him the most damning details yet. How Rabbit had mysteriously bunked off work in the aftermath of that party. How he was conducting shady business with someone, doing something he didn't want his mom to know about. How even Rabbit's own mother suspected he was up to no good. I pushed my remaining food away. First the insinuation about Jonathan and now this. Was there anyone in my circle who Capone didn't suspect of murder? Turned out there *were* problems that even the most delicious of pastries couldn't solve.

CHAPTER 10

My conversation with Capone ended abruptly just after he dropped that bombshell, when a text summoned him back to the proverbial Bat Cave. That was probably for the best, since by then I was too unsettled to speak. He departed with a perfunctory kiss, and no intimation of when I might see him again. I was left alone, staring at my half-eaten pastry and half-drunk cocoa. Jonathan was no killer. This was a man who slept in bed beside my sister every night. The weird feeling I'd had about him at the brunch was probably a figment of my imagination. And I knew Rabbit was beyond suspicion. Both men had been gone before the time-stamped video showed Natasha being pushed—a point I made sure to emphasize to Capone.

Still, my conversation with Maureen Blakemore echoed in my mind. When I'd asked her if she thought her son could be dealing drugs, she'd demurred. "Nothing in this world surprises me," she'd said. Rabbit's own mother doubted him. But murder? I thought of myself as a worldly woman. A cynic even. But try as I might, I couldn't see Rabbit as a murderer. Was it possible that I was blinded by loyalty? Could one of my own staff members be up to something nefarious right under my nose?

"*Jefa!*" Daniel's voice rang out across the restaurant.

I looked up to find him walking toward my table. I rose to greet him. "What brings you to the Grand Bay?"

"I'm giving my mother a sightseeing tour, well, mostly a driving tour," he said, gesturing to the arctic landscape outside the glass. "And now we're going to get facials in the spa."

My mouth curved into an amused smile as I pictured my ex-Army, ultra-buff bartender with a hot towel around his head and cucumber slices over his eyelids.

Reading my thoughts, Daniel tsked and waggled his finger at me. "Don't be sexist. One of the benefits of being raised by a widowed mother and three older sisters is that I learned to appreciate pampering. Most men never discover the value of moisturizer, and their complexions show it." He looked around. "What are you doing here?"

"I had breakfast with Capone. Did he reach out to you?"

"Yeah, but I've been busy with my mother," he said. "Do you know what it was about? The message said he needed to ask some questions about that party we catered?"

I figured there was no point trying to soften the news for him. Delicate flowers don't serve six years in the Army Reserve. "You heard about the body they found at the snow sculpting competition?"

He nodded.

"It was Natasha La Cotti." I paused. "You knew her, right?"

Beneath his look of surprise, there was another emotion—the strange look I'd seen on his face the previous day when her name was mentioned. Recognition. But also deep unease.

"Junior! There you are!"

We turned to find an attractive older woman making her way toward us. Her dark, wavy hair was sprinkled through with gray and cut into a shape that framed her strong jaw. Her makeup, although heavy, wasn't over the top—she was clearly a woman who knew how to play up her best features. And, like her son, good features were in ready supply. Dark, playful eyes, straight teeth, and a golden skin tone. She had a candy-red coat slung over her arm.

I did a double take and felt my facial muscles go slack. This was the woman I'd seen at the snow sculpting festival. The woman who confronted Adrian just moments before Natasha's frozen feet had been uncovered. It had never occurred to me that a woman nearing seventy with a New York accent could be Daniel's mother.

I hurried to arrange my face into something resembling a smile as Daniel introduced us.

"*Mamá*, this is my boss, Delilah O'Leary. *Jefa*, this is my mother."

"Angie," the woman said, laying a hand on her chest. "I've heard so much about you, the restaurant, everything."

"Good things, I hope?"

"Of course, though to be honest, I wasn't sure he'd like it here. I grew up in Queens, you know, so I know from cold weather, but he's never lived anywhere like this." She nodded toward the window. "I thought he'd freeze. But he loves it. And I gotta admit that it's beautiful. I didn't realize how much I'd miss the snow, living in PR all these years; it's been forever since I saw any. Guess you don't know what you got 'til it's gone."

She spoke quickly, barely stopping for breath. Other than the lightning-quick cadence of her speech and an accent as thick as East Rivah sludge, the woman before me bore little resemblance to the woman I'd seen threatening Adrian Hoffman. Where before she'd seemed like a powder keg ready to detonate, now she was warm and friendly, drawing me in with a wide smile.

"You must've gotten your fill of seeing snow the other day at the snow sculpting competition. You were there, right?" I prodded.

"Yeah, it's awful what happened, that a dead body could end up in such a beautiful place. Junior told me the police gave the sculptors the all-clear to start again tomorrow so they can finish before Christmas. Personally, I don't know if I could go anywhere near a mound of snow if I'd found that. That's what you said though, right, Junior? That they're restarting tomorrow."

I turned toward Daniel. "Junior?"

Daniel rested a hand on his chest. "*Sí, soy yo.* Daniel Alfonso Castillo, Junior."

"I lost Daniel Senior when Junior was only two years old. He had a heart attack." Angie made the sign of the cross.

"I'm sorry for your loss," I said.

I'd known that Daniel's father was no longer living, but not the exact circumstances. I hadn't come across many people who knew the particular kind of black hole an early loss like that created in your heart. Although losing a parent was one of the first things Daniel and

I bonded over when we met, we handled our losses in a similar way, which is to say burying the pain and rarely letting our feelings see the light of day.

"It really was awful to lose him like that," Angie agreed. "My Daniel retired from the Navy, and then less than a year later, he was dead. Very sudden. Junior joined the Reserve to follow in his father's footsteps." She touched her son's arm. "The military is a good career. I don't understand why you left."

"*Mamá, ¡Ay bendito!* We've been through this. It wasn't for me." Daniel's voice was weary. I got the impression that this was a well-worn conversation.

"Junior looked so handsome in his uniform," Angie continued. "You shoulda seen. He's every bit as gorgeous as his father was. *Rompecorazones*, like his father." She patted Daniel's cheek. "I still remember the first time I saw your papa. He was on leave in New York. I was friends with a cousin of his."

"How did you end up in Puerto Rico?" I asked.

"It was Daniel Senior's idea to move back to PR. I'm Nuyorican, from Queens, like I said, but he grew up on the island and he always planned to go back there. At first me and the girls moved around with him wherever he was stationed, but then we decided it would be better for us to live in PR, near his family. My grandparents and some cousins were still there, too. Then Junior came along, our surprise baby, and we built a bigger house. Daniel had retired, and we were finally all living together in our dream house when he keeled over at our Silvie's *quinceañera*, in the backyard. He hadn't even lived there a year." She reached out and squeezed her son's hand.

I'd been waiting for a pause in the conversation, hoping to steer her back around to her run-in with Adrian

Hoffman. I also wanted to see if I could get any details about the man Daniel had seen on the night of the party. Before I could get another word in edgewise, though, Angie was talking again. It was no wonder her son became a professional listener.

"And then in 2017, the hurricane destroyed the house. *¡Qué horror!*" She crossed herself again. "We've finally got it almost back to what it was, but it's taken all these years. Once all that's paid off, maybe next summer, then Junior's gonna come back home."

"I told you, *Mamá*," Daniel said. "I'm happy here. There's no reason for me to rush back."

His tone made me think that maybe the idea to return to Puerto Rico wasn't so much a fixed plan as a product of his mother's wishful thinking.

"Your mother and all your sisters aren't a reason? And with Roxy pregnant again, you want to have another little niece or nephew who barely knows their uncle Junior? And you haven't met Anabel's new boyfriend—piece of work that one, I need you to talk her out of it." To me, she added, "Things at home aren't the same since he left. Since his father died, Junior's been the man of the house. Only man in a family of women."

Daniel's smile had tightened more and more as his mother spoke, his black eyes as glassy as marbles. I'd already known that he was good at keeping his emotions in check and holding his tongue, but now I understood that he hadn't been born with those skills—he'd achieved mastery through long hours of painstaking practice. He glanced at his watch. "We better go, *Mamá*. We don't want to be late for our spa day."

Angie threaded her arm through her son's and pulled him away. So much for my chance to quiz them.

As I watched them walk down the hall, I couldn't help but notice that one by one, "Junior" turned the head of every woman they passed. *Rompecorazones*. A heartbreaker.

CHAPTER 11

As I rounded the curving driveway toward my house about three o'clock that afternoon, the wan daylight was already fading. It looked like evening, and it felt like it, too. I'd packed more into the day than seemed possible. Giving a witness statement, theorizing with Capone, running into Daniel and his mother. Since I left the resort, I'd been stuck in a meeting with our meat suppliers, trying to sort out issues with deliveries and invoicing. And my workday hadn't even really begun. I needed to make a quick in-and-out dash home before heading back to the restaurant to start dinner service prep for our five o'clock opening.

Thankfully, the wind had finally died down, but now snow-bloated clouds loomed overhead—heavy and sinister. The events of the past few days felt equally leaden, filling the entire horizon of my mind. When I'd woken up that morning, my biggest issue was disappointment over the sudden, macabre end to my date with Capone. Now the perplexing details of Natasha La Cotti's death sent any concerns about my love life so far to the back burner they had fallen off the stove entirely.

I was especially freaked out by the possibility that Rabbit could be implicated in the murder. I was worried about Jonathan, too, but he had resources behind him—a clean criminal record, a good education, rich friends, and my bull terrier of a sister. For Rabbit, even the merest whiff of wrongdoing could derail his life. Parolees skate on thin ice.

My encounter with Daniel and his mother had piled worry on top of worry. Daniel had already admitted that he was acquainted with Natasha La Cotti. At the time, I'd thought little of it. In retrospect, it seemed significant. When we chatted at the snow sculpting competition, her dead body was hidden just a few feet away. Capone had been there, too, and knowing him, I was sure the wobble in Daniel's expression wouldn't have gone unnoticed. As if that wasn't bad enough, Daniel hadn't said a word about his mother being, apparently, an archenemy of Adrian and, by extension, Daffi. Could Daniel's entanglements with the party guests go deeper than it appeared?

After I left the resort, I'd immediately composed a text to Capone, letting him know that I'd discovered the identity of the woman who'd confronted Adrian. I sat in my car for a full five minutes before deleting it. I justified the omission by telling myself that I'd mention it to Capone next time I saw him. That would allow me to control the messaging a little better, make it seem a bit less shady. In reality, though, I couldn't bring myself to throw Daniel, my faithful friend and consigliere, under the bus. Capone and I had only been quasi-dating for a few months. I'd known Daniel much longer and had worked side by side with him six days a week for almost a year. And frankly I was miffed by the casual way Capone kept throwing out homicidal theories about people I cared about. If I could keep Daniel out of the firing line, I would.

Despite the swirling flurry of confusion and unanswered questions, as the whimsical turret and ornately carved porch railings of my house's Queen Anne façade rose into view, my dark mood lightened. Coming home always made me feel better. I'd chosen authentic period colors for the exterior—moss green, khaki, and ivory. Against the muted backdrop, the reds, whites, and greens of our Christmas decorations popped to vivid life. To my mind, the effect was a picture of tasteful elegance. Auntie Biz, though, wasn't content with the display. This was our first Christmas sharing a living space, and we were finding it tricky to strike a compromise between my "Victorian Christmas" aesthetic and her "Santa in Vegas" vibe. More than once, Melody and I had caught Biz, who was north of eighty and prone to dizzy spells, on a ladder trying to festoon the place with a herd of inflatable reindeer vast enough to fill half of Norway or an array of flashing colored baubles the likes of which could be seen from near-Earth orbit. We'd reached an uneasy compromise—adding giant red bows to the bunting and running rows of candy-cane lights along the paths.

An unfamiliar Ford SUV was parked in front of the house. *Ugh.* I didn't think the workers who were renovating the bathroom were supposed to be there that day, but maybe I'd gotten the schedule mixed up. Or maybe Biz or Melody had a visitor. Whoever it was, I hoped they'd leave quickly.

Usually the prospect of gearing up for service would've enlivened me. Tonight, though, I wanted nothing more than to slump into my sweatpants and spend the evening with Butterball on my lap and an IV drip of wine hooked up to my arm. Thank goodness we only had two more days to get through before we had a break for the holidays. I'd been working nonstop for more than six months, sometimes putting in seventy-hour weeks, so the prospect of the less-busy winter schedule came as something of a relief. If we didn't need the cash flow so badly, I would have closed for the entire Christmas week. I sighed. I'd have to dig deep to muster the requisite holiday cheer to get through the next few days.

I opened the front door and was greeted by the warm, spicy aromas of mulled cider and gingerbread—scents straight from "happy holidays" central casting. I called out a hello as I took off my boots and hung my coat in the closet. The house was mammoth, but the open doorways were wide enough to allow my voice to carry between the main downstairs rooms.

"In here." Biz's reply was leavened by uncustomary cheerfulness. She wasn't known for being hospitable to unannounced visitors. I supposed this was another aspect of her personality that was on temporary hiatus.

I followed voices to the kitchen. There, I found Biz standing over a pot at the stove, ladling cider into mugs. She wore one of the many Christmas-themed sweaters she'd accumulated during her long career as a high school teacher. During the holidays, her typical wardrobe of buttoned-up (literally and figuratively) blouses and pressed slacks gave way to an avalanche of holiday mawkishness. The sweaters started appearing in heavy rotation around Thanksgiving and didn't go back into storage until the new year. Today's specimen was especially *festive*, with embroidered bunnies smooching under mistletoe.

Biz turned to me and said, "Look what the cat dragged in." She gestured with the ladle to the stools at the island where, like the Ghosts of Chrismukkah Past, sat my niece and brother-in-law.

"Well, the cat didn't *drag* us, but he was a big draw for me," Piper said. Butterball lay curled in her lap. Considering his curvaceous sixteen-pound frame, it never failed to amaze me how he could make himself fit into tiny spaces. If he wanted to get inside a tube of toothpaste, I was convinced he'd do it. "You're my favorite cousin, aren't you, buddy?" she asked him, lifting him so that their foreheads touched.

The cat purred his agreement.

While Piper appeared to have made herself happily at home, Jonathan perched on the edge of his stool, looking about as comfortable as a patient in the waiting room of a proctologist's office.

I set my purse on the counter, almost too bewildered by the scene to form words. "I thought you'd be heading back to California by now," I said. "Weren't you supposed to leave this morning?"

"We missed our flight," came Jonathan's stiff reply.

"Well, we haven't technically missed it yet, but since we're here and the plane is an hour's drive away in Chicago and takes off in a few minutes, we're definitely going to," Piper said.

Melody hustled in from the dining room, carrying a stack of china side plates. "Are these the ones you wanted, Biz?" she asked. "With the holly border?"

"No, dear, the ones with the nutcrackers are for teatime. The holly pattern is for Christmas eve dinner."

Melody waved an awkward hello to me and shuffled back out to the dining room, in search of the "right" china for the occasion. Biz was clearly pulling out all the stops. I winced as I thought again of Shea saying that me and Biz were "too extra" around the holidays. I took in the glowing lights, the holiday tea towels, the scent of freshly baked gingerbread cake, and the dulcet strains of Mel Tormé's "Chestnuts Roasting on an Open Fire"—it was hard to argue that it wasn't over the top. We'd brought a Norman Rockwell painting to life and then dialed it up to eleven. But isn't that what the holidays were for?

"Do you remember Natasha La Cotti from the party?" Piper asked, pivoting to face me. "Turns out she died there. Like, *at* the party. She fell off the balcony. That's why she didn't pick up her coat." Her brown eyes widened at the improbability of it.

"Actually, I know. I had to give a statement to the police this morning," I said.

Jonathan shifted in his seat. "We had to give statements, too."

"Isn't it crazy?" Piper said.

"Terrible," I said, watching my brother-in-law's face. Jonathan's grooming was usually as impeccable as a Ken doll's, not a sandy blond hair out of place, not a follicle of stubble on his chiseled jaw. Just then though, his clothes were rumpled and the shadow on his chin was giving the time as well past five o'clock.

"You were friends with Natasha, right?" I asked him, remembering the meaningful looks they shared in the wake of Hadley's plate-throwing temper tantrum.

His eyes struggled to meet mine. "We moved in the same circles."

In his face, I saw an echo of the expression I'd seen on Daniel's when Natasha's name was mentioned. Discomfort. In Jonathan, though, it was amplified. In fact, it looked a lot like guilt.

"I still haven't heard how you managed to miss your flight," Biz said, handing Piper a mug of cider.

"Oh, yeah, I was just starting to tell the story before you came in, Aunt Dee," Piper said. "It was so crazy. We were loading the rental car with our luggage to drive to O'Hare. We were early because Dad likes to leave, like, a week in advance for the airport."

Jonathan perked up a bit at his daughter's affectionate ribbing. "It's good to have a buffer. It's an hour drive," he said, "and we had to return the rental car. Plus, Chicago traffic and the security lines when you're flying around the holidays . . ."

She held up a hand to cut him off. "Hashtag Airport Dad." Jonathan returned her smile. "Anyway, we were getting into the car and this sexy cop who looks just like Shemar Moore walks out of the hotel. You know Shemar Moore? The smoking-hot buff guy on *Criminal Minds*? Anyway, Shemar Moore's stunt double comes up to us and is, like, 'Are you Piper and Jonathan Savage?'" She lowered her voice in a dramatic imitation.

"This was today?"

"Yep."

"Just after eleven," Jonathan clarified.

I gaped for a moment before managing to squeeze out a single word. "Wow."

My shock was genuine, but not for the reasons they might've thought. From Piper's description, I could be fairly certain Capone was the officer who'd stopped them in front of the hotel. What shocked me was the timeline. He'd left our impromptu brunch around eleven. That meant that he'd marched straight out of the restaurant and accosted them in front of the hotel. Had he been planning that all along? I thought back to the text that summoned him back to the station. As he read it, his expression had soured. When I'd asked him about the content, he fobbed me off. Had he received some information that caused his vague suspicion of Jonathan to crystallize?

I was familiar enough with Capone's modus operandi to know that he tipped his hand only when there was a calculated, strategic reason for doing so. But now that I was his actual girlfriend, I thought he might finally be starting to trust me. After all, hadn't we just spent a good chunk of time theorizing about the murder? What did it say about our future as a couple if he'd kept this—the questioning of my family members— under wraps?

Heedless of my percolating pot of irritation, Piper continued, "I know, right? So we were, like, 'Uh, yeah, that's us.' And he was all, 'I need you to come down to the station.' Isn't that wild?" Caught up in the drama of the retelling, Piper had stopped petting Butterball, an oversight that elicited a mewl of protest from the cat. "Sorry, honey," she said, taking a moment to nuzzle him. "I didn't mean to forget about you."

Melody had come back into the kitchen during Piper's recounting. She turned to me during the pause and said, "Do you think it was Detective Capone?"

Piper snapped her fingers. "Capone. Yeah, that was his name."

"You know him?" Jonathan asked.

"Of course." Melody shot a thumb toward me. "He's her boyfriend."

"Really." Jonathan's eyes narrowed, funneling a look of distrust in my direction.

Piper, by contrast, seemed impressed. She snapped her fingers and said, "Get it, girl. He's a straight-up snack."

Biz examined the plates that Melody had brought in. "These aren't right, either," she grumbled. "These are snowmen, not nutcrackers." She took hold of the stack and marched past Melody with an irritated huff. "If you want something done right . . ."

"Sorry," Melody squeaked.

You had to hand it to Biz. Her obsession with flawless holiday entertaining was so all-encompassing that, in her mind, having the right dinnerware trumped a murder investigation. Prior to moving to Geneva Bay, I'd have been right there with her. But my recent brushes with death and my deepening sense of connection with my friends here had brought a subtle shift. Maybe starting to prioritize personal relationships over perfect china patterns might not seem like a revelation to other people, but it felt like a tectonic shift to me.

"Did you explain to Capone that you'd miss your flight if you went with him?" I asked, hoping Biz's perfectionist grousing would give me cover to avoid any follow-up questions about my relationship with Capone. "I wonder why he didn't offer to take your statement over the phone."

"That's what I'd like to know," Jonathan sniffed. "I really should've refused, or called a lawyer, but that seemed excessive."

Piper chuckled and leveled her gaze at her father. "Yeah, right." She turned back to the rest of us, a smile still tugging at the corners of her mouth. "Dad was all 'yes, sir' 'anything you say, sir.' Your boyfriend made it pretty clear that it would be best for us to 'cooperate.'" She air-quoted the last word. "I thought he was going to arrest us. Seriously, it was that intense."

"Seems like he really wanted to talk to you," Melody said. "They asked me to come in, too, but it seemed more like a suggestion, like I could stop by whenever I had time."

Despite Melody's blond baby doll looks and farm girl inflections, she had a sharp mind. The frown line between her eyebrows indicated that her wheels were turning. I wondered if she, too, was speculating about why Capone had been so zealous in his approach toward Piper and Jonathan. There was a fine line between giving a witness statement and being questioned as a potential suspect. We'd both seen Capone in action enough times to know that he used his "bad cop" persona sparingly. Why had he used it on them? Even Daniel, who potentially had evidence in the form of a more detailed description of the mystery man he'd seen on the night of the party, hadn't been dragged down to the station.

"I'm sure it's just a formality," Jonathan countered. "They probably treat sudden deaths as suspicious whenever the cause is unknown."

"Unknown?" Piper said incredulously. "Hadley told me that the police told her that Natasha fell from their second-story balcony. I think we can imagine how a person could end up dead from that."

"I mean that it was a freak accident," Jonathan said. "So the police probably feel obliged to look into it. Natasha most likely had a bit too much to drink, slipped on some ice, and fell."

"I don't think they would've sent a detective out to get us if they thought it was an accident." Piper planted her elbows on the counter and leaned toward me and Melody. "Just by how serious the detective was and how everyone at the station was acting."

"Whoa," Melody said. "They only asked me a few questions. Same with Sonya. Detective Capone wasn't even there. I didn't realize it was so serious." She paused midway through wiping the countertop clear of cake crumbs and turned to me. "Do you think the body inside the snow sculpture is connected to Miss La Cotti's death? Maybe there's a serial killer on the loose!"

"What body in what snow sculpture?" Alarm and confusion imbued Jonathan's question.

"Didn't Delilah tell you?" Melody looked from Jonathan and Piper to me. "They found a dead body in one of the snow sculptures at the festival yesterday. She was there when it happened."

"Oh my god," Piper gasped. "That's crazy. But it can't be Natasha, can it? How would she have gotten over to the park if she died falling from the Hoffmans' balcony?"

"I'm sure it's not a serial killer," I cut in quickly. "Geneva Bay is very safe."

From what Piper and Jonathan had said so far, it seemed likely they weren't privy to the same information I was about Natasha being pushed. More to the point, it seemed like hardly anyone knew that Natasha and the snow sculpture corpse were one and the same. If Capone was trying to keep some of the evidence out of the public domain, I didn't want to be the one to let anything slip. I'd already told Daniel, but beyond that, I'd leave the town crier role to Officer Stanhope. I assumed the police would've told Daffi, Adrian, and Hadley *something* about why they were searching their house, but clearly not the whole truth.

Biz had returned with the "correct" plates, and she chimed in, saying, "What a shame about all of this. And you said you can't rebook another flight until after Christmas? So you'll be here?" Her fixation on the holidays once again offered a timely change of subject.

"That's right," Jonathan said. "By the time we left the station, I knew there was no way we were going to make our flight. I checked flights out of Milwaukee, O'Hare, Midway—everywhere within driving distance. No seats to be had until December twenty-sixth. Apparently there's bad weather out West, which is scrambling everything. And our hotel is booked up, too, so we can't check back in there. I called around, but everywhere is full."

Addressing me, Piper said, "When we realized we were going to be stuck here and get the boot from the Grand Bay, we called your house to see if you could put us up."

"Well, luckily we have more than enough room," Biz said. "Melody and I sprang into action to get everything ready, isn't that right?"

"Uh-huh." Melody smiled, tucking a stray curl behind her ear. I couldn't help wondering how she felt about getting commandeered into preparing for last-minute houseguests and ordered around like a skivvy.

"Is Shea going to try to get a flight here for her and Caleb?" Biz asked. "Since you can't get home?"

"It'll be tough," Jonathan said. "I don't see why there'd be flights *from* California if there's nothing going *to* California."

"Won't that be nice, though, if it works out?" Biz said. "We've barely been able to get to know little Caleb, and now we may get to spend the holidays with him."

Her joy was barely suppressed. Sure a woman died a violent death, but what was that next to the prospect of a forced family holiday?

I looked at the time and grimaced. "I'm sorry to break up the party, but I've got to get to the restaurant.

Rabbit's out and Jarka doesn't get back from Bulgaria until Christmas Eve. We're seriously shorthanded."

"I can lend a hand with hostessing if you want," Piper said. "I did that for our sorority's casino night, and I learned silverware placement in the etiquette classes Shea made me take before my bat mitzvah." She threw an arm over Melody's shoulder. "I'm sure Mel here can show me the ropes."

Melody smiled, looking pleased but a bit over-whelmed. I, too, felt a little kernel of unease. I loved my niece's all-in gusto, but it seemed like she was treating a single night showing glammed-up coeds to their tables as the equivalent of Melody's years of hospitality experience. Would Piper be up to the grueling pace of a busy dinner service?

"You really don't mind helping?" I asked.

"It'll be a blast!" Piper said. Her smile suddenly fell. "Shoot, I told Hadley we'd go night skiing together."

"You can leave early to meet your friend. Right, Delilah?" Biz said. "I'll pitch in if you're shorthanded." Turning back to Piper, she added, "It's wonderful that you're willing to help."

"That'll work," I said. "Once we get past the seven o'clock seating, things tend to ease off. Can you come over around four-thirty and Melody will go over the basics with you?"

We had a steady stream of tables booked, and we were down not one, but two, key staffers. Piper pitching in would help, allowing Melody to shift into a server role, but my niece was untested, and Melody often got flustered when she had too many things to juggle. Still, looking at Biz's beaming face, I felt I had no choice. She was happy, and I didn't want to say or do anything that would rock the boat.

The holidays had always been Biz's release valve—
the one time of year she let herself smile. The past few
years, though, with Shea steering clear and my dad's
illness and death, our smaller celebrations hadn't given
her the same boost. She still went all out, but the festivities had felt forced and empty. I watched in wonder as
Holiday Biz reached across and gave Butterball a fond
pat on the head. I'd heard of ghosts possessing people.
Judging by Biz's wholesale transformation, it seemed
the Christmas spirit was capable of the same feat.

"Well, I've really got to get going," I said. I scooped
Butterball off the island countertop. "Just got to get this
monster loaded into his cat carrier."

"Butterball goes to the restaurant with you?" Jonathan asked. "I assumed that was a one-time thing."

"He stays in the upstairs apartment. I started taking
him a few weeks ago to get him out of the way while
the work's being done on Biz's bathroom. He used
to *hate* car rides. But I managed to bribe him with
enough treats that now he gets pissed off if I *don't* take
him. I guess I'm going to have to make it a permanent
arrangement."

I gave the cat a gentle noogie. In truth, I benefit-
ted more than he did. Having him in close proximity
meant that I could pop upstairs for a restorative cuddle
whenever I needed one.

"Melody and I will go up and finish getting your
rooms ready," Biz said.

Watching them leave, it struck me how, when we
had guests, Melody inhabited some weird limbo between being our employee and our housemate. Her
eldercare duties with Biz were light—mostly driving
her to appointments, organizing her prescriptions, and

taking her shopping. In exchange, she got free rent. I didn't expect her to do anything other than pull her own weight with household chores. But at the restaurant, she clearly worked for me, and her job was to run the front of house and ensure a pleasant experience for our customers. She seemed unsure of what her role was now. Was she supposed to feel at ease, make small talk, kick back and pour herself a mug of cider? Or was she supposed to fade into the background, emerging only to serve the whims of our guests?

"I'm going to bring in the rest of my stuff," Piper said. She gave Butterball a kiss as she passed us on her way out the front door.

"I'll be at the restaurant until late, but I'll see you in the morning," I said to Jonathan. "Make yourself at home."

I swung Butterball onto my hip and slung my bag over the opposite shoulder. Before I could head out, though, he cut me off. "You know, you could've given us a heads-up about your boyfriend questioning us."

I weighed my options, and landed on telling the truth. "I didn't know."

He sniffed, seeming unconvinced.

"What do you think happened to Natasha?" I asked.

"No idea," he said. "For all I know she jumped."

I tilted my head, taken aback. "You think she killed herself?"

"No, of course not," he said, and then corrected himself. "What I mean is, anything's possible. She seemed fine that night, but what do I know?"

"Was there something going on between you, her, and Adrian when you came up the stairs at the party? You said something about a problem?" I hoped my question came across as natural rather than meddle-some. I was struggling to quell the burning flames of my curiosity.

"Look, Delilah." His tone sharpened. "I've had a long couple of days, and I've certainly had enough of being interrogated." He huffed in annoyance. "You're as bad as Shea. She gave me the third degree over the phone earlier. I'll tell you what I told her and your *boy-friend*. I went to a party. A woman I barely know had some kind of accident and died. What else does every-one want me to say?"

How about the truth? The thought surfaced so quickly that I only just had time to clamp my lips shut to keep it from tumbling out.

CHAPTER 12

On my way out the door, my thoughts shifted to Capone. He'd derailed my family's holiday and put me in an awkward position. Sure, I had suspicions that Jonathan might be hiding something, but they were just vague inklings. He and Piper didn't deserve the third degree. The guy wasn't a murderer. Plus, didn't my family merit some special consideration from my boyfriend? Didn't I?

I fired off a text to Capone. *So you have breakfast with me and then immediately turn around and question my family without telling me?!*

The act had been reflexive, almost primal. How dare he cozy up to me, allow me to feed him *my* croissant, and then turn around ten minutes later and mess with my family? My phone rang through the Bluetooth just as I was pulling into the restaurant parking lot.

"Look, Delilah," Capone began. "The text I got while we were at the Grand Bay that made me leave suddenly? It was from Rettberg, telling me that there were at most ten or fifteen people at the party fit enough to move a body without help. I was heading back to start drilling down on those people. Jonathan Savage was one of them."

"Then why didn't you tell me you were going to question him? You blindsided me."

"At that point, I wasn't sure what my next move was," he said. "Then, I walked out the front of the hotel and there he was, one of my top suspects, loading up a car and getting ready to fly out of my jurisdiction. I couldn't let him slip through my fingers without questioning him."

"You didn't have to be so harsh with them. Piper said she was afraid they'd get arrested. She's only nineteen."

"But your brother-in-law is a grown man. I've been doing this a long time, Delilah," he said. "Jonathan's reaction seemed off to me, so I turned up the heat. On him, not her. I had a hunch."

"This is my family we're talking about. My niece was collateral damage to your hunch. They missed their flights because of your hunch," I pointed out. "My sister's family might not be able to be together for the holidays."

Capone let out a weary sigh. "And I missed my family cruise," he said. "I'm trying to solve a murder. I don't have time to be your family's travel agent or manage your emotions right now."

"Manage my emotions?!" I shouted. "What's that supposed to mean?"

"First you complain that you're not that close to them, now you come at me with guns blazing because I dared to approach them without your say-so."

My reply came out in sputtered syllables. My brain was too angry to form actual words.

I heard voices in the background, and then Capone came back on the line. "I've got to go. I'll talk to you later."

As the call dropped, I was fuming. I longed for the old days when phones could be slammed down. I cut the engine and sat in the empty parking lot, stewing. Butterball, who was in his crate in the back seat, let out an interrogatory *mew*?

I swiveled in my seat to face him. "How dare he, right?"

Mee-ow, he responded. There was commiseration there, but not necessarily agreement.

"He's making it sound like *I'm* being crazy, when *he's* the one who ambushed my sister's husband and kid and wrecked their holiday," I protested.

Butterball let out a string of chatter that I didn't like the sounds of. I knew he couldn't talk, but sometimes he seemed preternaturally able to play devil's advocate. *Did you expect Capone not to do his job?* he seemed to be asking. *Wasn't his competence and moral fiber one of the things that attracted you to him in the first place? And did you really want him to ignore a lead just because of your relationship?*

I got out of the car and hefted the cat carrier aloft, holding it so Butterball could see my face. "Remind me not to come to you for relationship advice anymore."

Dinner service kicked off with the usual flurry of activity. Midwesterners tend to eat early in the winter, so by six o'clock, Delilah & Son was slammed. For the next two hours, I could think of nothing but pulling the next ticket off the printer, expediting the next order. Being forced to focus on cooking was a blessed respite from the dark events of the previous days. Without Rabbit around to bus tables or Jarka to serve, Piper and Melody had been flitting in and out at a breakneck pace, trying to keep on top of seating, serving, and clearing. Meanwhile, Sonya and I were frantically fitting dishwashing duties into our routine. I'd given her a condensed, piecemeal update of my day's sleuthing as we rushed around filling orders, with a promise to meet up for a proper debrief the following morning.

When the rush finally began to die down around eight, I turned to Sonya. "Can you handle the kitchen for a bit? I'm going to see how everything's going out front."

"Ten-four, boss lady," Sonya said, pulling a piping hot eggplant deep-dish from the oven.

I walked into the dining room and surveyed the scene. All seemed calm. Delilah & Son was designed with a Chicago theme, evoked both by the deep-dish-heavy menu and the décor, one element of which was a series of colorful, oversized portraits of famous Chicagoans suspended from the high ceiling. An Art Institute student had created the works, which rendered leading figures of Chicago history. The artist's creative spin was to show upright citizens, like social crusader Jane Addams, in beautiful, vivid colors, while depicting some of the city's less-savory characters, like Al Capone, as tiny, diaper-wearing babies. Of course, I'd commissioned the art before I hooked up with Scarface's great-grandson. Thank goodness *my* Capone took his villainous ancestry mostly in stride, and considered it motivation to try to redeem the family name.

For the holidays, the paintings had been dressed in white twinkle lights, and I'd hung dozens of oversized Christmas baubles in shades of glittery gold, mirrorball silver, and deep crimson alongside the artwork. Above Daniel's domain—the beechwood bar that extended along one entire side of the room—an abstract gold-wire sleigh and team of reindeer seemed ready for Santa to spur them on their way. The centerpiece of the space was the large picture windows that faced the lake. While in summer they offered views of passing boats, kayakers, and other open-water revelry, on a frigid night like tonight, the windows allowed guests to gaze out into the inky darkness from their snug vantage point, watching as the snow fell in gentle, downy feathers.

Everything looked Hallmark-movie perfect, but as my eyes panned the room, I began to see cracks in the holly-jolly veneer. Piper grabbed a tray of apps from the pass-through and brought them to a table. She gave me a little nod of acknowledgment when our eyes met. She'd made a few mistakes, but her ready wit and friendly smile seemed to have smoothed them over. I gave her a thumbs-up, but as I turned, my eyes caught Melody, who was punching an order into the dining room kiosk. No, "punching" understated the action. Her finger moved with a force that went well beyond punching. Her index finger was the stone-faced Russian from *Rocky IV* trying to commit actual homicide in the ring. *Uh-oh.*

I followed Melody's murderous gaze toward the bar and saw the source of the trouble. Hadley Hoffman perched on one of the barstools, leaning so far forward that her boobs could practically be plated up as a menu item. Hadley had gathered her striking ginger curls into pigtail braids, which stood out against her tight, baby blue sweater like maple leaves against the autumn sky. Daniel, meanwhile, mixed drinks in a cocktail shaker for a pair of elderly ladies. He said something to them and Hadley, setting off peals of laughter and another wave of kiosk finger punching from Melody.

I veered sideways. "You good?" I asked her.

"Yes, chef," she replied curtly, not taking her eyes from the screen.

I knew it was far from the truth, but I didn't want to delve into it when we still had two hours until closing. "Keep up the good work," I said.

"I will. I always do," I heard her mutter as Piper crossed toward us. Yeesh, maybe I could arrange a little girl talk between her and Sonya later. Sonya would know what to say. Lord knew that Biz and I were of little help when it came to that kind of thing.

"Still okay if I take off early to hit the slopes?" Piper asked.

"Sure," I said. "I can't thank you enough for pitching in. I don't know what we would've done without your help."

By now, Hadley had crossed over to join us. "You ready?"

"Yep," Piper said. "I left my stuff upstairs in the apartment. Do you want to come up and say hi to Butterball while I change?"

Hadley cast a glance toward the bar, where Daniel had returned to serving other patrons. Her forehead creased, as if she was weighing something up in her mind. But the expression quickly faded, and she said, "Sure, let's go."

I walked through the kitchen with them and was still there when they came back about ten minutes later. "Okay, we're gonna bounce," Piper said, shrugging on her ski jacket.

Melody walked in just then, carrying an armload of

plates. I took them from her and transferred them to the sink for a rinse.

"You sure it's okay if I leave?" Piper asked. "Looks like there's still a lot to do."

"You're on vacation," I said. "You've already done a lot to help."

"Do you want me to do your tip out now or give it to you later?" Melody asked.

Piper smiled. "You keep it. I had fun. I should be paying you."

I knew Piper meant her comment to be lighthearted, generous even, but as I saw Melody's cheeks redden, I realized that to her, it probably felt condescending.

"Well, we better go if we're going to get any runs in. It's super fun after dark," Piper continued. "The slopes are all lit up, and just before they close at ten every night, there's a light show. Everyone stands at the bottom of the slope and watches."

Hadley twirled the end of one of her braids. "It's really wild. Psychedelic."

Piper put her arm around Melody's shoulder. "Hey, you should come skiing with us tomorrow!"

Melody's eyes brightened, but she cast a wary glance at Hadley and the spark of excitement immediately dimmed. "I don't ski very well."

Piper flicked her wrist dismissively. "You can hire an instructor."

"I don't have skis or the right clothes," Melody said.

"You can just rent everything," Piper said.

"Yeah," Hadley said. "They have a really great ski shop."

I watched as clouds of emotion passed over Melody's

face. Her jealousy made her guarded around Hadley, but she was also clearly delighted at being included in the "cool kids" plans. Then there was the matter of money. Ski rentals and lift tickets at the resort would cost hundreds of dollars. For me, and, I suspected, for Melody, the idea of blowing a week's wages on a few hours' snowy fantasy seemed like an impossibility. But saying so would drop a grenade of awkwardness.

More than that, though, witnessing Melody's inner turmoil allowed me to see her in a new light. Here was a young woman, Piper and Hadley's age, who had never enjoyed upper-middle-class ease. She'd mucked in on her family's farm since she could stand upright. She was chiseling away, credit by credit, at a community college degree in graphic design. While girls like Piper and Hadley were taking pouty-faced holiday selfies for their social media feeds, Melody was serving them canapes. Hadley's privilege gave her the confidence to flirt with Daniel, while Melody stood timidly in the background. I tended to have a tin ear when it came to touchy-feely sentiments, so the tidal wave of empathy I felt for Melody took me by surprise.

I cleared my throat. "Remind me to give you your holiday bonus check, Mel." I reached over nonchalantly to ladle some red sauce onto a waiting pie.

She looked at me in surprise, and I took the opportunity to mouth the words "Five hundred dollars" and flash the five fingers of my hand to make sure she understood.

Sonya, who'd caught the interaction, widened her eyes but said nothing. Five hundred dollars was more money than I'd intended to give out, and—when I gave the same amount to Rabbit, Daniel, Sonya, and Jarka— it was frankly more than I could afford. But I didn't want money to be the thing that stood in the way of Melody getting to cut loose for once and act her age.

Relief broke over her face as she turned back to Piper. "Um, okay, that would be fun."

"Great!" Piper beamed. Turning to me, she said, "Oh, Biz said it's okay if Hadley comes for Christmas dinner. That's cool, right? Neither of us usually celebrate Christmas, so it'll be fun to see what the whole deal is."

"Sure," I said, not sure at all. Not only was Hadley high on the suspect list for Natasha's murder, but I also was beginning to fear that she was in danger from the death rays Melody shot from her eyes whenever the girl got too close to Daniel.

Hadley hadn't played much of a part in the conversation up until that point and I'd thought she wasn't paying attention. But suddenly she livened up. "Ooh, and we should invite the hot bartender skiing, too, so we have some eye candy on the slopes."

"Good call," Piper replied.

"He's such a sweetheart," Hadley crooned. "His last name's Castillo, right? He said he was named after his father. And I think he said he's from Fajardo?"

"That's right." Melody's eyes narrowed. "Why do you need to know?"

"No particular reason," Hadley said with an innocent smile. Turning to Piper she added, "Let's stop by the bar on the way out and ask him."

Melody's smile congealed into something brittle. When she spoke, her voice brimmed with acid. "You know what? I just remembered I have some work to catch up on tomorrow." She reached one of the low shelves and pulled out a bin of clean silverware. "Have fun."

I caught a glimpse of her thundercloud expression as she rushed out of the kitchen. I wasn't sure if the gathering emotions would burst forth as tears or fury, but I *was* sure it wasn't going to be pretty.

CHAPTER 13

"What's with her?" Hadley asked, looking after the retreating hostess.

"Yeah, she *seemed* cool." Piper gave a shrug and flicked her dark blond hair over her shoulder.

I wanted to say something to them. To grab them by the scruffs of their pretty necks and tell them how much they'd hurt Melody. But really, what had they done? Piper went out of her way to try to include Melody, and Hadley probably had no clue that Melody had spent the better part of a year pining after Daniel. To Hadley, he was fair game—a single, twentysomething "hot bartender." Maybe they'd displayed a "let them eat cake" level of obliviousness about the luck they'd been born into, but I suspected that life hadn't afforded them many opportunities to see firsthand how the hoi polloi lived. They had money, beauty, and youth by the Gucci bag load—along with all the swagger that combination of attributes afforded.

Piper gave me a little wave. "See you later tonight, Aunt Dee. Can you leave the door unlocked? Not sure what time I'll be back."

After they'd left, Sonya observed, "That's not going to end well."

"I should do something," I said.

"Do you really want to get in the middle of it?" she asked.

"Someone has to."

"Really? I think you should butt out," Sonya said, "but I've never known you *not* to take the reins, if reins are available for taking."

"When it comes to the matters of the heart, even I have to admit some things are out of my control."

She gasped and clutched her chest in mock surprise at my admission.

"If there were an easy way to stop the people I love from getting themselves into romantic trouble," I continued, "I would've put the kibosh on about ninety-nine percent of *your* relationships."

Sonya picked up an olive and used her middle finger and thumb to flick it at me. I caught it midair and popped it into my mouth. I wasn't particularly sporty, but through cooking, I'd developed excellent hand-eye coordination.

My phone buzzed and I removed it from my pocket. A text from my sister that simply read: *Arriving tomorrow*.

I nearly choked on the half-chewed olive as my heart bolted into a gallop.

I'd opened a Bordeaux to add to the beef stock for tomorrow's soup special, a hearty, garlicky Italian meatball stew. I pulled a clean mason jar from the shelf and poured myself a glass of what remained.

"What was *that* about?" Sonya asked, nodding toward my phone.

"Nothing." Even as I pocketed my phone, I was unsure why I hadn't told her the truth.

Turning back to her chopping, she asked, "Do you think he'll go skiing with them?"

"Who?"

She raised her eyebrows at me. "Daniel," she prompted.

"Oh," I said, taking another swig of wine. "Well, his mom's in town, so I'm guessing he'll want to spend time with her. I don't think Daniel would go for Hadley anyway," I said. "She's twenty-one. He's hardwired to flirt with anything with a pulse, but for actual dating he always goes for older women. I think that's one of the reasons he's never shown much interest in Melody." I took another glug, then another. "Daniel and his mother are coming for Christmas dinner," I continued. "Now Piper invited Hadley. I don't know if Melody will stay away or subject herself to it."

"That's not going to be easy," she observed.

I went silent. *Shea is coming.*

"Dee, what's wrong?" Sonya asked. "Your hand is shaking and you're chugging that wine like there's no tomorrow."

I looked down and saw that, instead of the usual perfect spiral of marinara, I'd practically drowned the hapless pizza I was making in sauce. Reluctantly, I held up my phone to show her the text.

She took it and read, "'Arriving tomorrow.'" She looked at it again, scrolling up and down, her eyes widening. "Wait, is this really the only text you and your sister have exchanged since October? She didn't reach out to you about Piper and Jonathan coming to Geneva Bay? Or them getting stuck here? Nothing?"

"Nope." I sprinkled a handful of bay leaves into my stockpot and turned up the flame.

She shook her head. "I can't imagine what it would be like to have relatives who aren't fully inhabiting your business hole twenty-four-seven three-six-five. My mom texts me a picture of her breakfast every morning. My uncle Avi forwarded the results of his colonoscopy to the family group chat the other week. Apparently he has the digestive tract of a man half his age."

"Talk about a business hole," I said, raising an eyebrow. "I don't want to know about Shea's colon."

"Okay, that's an extreme example, but this"—she pointed to my phone—"is bizarre. First, she doesn't even tell you that Jonathan and Piper are here, and then she sends this zero-context message." She clicked her tongue. "Does she think it's a telegram and she's being charged by the word? I don't get why she's so standoffish. Are you sure you didn't murder her hamster when you were little or something?"

"We were pretty close until our mom died. I'd just turned twelve and she was already sixteen. I think any age is a bad age to lose your mom, but it seemed like she had a harder time coping with it than I did."

"I think the problem is that you two are both Elsa," she said.

"Elsa who?" I asked.

"You know, from *Frozen*."

"Didn't see it."

She sighed. Sonya knew me well enough to know that I was clueless when it came to culture. Didn't matter if it was a highbrow novel or a lowbrow sitcom—I probably hadn't read it or seen it or heard of it. Occupational hazard of spending my entire adult life as a workaholic chef.

"Surely you at least know the song?" She mimed

a motion that looked like throwing confetti and sang, "Let it go!"

A glimmer of recognition flickered in my brain and I belted out, "Let the storm rage ooooooooon! The cold never bothered me anyway."

She took a minute to recover from my attempt to hit the high note before elaborating. "Right. It's about two sisters, who are of course princesses because this is a Disney movie. They lose their parents in a tragic boating accident. They're orphans. But instead of banding together, Elsa shuts her sister out. Like, literally stops talking to her."

"So I'm the other sister?" I asked.

"No. Anna is ditzy and naïve and befriends woodland creatures. She's emotionally vulnerable and open. Very much the anti-Delilah. You"—she pointed to me—"are also an Elsa. In addition to being emotionally frigid and closed off like Shea, Elsa also has monumental control issues." She paused to clear her throat, eyeing my spotless workspace, my perfectly organized *mise en place*, and the magazine-worthy salad I was plating. "Basically, you're both coping with your grief and trauma by becoming versions of Elsa. For your relationship with Shea to work, you both need to be a little more Anna."

"Befriend woodland creatures?"

She put her head in her hands.

"Look, I appreciate the 'Dr. Phil goes to Disneyland' family therapy you're trying to provide," I said. "But I've given up on having a real relationship with Shea. She's made it pretty clear that she's not interested."

"I just think—"

"I don't want to talk about it," I said firmly.

Sonya shot me a meaningful look. "What's that? You want me to *let it go*?"

We managed to get through service without further incident, but I let out a heavy sigh as I flipped the sign on the front door to Closed just after ten o'clock. Today was December 22. Just a few more shifts to get through until our Christmas closure could begin. At least some relief was in sight. If we could survive that long, that is. We were still down two staff members. Normally, as the "campers," i.e. lingering guests, departed, Jarka would have been changing out tablecloths, refilling salt and pepper shakers, and resetting the tables for tomorrow's service. Rabbit usually would've already mopped, restocked, and sanitized the restrooms and taken out all the trash. Now those, along with the million other heroic little tasks the two of them performed every night, would need to be divvied up among the rest of us. Again.

Plus, I'd already promised Daniel he could leave after he finished his closing tasks. Usually, he would've pitched in to cover the extra work, but he understandably wanted to spend time with his mother. By 10:15, he was gone, leaving me, Melody, and Sonya to tackle everything else. The three of us were in the dining room now, repositioning tables that had been moved during the night.

"You know," Melody said, scooting her end of the table into place. "I heard from my cousin, whose boyfriend works as a nine-one-one dispatcher for the county, that the body in the snow sculpture was Natasha La Cotti. You know, the lady who died at the party? Nobody knows how it got there."

I bit my lip. I'd given Sonya the lowdown at the

start of service, but I hadn't yet decided how closely to guard that information. In fact, I'd been trying hard to put the whole macabre business out of my mind. But it came flooding back—my friends and family, all on the suspect list.

Seeing my expression, Melody said, "You already knew?!"

I nodded, vowing to work on my poker face. "I didn't think it was my news to spread, but I guess if the word is out, there's no point in trying to keep it secret."

"You could've told me," she grumbled. "I was scared that there was a serial killer."

"I'm trying to keep all of you out of it. Capone has floated everyone and their grandma as suspects."

"Like who?" Melody asked.

"The less you know, the better. In fact, if you want to clock out, I can finish up."

"You'll be here until two a.m. if you try to do everything by yourself," Sonya said. "Although I really *should* hit the town with this fabulous thing."

I looked over to find Sonya with a designer bag slung over her shoulder. The thing was enormous, practically a piece of luggage, made of brown shearling.

Melody noticed it at the same time. It was not a subtle accessory. "That's Hadley's," she said. "She must've left it."

"Found it hanging on one of the hooks next to the bar stools," Sonya said. She held it up to examine it more closely. "Bottega Veneta," she observed with an appreciative whistle. "Probably worth beaucoup bank, although it's very much not my style. It looks like someone skinned Fozzie Bear and fashioned this from his pelt."

I ignored her vivid description. "Is her phone in

there? I can't believe she'd leave without it," I said. "It's practically glued to her hand."

"True," Sonya agreed. "She'd die of validation deprivation before she got three steps away."

"She was holding her phone and keys when they walked out," Melody said. She stepped toward Sonya and peered inside the bag. It had only a small fastening at the top, but was otherwise open.

"Melody . . ." Sonya's voice held a note of caution.

"If Capone's looking for suspects, why not her?" Melody's voice carried an unaccustomed petulance. "There's definitely something shady about her."

I stepped closer, warming to the idea. "Hadley *was* extremely angry that night, possibly about something Natasha La Cotti had said or done. Maybe she pitched such an over-the-top fit about the broken glasses to give her an excuse to go upstairs and confront Natasha. Maybe she even ran into Rabbit on purpose to cause a scene. Does she have an alibi for the time of the murder? Once Daniel left her, she was in her bedroom. Alone. Allegedly."

Melody bit her lip. "Although we probably shouldn't snoop," she said, her Midwestern morality getting the better of her jealousy. "Besides, don't cops need probable cause or something to search a person's stuff? Even if you found something in there, could Capone use it as evidence?"

"It would be iffy," Sonya confirmed. "Unless the evidence was in plain view."

I grabbed the purse and tipped the entire contents onto the fresh, white tablecloth. "Oops. Clumsy me knocked it over and spilled everything into plain view."

Sonya gave the bag a couple of good shakes just to be sure I'd thoroughly "knocked it over," and Melody helped us sift through the accumulated flotsam and jet-sam of Hadley's life.

"Looks like the usual college girl stuff," I said, nar-rating as I raked through the pile. "Palisades Sweat-shirt. Nine thousand lip glosses. Ten thousand hair ties. Tampons. Mints. Sunglasses . . ." My eyes caught on a piece of black fabric. I used one of the lip glosses to spear the object and hold it up. "And some dude's underpants?"

I examined the item. A pair of tight-fitting hip briefs. The cut of the fabric left no doubt that they were men's underwear and that they were designed for maximum sex appeal.

"Maybe Hadley wears men's clothing sometimes?" I ventured, leaning in as close as I dared. "Or has a kinky boyfriend?"

Sonya grabbed the underpants and raised them toward the light. "Those are Daniel's." Her statement was definitive.

Melody blushed crimson and took a step back from the table.

"How do you know what Daniel's underpants look like?" I asked.

"Sometimes I'm up there doing my makeup while he's getting ready."

"And he just walks around in his underpants in front of you?"

"We have an understanding. He knows I'm not in-terested in his"—she flicked her fingers dismissively—"wares. Plus, not everyone's as uptight as you are, Dee. Some of us are more comfortable with the full range of human expression."

"'Expression'? This isn't the Age of Aquarius. I'm instituting a dress code for that apartment," I said.

"Starting tomorrow, everyone is fully clothed at all times."

"Pants *and* tops?!" came Sonya's affronted reply. "What are we, monks?"

Melody waved her hands around her ears, apparently trying to purge all the imagery this conversation had conjured. "I don't want to know this."

"Sorry, Mel," Sonya said.

"Let's get back on track," I said. "We need to figure out how Daniel's underwear got in Hadley's bag."

"Well . . ." Sonya cast an apologetic glance at Melody and lowered her voice. "One obvious way is if *he's* Hadley's kinky boyfriend."

"He wouldn't be interested in a girl like that." Melody's voice was shaky as she struggled to keep her emotions in check. Then, less assuredly, she added, "Would he?"

"No. Hadley seems emotionally fragile. He wouldn't take advantage of that." *My* tone held no hesitation.

"Maybe she stole them while she was up there with Piper to visit Butterball?" Sonya speculated. "Daniel showers up there. They could've been laying around."

"Don't you think he'd realize his undies were missing when he was getting dressed?" I asked. "Would he walk around commando all day and not notice?"

Sonya gave a noncommittal shrug. "Daniel is Daniel."

"Daniel is Daniel," I repeated.

Yes, Daniel was Daniel. Fun, carefree, flirtatious Daniel. The same Daniel who seemed to know a murder victim better than he was admitting. The same Daniel who seemed to have hidden the fact that his mother had a vendetta against Adrian Hoffman, in whose house the murder took place. The same Daniel who was one of the only people at the party strong enough to carry Natasha's dead body from below the balcony all the way to bottom of the ski slope.

I couldn't meet anyone's eyes as I began to replace the contents of Hadley's purse. Each item seemed to grow heavy in my hand as the realization of Daniel's plight settled over me. I'd hoped that, when I eventually got around to talking to Capone about the connection between Daniel's mother and Adrian Hoffman, I could mention it in passing, no big deal. I'd hoped that I'd find something in Hadley's purse to distract Capone and throw him off the scent of the people I cared about.

Instead, I'd singlehandedly made everything worse.

CHAPTER 14

A fresh blanket of snow greeted me the next morning when I came downstairs just before nine o'clock. After the underpants discovery, we'd given up on our usual cleaning and closing routine, deciding it was best to come in early today and finish everything before service. Thank goodness we were on an abbreviated, dinner-only schedule.

Biz had apparently been up early, as a tray of fresh-baked cinnamon rolls was laid out on the island. A note on the counter informed me that she, Piper, and Jonathan had already headed over to the lakefront park to watch the snow sculpting resume. I stood in the kitchen's bay window, enjoying the quiet of the house. More of the white stuff continued to fall at a steady clip, obscuring the view of the lake. I felt sorry for the sculptors. Although the weather was warm compared to the day of their previous attempt, I wondered how the fast-falling snow would play out for them.

The light coming in from outside was barely enough to see by, but rather than flip on a lamp, I lit a fire in the living room. I'd just settled into an armchair with a big mug of coffee and a cinnamon roll when Sonya bustled in.

She wore a short faux-mink jacket with a coordinating hat perched atop a Jackie O–swoop of shellacked black hair. She planted herself in the chair next to me and without even greeting me, said, "So let's figure out this murder."

Since yesterday's recap of the theories had been such a stuttering, interrupted affair, I filled her in on the basics—the time-stamped video of Natasha's fall, everyone's whereabouts at the time, the partially disrobed body that had somehow been transported from where it fell to the bottom of the ski slope and then trucked from there to the lakefront park. Then there were the matters of Rabbit's disappearing act and Daniel's mother's run-in with Adrian Hoffman. I finished by recounting the odd sense that both Daniel and Jonathan were concealing the nature of their relationships with the dead woman.

She let out a long whistle, then added, "Plus, the underpants."

"Plus, the underpants," I repeated. "My best theory on that is that Daniel left them in the apartment and Hadley stole them when she went up there last night. She clearly has a crush on him. She was asking all those questions about his name and where he's from. It's all a little stalker-y."

"How would she even have known they were his, though?"

I shrugged. "Maybe she truly is a little unhinged, like Jonathan implied, and just steals random undies? For all we know, she has a whole secret lair full of stolen underpants."

Sonya gave a skeptical tilt of her head. She rose and took hold of my cup of coffee as she paced back and forth in front of the fire. "Well, underpants notwithstanding, let's rule out Daniel and Rabbit. I can't bring myself to suspect them." She took a thoughtful sip from my mug. "You said you think Jonathan is lying about how well he knew Natasha. Let's drill down on that."

"You *can* get your own coffee, Son," I pointed out. "There's still half a pot."

She shook her head. "I already had two cups and I don't want to be jittery." She put my coffee back down, unpinned her hat, and set it on the end table. "We both know Capone wouldn't accidentally-on-purpose keep the Savages in town unless he thought they were involved in some way. And you said Piper was acting totally normal but Jonathan seemed nervous."

She picked up my mug and took another sip.

"Do you want me to make a pot of decaf for you?"

"Nah, I can't stay. I'm on my way to the Jewish Community Center in Kenosha for a Hanukkah brunch. There's a new cantor I have my eye on."

When Sonya came in, I'd vaguely registered that she was extra dressed up. But considering that her usual attire was a fit-and-flare rockabilly dress with kitten heels and a full face of retro-style makeup, it would take her wearing an actual tuxedo and top hat for the level of glamour to be truly remarkable.

"Please tell me cantors are allowed to date," I said. "I don't want a repeat of that time you fell for the Buddhist nun who'd taken a vow of celibacy." Sonya was notorious for setting her sights on a wide variety of unsavory and unavailable women. A gainfully employed clergywoman didn't seem like her type.

"The cantor is single, but I'm not positive she dates women," she said. "I don't have much to go on besides her haircut and the fact that she played college softball."

That was more on-brand. I raised an eyebrow.

"Whatever," she said, waving away my unspoken doubts. She lifted the cinnamon roll from my plate and took a bite. "I'm almost afraid of what would happen if it works out anyway. My parents find out I'm dating a nice Jewish girl, they'll be following us around with a chuppah and picking out their grand-dogs' names before the end of the second date. Anyway, back to business. You still haven't given me the full lowdown on your visit to Rabbit's house."

"There's not much more to tell. I confirmed that he's not sick," I said. "He wasn't home and his mother didn't know where he was. She overheard a snippet of him talking to someone on the phone, late on the night of the Chrismukkah party."

"A romantic interest?"

"Could be, but they were talking about money. Sounds more like business than pleasure, don't you think?"

She nodded and stuffed the last piece of cinnamon roll into her mouth.

"There are more cinnamon rolls on the counter," I said.

"I'm not hungry," she replied, licking the icing from her fingers. "So, there seems to be a lot of lying men and mysterious women floating around," she observed. "First, Rabbit had some kind of rendezvous when he snuck off during the party, following those high-heeled footprints. Could that be the same woman his mom overheard him on the phone with later that night?"

My shoulders rose and fell. "Seems unlikely that Rabbit would move in the same circles as the Hoffmans, but who knows? *Something* at that party spooked him. And all of these little problems are a sideshow to the main event—Natasha La Cotti's murder."

She walked into the kitchen and came back a moment later, having topped up my beverage and replaced my cinnamon roll. She took another drink before handing the mug back to me. "And then Daffi and Adrian got into an argument with Daniel's mom at the snow sculpting competition. What did Capone say when you told him the angry woman was Daniel's mom?"

"I haven't told him yet." Before she could chastise me, I raised my hands. "I will. I will. I just need to figure out . . ." I searched the air with my hands.

"How to keep it *brief*?" she offered.

I shot a withering gaze at her. "No. A way to make it look less bad. Do I tell him about the underpants, too? Maybe I can find out what it's all about and then tell him. If there are innocent explanations, there's no reason for Capone to go all . . . *Capone* on Daniel."

"Innocent? Like his underpants *innocently* vaulting into Hadley's bag, and his mother *innocently* strolling up to the Hoffmans to tell them she hoped they burn in hell."

I took a sip of my coffee and frowned into the glowing fireplace.

Sonya bit into the fresh cinnamon roll. "Any chance you can find out from Capone what his working theory is? Maybe take him to a dark room and pump him for information?" she suggested with a lurid wink.

"I wish. We're currently in a fight, though."

Butterball, who'd been lying on the arm of my overstuffed chair, rolled onto his back and began making a series of impossible pretzel shapes with his body. He slow blinked and mewed at Sonya. As she reached out to stroke his tummy, I caught her wrist.

"Don't you know by now that his tummy is a trap?" I chided. "He'll lure you in with those seductive green eyes and then scratch the bejesus out of you when you try to give him a tummy rub."

She leveled her false eyelashed gaze at me. "This wouldn't be the first time I've had a potential love interest scratch the bejesus out of me. Sometimes, it's a sign of affection."

"And sometimes your uncle Avi has to help you take out a restraining order. For your sake and mine, I hope this cantor isn't a scratcher."

Butterball, annoyed that his come-hither ploy hadn't worked, languidly flipped over and jumped down. He made a beeline for the back door and began to paw at it. I tried to ignore his demands. I'd put him on house arrest a few days prior after he deposited a series of increasingly gruesome avian corpses around the house. His version of the Twelve Days of Christmas.

"Speaking of tainted love," she said, lowering her voice and casting a glance over her shoulder. "How's Melody? She seemed really upset by Underpantsgate."

"Not good," I said.

It was going on ten o'clock, but Melody had yet to emerge from her room. I'd heard the distinct sounds of her slamming things around, though, followed by some very moody Olivia Rodrigo songs. Sharing a house with a twentysomething, an eightysomething, and a very opinionated cat meant that there was truly never a dull moment.

While Sonya and I were talking, Butterball's relent-less campaign of door scratching had continued un-abated. He now added a chorus of dissonant meowing. He usually didn't like going out when it was snowing.

"For heaven's sake, B-Man." I rolled my eyes to the ceiling, my resolve defeated. "Just a sec, Son. I've got to let this homicidal maniac out."

Sonya sat on the now-vacated arm of my chair and stuffed the last of cinnamon roll number two into her mouth. "It's okay, I need to head out anyway. The foxy cantor awaits." I rose to walk her toward the door, but she waved me away. "I'll see myself out. Go attend to His Royal Buttness."

I crossed the kitchen and opened the door that led onto the sunporch. Butterball immediately rushed from the kitchen door to the porch door, pawing it with the same level of intensity. I'd enclosed the space when the house was renovated, wanting to eke out a few more weeks of evenings on the porch in the spring and fall and offer a bit of protection from the summer's maraud-ing mosquitos. Both the kitchen door and the sunporch door had cat flaps carved out, but I'd locked them to keep Butterball inside.

The sunporch wasn't heated, and as I entered the space, I felt the familiar chill that I associated with trooping in and out of the restaurant's walk-in freezer during service. Sometimes, going into the walk-in was the only moment of respite from the clamor of the kitchen. With the sun invisible through the heavy snow, the gloom further evoked the dimly illuminated silence of those stolen moments of freezer zen. I opened the porch door to release Butterball into the wilds of the Geneva Bay's lakefront mansions, but he instead beelined it to a clump of bushes next to the porch. Odd, but then, he was an odd fellow. He emerged after a moment and bounded back up the porch steps, through my legs, and into the house.

"What was all that about, B-Man?" I called after him.

Rather than immediately following him, I breathed in, letting the cold air tingle inside my lungs. Icicles, dangling from the edge of the wraparound porch, glinted like metal against the heavy gray clouds. A whiteout blur of snow blanketed the yard, further deadening sound. I inhaled again. Yes, this was my moment of zen. I hadn't figured out even one of the multitude of mysteries, but a fire and fresh coffee awaited me.

Suddenly, the sharp crack of a snapping twig sounded from the clump of bushes Butterball had just vacated. "Butterball?" I wasn't sure why I called out his name. I'd just watched him go back inside. I took a few steps along the porch. "Sonya?" I'd done it again, calling out a name when the possibility was clearly nonsense. As if Sonya, who'd sashayed out the front door in her pretty clothes a moment earlier, would've snuck around back to lurk in the bushes.

Most likely a wild animal. I prayed a skunk wasn't nesting there. The last thing I needed was for Butterball to challenge Pepé Le Pew to what would doubtlessly be a losing battle. Before I could take another step, though, a person sprang out and legged it down the lawn toward the lake.

"Hey!" I cried out. I took off after the retreating figure, racing through the snow in only my house slippers. It was clear within a moment that I didn't have a snowball's chance in hell of catching up. All I could do was stand, slack-jawed in my slippers, ankle-deep in snow, watching as the intruder disappeared into the storm.

CHAPTER 15

"And you have no idea who it was?" Sonya asked.

I shook my head in frustration. "None. I'd guess a man, but it could've been a tall woman. The person had a thick coat on. The snow was really coming down, and I was so surprised."

I'd been fretting on and off all day about the backyard lurker, but if I'd been waiting for some sort of epiphany that would reveal the person's identity, it never came. Whoever it was had been facing away from me during the whole fleeting encounter, with the hood of a dark coat pulled over their head. They'd moved well through the snow, which made me think they had to be youngish, or at least in good shape. The prints their boots left in the yard were quickly covered by the snow, but my quick assessment was that they were a little bigger than my size elevens. That was all I had to go on.

Repeating the info now under Sonya's questioning hadn't jogged any new recollections loose. She and I, plus Auntie Biz, were in the restaurant's kitchen, deep in the throes of dinner service. We'd been hammered since we opened, but a brief lull finally gave me a chance to fill them in.

"I can't believe you're only telling us about this now," Biz huffed.

I mounded grated Gouda onto one of our signature pies, the Deep Dutch, topped it with sauce, and popped it into the blazing-hot oven. "We were so busy during prep," I said.

In fact, "busy" didn't cover it. I'd come in at noon, with Daniel, Melody, and Sonya joining me shortly after. But even with all of us arriving early, we'd still been in headless-chicken mode trying to catch up on the unfinished tasks from the previous night, plus all of Jarka's and Rabbit's usual prep work. And it didn't help that we had a last-minute reservation to squeeze in. Biz had proposed hosting a welcome dinner for my sister and nephew, and Jonathan and Piper had extended the invite to the Hoffmans. They were booked for six thirty. Every table was booked at that hour, so not only would I have to get creative with the furniture to accommodate extra people, but I'd also have to whip up a feast, under pressure, that was good enough to impress my judgmental sister.

"Yeah," Sonya agreed, pulling an incoming order ticket off the printer. "Why didn't you call me as soon as it happened?"

"I didn't want to interrupt you in case you were getting somewhere with the cantor."

"She has a boyfriend, if you can believe that." She blew a disgusted raspberry.

"That's never stopped you before," Biz pointed out.

"Exactly. I'm not counting her out. Her haircut gives me hope, plus she was wearing Doc Martens. Anyway, don't steer me off topic. You should've at least called the police."

"I thought about it," I said, "but the Geneva Bay cops

have enough on their hands without me asking them to run around my yard in the midst of a snowstorm. They'd be looking for a person who I wouldn't even know if they walked in right now and sat on my lap."

Calling the police had been a tantalizing prospect, and I'd entertained a brief fantasy of Capone rushing over, begging my forgiveness for our fight, and folding me protectively in his arms. I had an uneasy feeling, though, that I might be the one in the wrong, and apologies didn't come naturally to me.

Besides, I couldn't, in good conscience, waste police time on the matter. The only crime that had been committed was trespassing, and there was no suspect. My house, like all properties around Geneva Lake, was intersected by the shore path—a public footpath that ringed the entire twenty-mile circumference of the lake. It was a quirk left over from the time before European colonization, when a footpath led from one lakeside Pottawatomie settlement to the next. As more land was developed along the lake, the path persisted. Every lakeshore landowner was required to maintain their section of the path, and allow it to remain open for the public to walk on. Most homeowners took the peculiarity of hosting a public thoroughfare in their backyard in stride, accepting it as part of the area's unique charm. Some even installed amenities for walkers, like benches and dog water stations. Others swung far in the other direction, erecting privacy fences, walls, and menacing signage.

My approach to the path's proximity fell somewhere between those extremes. Most of the time, I liked greeting random dogwalkers and sunset strollers when I sat on my dock. The house had a wide expanse of grass between it and the lake, and I was far enough out of town that foot traffic was fairly limited. Plus, my backyard was dotted with clumps of oaks and evergreens that provided a visual buffer. In the interest of security, my ex, a keen techie, had installed a camera at the back of our property. I'd checked it after my encounter with the stranger, of course, but it picked up only a brief, unidentifiable flash as the figure ran across the camera's frame. So, while the experience had spooked me, there didn't seem to be much more I could do, short of digging a moat.

"Probably just a shore path lookie-loo," Biz said. Indeed, while most people respected the boundary between the public path and the private land it crossed, it wasn't uncommon for snoopers to venture nearer to one of the lake's magnificent mansions to get a closer look. And every once in a blue moon, a tipsy tourist would be found frolicking in someone's patio pool or on their private dock. "I'll start walking around the house naked," she continued. "If they're going to peep, might as well give 'em something to write home about."

Sonya burst out laughing, but I could muster only a sliver of a smile.

I'd shaken off the worst of my jitters after the frightening encounter, but I still felt uneasy. Our ticket printer was slowly ratcheting up again as another wave of diners was seated. I pulled the latest order—a small Red Hot Mama and a Curried Cauliflower Calzone—my stress building. The whole day, I'd tried to distract myself with positive thoughts—the holidays, the prettily falling snow, a fully-booked restaurant. But nothing seemed to drown out the drumbeat inside my brain, which seemed intent on hammering out the rhythm of impending doom.

We were busier than usual, but Piper had offered

to help out again, and she seemed to be pulling her weight. The kitchen was under control. Nothing external seemed to justify the tightening stricture of anxiety in my throat. There was the murder investigation, of course. And my fight with Capone. Yeah, that must be it.

I glanced at the clock. Shea, Jonathan, Caleb, Daffi, and Adrian would be arriving any minute.

Shea is coming.

My thoughts screeched to a halt.

Shea. Is. Coming.

I could almost feel a cortisol spike. The fingers of dread around my throat constricted with every inhale. The steady beat in my head crescendoed into a full-on, Led Zeppelin–style, cymbals-and-bass drum solo, and the only lyrics to the song were "Shea is coming."

Not being particularly blessed with emotional introspection, I struggled to fathom the mix of feelings my sister conjured inside me. I loved her. I hadn't seen her since our dad died, and soon we'd be reunited. So why was the dominant feeling inside of me not excitement, but dread?

"Why are you adding oregano to the sauce for the Curried Cauliflower Calzone?" Biz knocked my hand aside before I could scatter the herb into the wrong pan.

"Oh . . ." I stammered, drawing my hand back and blinking.

Tonight, my nerves had me making a mountain of tiny mistakes. The oregano near-miss was just the latest. I breathed in the familiar scents of my kitchen, trying to calm myself. The piquant tang of garlic, mellowing into an aromatic perfume as it hit a pan of hot butter. The sweet, yeasty warmth of crust baking. The tantalizing aroma of mozzarella, which was, at that

moment, crisping to a caramel char under the broiler.
My eyes fell on each item in my workspace. My knives.
My spoons. My pans. The tools of my trade. My armor
of competence. *You can cook. This is what you do.* I
took in another breath. *You're in your own kitchen, in
your own restaurant.* My deep breathing steadied me
for about a millisecond before another thought crept in.
Shea is coming.

As if I'd summoned her with my thoughts, my sister
entered the kitchen. "Figured I'd find you back here."

Biz, who'd been sitting on her usual stool, slapped
her hands down on her thighs and rose. "Well, look
who's coming to dinner!"

The O'Learys aren't huggers, and Auntie Biz in particular was decidedly uneffusive in bestowing signs
of physical affection. Her typical gesture of familial
tenderness was an approving nod, swiftly delivered.
For her part, Shea was a rosebush—pretty to look at,
but prickly if you tried to get too close. My own relationship with Biz could sometimes be strained, but she
and Shea hardly had a relationship to speak of at all.
That's why, even after such a long absence and even at
Christmastime, I wasn't sure what would happen when
they first encountered each other.

My sister smoothed her fitted black cashmere sweater
as Biz walked toward her. Shea's taste in fashion was
understated elegance, bordering on austerity. Tonight,
she paired the sweater with wide-legged, camel-colored
slacks and a slender gold chain belt. There was a tense
moment when it looked like she and Biz might shake
hands or exchange business cards, but then Biz opened
her arms and embraced my sister. Shea stood about
an inch taller than me, while Biz skimmed the bot-

tom of the five-foot mark. In Shea's arms, she looked childlike and fragile.

"I'm so glad you came." Biz's words were muffled. When she pulled out of the embrace, her eyes glistened.

I felt a Prodigal Son–style pang of jealousy. Why did *I* have to deal with Normal Biz's day-in, day-out curmudgeonly-ness fifty-one weeks out of the year, while Shea and her family waltzed right into smiles, warm apple cider, and hugs from Holiday Biz?

My sister seemed to be thrown slightly off-kilter by the hug, but she quickly recovered. "Thanks." She gestured to our surroundings and met my eyes. "Finally, you got your own restaurant."

My brain immediately began to rip apart the sentence, turn it over, dissect it. Why had she said "finally"? Did she think I should already have achieved this milestone before now? Did she consider thirty-five too old? And why "you got" your own restaurant instead of "you opened . . ." or "you're running . . ."? Was she implying that because my ex had bankrolled it, it had been given to me?

I pushed the thoughts back down to whatever wellspring of self-doubt they'd bubbled up from. *You are a grown-ass boss lady. Stop. Freaking. Out.*

"Hi, Shea. Good to see you."

I put down the flaming-hot pan, although part of me wanted to cling to it for self-defense. As I crossed the room, Biz turned and pulled the two of us into an awkward, three-way hug. I felt the gym-toned solidity of my sister come up against my soft curves.

"If hugs are happening, I want in," Sonya said. She threw her arms around the three of us and squeezed. She released us and stepped back with a sharply appraising look. "Man, your cuddle game needs work. That was like hugging a pile of driftwood."

It was true. The O'Leary women were out of practice, as shy with one another as sixth graders at a coed dance.

Shea smiled primly. "I didn't realize we were being scored."

"Well I, for one, thought we stuck the landing," I said, trying to inject some levity.

No one laughed. Biz broke the uncomfortable silence. "How was your flight?"

"The usual nightmare." Shea waved her hand wearily. "Crazy busy in Denver. We barely made our connection."

"You were probably at the Denver Airport the same time as my uncle Avi," Sonya said. "He's on his way back from a pickleball tournament in Palm Springs. He almost beat Kourtney Kardashian."

"How fun." Shea's face showed interest, yet her tone somehow managed to convey that she couldn't care less about Uncle Avi's pickleball prowess.

"I don't understand why you and Caleb didn't come with Jonathan and Piper in the first place," Biz said. "Caleb's the perfect age to start learning to ski on the bunny slopes."

"I had a lot of work to catch up on before the holidays," Shea replied.

"If it hadn't been for that woman dying, you wouldn't be here at all," Biz said.

"Yes, well, we're all here now."

Once again, Shea displayed an impressive ability to give off two meanings at the same time. At face value, her words could be taken to mean that all's well that ends well. But beneath the surface, she was emitting a strong signal that this topic of conversation was closed.

"Is everyone else here?" I asked. I examined the ticket for the order that had just come through. Artichoke dip and garlic knots.

"Those were our apps," Shea replied, indicating the ticket. "Piper took our order. I see you roped her into waitressing."

"Yeah, she's been a big help," I said.

"I'm sure this is a fun little hobby for her," Shea said.

I took in a deep breath as I filled an ovenproof skillet with the heavenly mix of dairy and vegetables that comprised our artichoke dip. We always made a big batch during prep so all we needed to do when an order came in was broil it until the top was golden and bubbling. *Stay in control. Focus on the food.*

"How do you and Jonathan know the Hoffmans?" Sonya asked.

"I don't know them. The girls are sorority sisters, but I've never met Hadley in person. Jonathan knows them through a mutual business associate, Natasha La Cotti." Shea's eyes brimmed with revulsion as she said the woman's name.

"That's the lady who died, right?" Biz asked. I realized with a start that she had been insulated from the investigation, and, unlike me, hadn't been obsessing over the details.

"Yes," my sister replied. "The dead woman."

Was I crazy, or did I detect a hint of satisfaction in Shea's tone? Sonya, who'd gone back to cooking, seemed to notice the same thing. She caught my eye over my sister's shoulder and raised her eyebrows.

"What sort of business was she in?" I asked.

Shea gave a careless flick of her wrist. "No idea."

I looked at her closely, trying to read her expression. Despite repeated attempts at questioning Jonathan, I hadn't succeeded in understanding the connection between my brother-in-law, the Hoffmans, and Natasha La Cotti. Jonathan was a tennis coach. Adrian was in property. Natasha was some kind of consultant, a highly paid one based on how she dressed. Yet, the connection between them seemed to run deeper than casual acquaintanceship.

"So, you didn't know Natasha?" I asked.

"I don't see why we're talking about her. She's dead." Her jaw was firm, almost daring me to ask another question.

Biz preempted the possibility. "Well, I'm itching to see Caleb," she said. "I bet he's grown up so much." She was already halfway through the door, her arm hooked through Shea's. "Come on, Delilah."

I watched them walk out. A moment passed. Then another. I hadn't budged. My gaze shifted to the order tickets waiting to be pulled off the printer. I looked around the kitchen, trying to remember what I'd been doing, trying to find some task that would occupy my hands and still my tumultuous emotions. I felt a strong impulse to go visit with my little nephew, who I, too, was dying to see. But *someone* had to ensure that the dinner service proceeded flawlessly. Maybe I should just stay in the kitchen. Yes, I was needed here.

Sonya followed my eyes to the ticket printer. She also followed my train of thought. "Work isn't going to protect you."

"I don't know what you mean," I lied.

"Some people hit the bottle to get through family engagements. Work is your drug of choice." She leveled a look at me. "We've got a good jump on these orders. Most of the pizzas are already in the oven. Why don't you bring out their apps?" When I didn't move, she threw some oven mitts at me, pointed to the skillet of molten dip she'd just pulled from the broiler, and shooed me out. "Go."

I made a move to grab the app order, but instead rushed over to hug her. Over the six-plus months since the restaurant opened, she had proved time and again that she had my back. She knew me, all of me, and she still liked me. With Sonya, I never had to pick apart the meaning of her words, looking for razor blades hidden in the candy. She made me feel competent and supported. I knew I'd never completely let go of my control-freak tendencies or my workaholism but, confronted with the roiling emotions stirred up by Shea, it was nice to be reminded that I had a pretty damn good substitute for a sister by my side every day.

"I love you, you know," I said.

When I released Sonya from the embrace, she looked slightly stunned by the ferocity of my gesture. "What was that for?" She peered into my face. "Are you dying?" She patted up and down her body, her eyes widening in alarm. "Wait . . . am *I* dying?"

"I'm just glad you're here, that's all."

I grabbed the appetizers, girded my loins, and walked out of the kitchen.

CHAPTER 16

As I came into the dining room, I tried to regain control of myself. When I'd designed Delilah & Son's interior, I tried to imbue it with a sense of enchantment and escape. Right then, though, I couldn't quite get its magic to work on me. At least it seemed to be working on the restaurant's guests. Conversations created a pleasant thrum, a background noise occasionally punctuated by a peal of laughter or the clink of a glass. Sonya and I had curated a holiday playlist that mixed festive standards with modern jazzy takes on the season by Jamie Cullum and John Legend. The mood was further heightened by the seductive aromas of freshly baked pizza and roasted garlic drifting from the kitchen.

I'd made sure to seat Shea's party at one of the window tables, the best table in the house. But as I approached, I could see that the best table was also the only table not having a good time. And really, how could they be? Shea had dropped everything and flown across the country to be with her husband and stepdaughter, who themselves had been questioned in a murder investigation. The Hoffmans' home had been searched; their party had become a crime scene. Just as my eyes couldn't help but be drawn to the view of the freezing, ink-black lake, the group at Shea's table must've felt unable to pull their attention away from looming specter of Natasha La Cotti's death.

Adrian glowered at the head of the table, Daffi to his right. Hadley sat next to them, her arms folded into a tight X over her chest, her lips fixed into a pout. Everything about her seemed pinched. Her shoulders rounded as if her body were curling in on itself. Every motion was staccato, as if her tendons and ligaments had suddenly grown too short to allow her to move freely.

Daffi's eyes were glassy and her cheeks had a ruddy glow that could have resulted from stinging wind or excess imbibing. Watching as she topped up her wine-glass in a practiced, weary way, I guessed it was the latter. When I'd seen Daffi the night of the Chrismukkah party, I'd been struck by her resemblance to her daughter. But it was as if she'd aged in fast motion since then, all the years hitting her at once, like gathering waves that had finally broken. And when the breaker drew back, it clawed away her protective layer.

On the other end of the table, my sister had taken her seat. Jonathan was next to her, and leaned in to murmur something in her ear. The two of them, each so attractive, looked even more so when sitting side by side, like a matching his-and-hers gift set of health and prosperity. But while Jonathan's attention was zeroed in on Shea with a devotion that bordered on desperation, her own concentration seemed fractured. She barely registered whatever he was saying. Her discontented gaze flitted around; her fingers drummed the tabletop.

Biz was the only one of the group in a holiday mood, resplendent in a Christmas sweater so loud it could almost be heard over the background music. She had pulled up a chair on the other side of Shea, next to Caleb. The precocious three-year-old, who had inherited ebony skin and curly hair from his biological parents, nonetheless bore a strong resemblance to my sister, his adoptive mother. Like her, he sat up straight, radiating intelligence. Shea had dressed him—a young child who'd just taken a five-hour flight—like a page from the toddler edition of *GQ*. Caleb held up a coloring book, showing Biz something. Probably algebra problems, knowing Shea.

Biz waved me over, and I plastered on a smile. *What could be merrier than an evening with my family in my very own lakefront restaurant at Christmastime?* I caught sight of the Al Capone painting as I passed beneath it. I'd fixed a little paper Santa hat on the portrait of old Scarface, covering his usual baby bonnet. The detail caught in my mind, an eerie echo of how I felt as I approached the table. As if only the thinnest veneer of fake holiday cheer was papering over something sinister.

I greeted the group and set down the appetizers. Daffi gave a feeble wave, while Adrian merely grunted and took a swig from his wineglass. I looked from the Hoffmans to Daniel, over at the bar, and tried to tune into the vibe between them. If he shared in his mother's grudge against them, surely the air would be thick with tension? But I saw nothing between them except, well, thin air. No stolen glances. No avoided eye contact. If they and Daniel recognized one another from somewhere other than the Chrismukkah party, they were all doing an Oscar-caliber job of concealing it.

"How's everything so far?" I asked.

"The wine's delicious," Daffi said.

"You've certainly sampled enough of it," Adrian muttered.

"This place reminds me of this little spot in Boca I sometimes hit when I'm down there coaching," Jonathan said, in an attempt at cheerfulness. "It has a patio right on the water, like yours." He looked out at the falling snow and laughed. "Well, like I bet yours is in the summertime."

Hadley, who I'd thought was zoned out, suddenly piped up. "I didn't realize you were still *coaching tennis*. You should give me some lessons sometime. I'd *love* to improve my game."

"Hadley, quit being a brat," her father snapped.

The sarcasm in Hadley's voice and the contempt in her father's caused the conversation to screech to a halt. I couldn't be sure, but her comment felt like an intentional dig at my brother-in-law's profession. And while I agreed it was a bratty thing to say, the tone of Adrian's rebuke seemed overly harsh. Hadley pushed back from the table and stomped over to take a seat at one of the bar stools.

Biz piped up to break the silence that followed. "You should come in August for the Venetian Festival. That's the best time of year." She turned to my sister. "Don't you remember, Shea? When you and Delilah would come up to my house and spend the whole summer?"

"I only did that once," Shea said. "While Mom was alive, we only came up for a week or two. It was only after she died that we came for the whole summer. To give Dad a break, I guess. Or get our minds off of it. I did it for one summer, and the next summer I had to start my ROTC training. You must be remembering your summers with Delilah."

Biz's expression crumpled, as if Shea had just wad-
ded up her happy memory and tossed it in the trash.
Shea made no move to relieve the awkwardness, instead sipping her wine with cool detachment. Jonathan
cleared his throat, but even his seemingly inexhaustible
well of small talk seemed to have run dry.

Finally, I cut in. "Jonathan, you said you were
doing some coaching down in Florida? Is that a regu-
lar gig?"

"Yeah," Jonathan said, peeling his gaze off his wife.
"I've been running some tennis clinics there and in
Montauk. I alternate about every six weeks. I'll be head-
ing to Florida again right after the holidays."

Adrian raised his glass in a cheers gesture. "Playing tennis in Boca and Montauk. Nice work if you
can get it."

"It would be, if it were real work," Shea said, an acid
hiss in her voice.

Whoa. I had certainly been on the receiving end of
Shea's pronouncements about what constituted acceptable work. She'd made it clear that she didn't think
cooking was a real career path. But previously Jonathan
had been immune from her tough assessments. She'd
always pulled in the larger salary, and her job was the
one that provided stability and benefits. Despite that,
I'd never once heard her hold it over her husband's
head. If anything, she always went out of her way to
talk him up, lauding him for being so dedicated to the
sport. But not only had she failed to defend him from
Hadley's snarky jibe, she'd doubled down by saying that
his profession wasn't even real work.

Jonathan looked stricken. "What's that supposed to
mean?"

"I think you know," came Shea's reply.

Jonathan rose, not looking at her. In fact, his attention had shifted entirely. Making pointed eye contact with Adrian, he said, "I need some air."

He pushed past me without excusing himself. Shea's hands trembled as she clutched the stem of her wineglass and raised it to her lips. Her eyes followed her husband as he crossed the room. I tried and failed to read her expression. Anger? Disdain? From her words, that's what I expected. But this was something deeper. Primal. Like she could barely keep herself from crying out in agony. I was shocked by her cruelty, but there was something so tortured in her eyes that I couldn't help but feel pity for her.

Adrian rose. He glanced at his daughter, who was still sitting at the bar, and then said, "I think I'll take a breather, too."

When the men had departed, I scooted closer to Shea. "You okay?" I asked quietly.

"Of course," came the curt reply, the words pushed out through clenched teeth.

In that moment, I barely recognized my sister. She'd always been driven and little aloof, caught up as she was in exuding an aura of effortless perfection. Those things, I understood all too well. But it was as though I were watching dangerous cracks fracture the surface of a frozen lake. As if maybe, right before my eyes, the whole enormous artifice of my sister's perfect life was about to break apart.

"You sure?"

"I said I was fine, didn't I?" she snapped.

If anyone else had talked to me like Shea did, I wouldn't hesitate to serve them a big, salty piece of my mind. But with her, my bluster was always replaced by fluster, as if I were still the left-behind kid sister.

I wanted so badly to make her happy, but it was a losing game.

I tried to exorcise the bad juju, taking a deep breath and squatting down to my nephew's level. "I don't know if you remember me. I'm your aunt Delilah. I got you a Nerf Super Soaker for your birthday, when you turned three in November," I added, hoping to jog his memory.

"Mommy says I can't keep it." Caleb gazed at me with solemn eyes. "We don't play with guns."

I grimaced. "It was more of a water cannon . . ."

Thankfully, Piper bounced over just then and saved me.

"Everything okay? You hanging in there?" I asked, rising and taking a few steps toward her.

"Totes," she said. "I was just telling Hadley that this work is weirdly therapeutic. You really have to be in the zone. You can't think about anything else. I think she'd like it. She's been so distracted lately, like she can't get out of her own head."

"Seems like Hadley's more interested in bartending than serving," I observed grimly.

At the bar, Hadley, for the second night in a row, had fallen deep into conversation with Daniel. I'd given her purse back to Piper that morning, underpants and all, and I saw it now, hanging from one of the hooks under the bar. On the other side of the dining room, Melody was also looking at them, twisting a napkin between her hands with such ferocity I wondered if she was forming it into a garrote. She was probably thinking the same thing I was: *How had Daniel's underpants gotten into that purse?* My interest was aimed at solving a mystery. Hers was aimed like a grenade launcher.

"Has Hadley said anything about Daniel?" I tried to

make my question sound nonchalant, not like the fishing expedition it was.

"Just that he's hot," Piper said with her usual throaty laugh. She snapped her fingers. "Oh, there *was* one weird thing. I saw her looking on her phone for info about Puerto Rico. I thought she was planning a beach vacay, but she said it was research. I thought that was weird, since our classes are all done for the semester, and anyway, Hadley, like, *doesn't* do research. I wondered if she was trying to learn some stuff about the island so she and Daniel would have more to talk about." Piper further lowered her voice. "But honestly, I bet she's just hanging out over there to avoid her parents. She's always had drama with her dad, but now she's pissed at her mom, too."

"Do you know what's going on?"

She shook her head. "She won't tell me."

The news of Hadley's conflict with her father didn't surprise me. He seemed like a Grade-A hosebag. But Daffi seemed devoted to her daughter, though perhaps worryingly deferential to her husband. Then I remembered the sharpened steel in her voice when Daniel's mother confronted her husband at the snow sculpting contest.

I looked at Hadley for a beat longer. I was too far away to hear what she and Daniel were saying, but it struck me that Daniel, instead of displaying the usual twinkle-eyed naughty schoolboy expression he wore when tending bar, had his face set into a mask of earnest concentration. He, like Sonya, was often playful even in serious situations, but like any good bartender, he knew how to calibrate his emotions to match the prevailing conditions. And these conditions looked stormy. I couldn't see Hadley's face, but the coy posture she'd displayed yesterday had disappeared. She sat straight, her fists clenched into balls on the top of the bar. Whatever the two of them were talking about was a topic that didn't call for flirtation.

Piper didn't seem to have picked up on the vibe. "Well, I better get back to work," she said.

"Why don't you join your family? I'm sure Melody can handle things for a while."

She untied her apron and took the seat her father had vacated. She snatched a garlic knot from the basket and took a big bite. "Will you and Auntie Biz teach me a couple of recipes while I'm here?" she asked. "I can barely make ramen."

"Of course, dear," Biz cut in, clearly delighted by the prospect. "We can start with crêpes Suzette tomorrow for breakfast. That's the first thing Delilah learned to cook on her own. The ingredients are all pantry staples and you only need one pan, so you can make it anywhere."

"Can I do it, too?" Caleb asked.

"Of course," Biz said. "And we can have hot cocoa and light a fire." Her eyes shone. Visions of sugar plums were clearly dancing in her head.

Piper and Caleb smiled happily, but when I caught a glimpse of Shea, her lips were compressed into a paper-thin line. What was wrong with her? Something major was clearly going on, but couldn't she muster a little bit of holiday spirit for Biz's sake? Or at least for her kids' sake?

"You'll love them," I told Caleb. "They're skinny pancakes with orange and caramel sauce."

"I don't like the pancakes at the hotel," he replied.

"What hotel, honey?" I asked.

"This morning, where me and Mommy were."

"This morning?" I repeated. Shea hadn't mentioned anything about staying in an airport hotel.

Before I could suss out his meaning, my sister rose from her chair so abruptly it screeched against the wood floor. "We should get going. It's past Caleb's bedtime."

"But you just sat down," Biz protested. "You haven't even eaten."

Shea lifted her son from his chair and hoisted him onto her hip. "You have food at home, I assume?" she said to me. "You always do."

I nodded. "There's coq au vin in the fridge. And a quiche. And meatballs."

"So we won't starve." She flashed a tight smile. "This little guy needs his sleep. His schedule is already messed up from the jetlag."

"Come on, Shea," Piper said. She stood up and gave her brother's head an affectionate rub. "You just got here, and Delilah and Biz have hardly gotten to see you."

The bell over the door jangled, and Jonathan and Adrian made their way back inside. Shea cast a venomous glance at them, but then turned back to the rest of us with a smile. "No, I'm going to head back. For some reason, I've lost my appetite."

CHAPTER 17

At last, the meal was over, and everyone went their separate ways. Piper and Jonathan took Biz back home, leaving me and my skeleton crew to clean up and close. I'd never been happier to see the last customer depart. Well, not since the previous night.

Under normal circumstances, my team worked with cheerful camaraderie. Tonight, though, Melody was alternating between bouts of (literally) furious activity and spells of staring sullenly out the window. Daniel, instead of cracking jokes as he usually did, seemed subdued. Sonya was keeping up a good front, but a combination of fatigue, mussed hair, and smeared eye makeup had given her the appearance of a frazzled panda. I, too, was worse for the wear. When I'd caught a glimpse of myself in the bathroom mirror as I scrubbed the sinks, I looked like a slightly melted wax figure version of myself.

Jarka, at least, would be back tomorrow to help with the Christmas Eve lunch service, which meant if we could get through tonight, the worst was behind us. Rabbit, though—who knew?

I looked at my phone. Rabbit was still ghosting me, and I was angry enough to fire him. The old Delilah probably would have. But my time living in Geneva Bay had softened me in ways that weren't always good for the restaurant's bottom line. I knew that if Rabbit lost his job, it would jeopardize his custody arrangements, his ability to support himself, and possibly his freedom. His parole was contingent on him being employed. Old Delilah would've chalked those dire consequences up in the "not my problem" column, but living in this small, tightly interconnected place, it was hard to ignore the impact a decision like that would have. Still, Geneva Bay hadn't turned me into a total mush bucket. I was going to give Rabbit an ultimatum. He had to meet me face-to-face ASAP and explain himself or he was out on his ear. I tapped out a text and sent it before I could talk myself out of it.

With that problem attended to, I turned to my next task—clearing the air between Daniel and Melody. I had no clue how to intervene in matters of the heart, so I beelined it to the kitchen to consult with someone who did. Sonya, despite her own bleak track record of romantic snafus, was surprisingly clear-eyed when it came to other people's entanglements. She was also adept at wading gently into emotionally turbulent waters, while I tended to steam in like a nuclear submarine with my warheads locked and loaded.

I found her prepping dough for the next day's crusts.

"We've got a Code Red Melody Situation," I said, bringing her up to speed on the latest front-of-house drama. "Daniel, Melody, and Hadley will all be at my house for Christmas dinner and I don't want her jealousy poisoning the atmosphere. It's bad enough that I have to deal with Biz's whole 'perfect Christmas' dream and whatever is going on with Shea."

"Yeah, I don't envy you," Sonya said.

"Most importantly, I can't afford to buy a new point-of-sale kiosk, and Melody seems on the verge of destroying ours by anger-entering orders."

Sonya's gray eyes became thoughtful as she poured a bag of flour into our huge mixer. "Personally, I'd let it blow over. Hadley will be gone in a few days. But if you feel like you *have* to do something, I guess the first step is to figure out if there's fire or just smoke."

"Meaning?"

"Hadley is crushing on Daniel," she said. "But as far as I can tell, he's been polite, in a brotherly way. I haven't seen him actively encouraging anything. Have you?"

I thought back to the interactions I'd witnessed. "He was in a pretty intense conversation with Hadley tonight," I said, "but he might've been trying to show empathy for whatever she's going through." I let out a heavy sigh. "But then there are the underpants."

"We still don't know what the deal is with those. If this is a one-way thing, though, then you could try to make it clear to Melody that she's not in competition with Hadley. Or, if Daniel's been encouraging Hadley, try to help him see that it can't be worth causing so much heartache over a few days of fun. Or—here's a novel idea—you could stay out of it."

"How can I? What about the beef between Daniel's mother and the Hoffmans? I still haven't said anything about it to Capone. I need to get to the bottom of that ASAP. That's going to involve figuring out what the connection is between his family and Hadley's."

Sonya tipped her head philosophically. "I would definitely tread gently when it comes to asking Daniel about his mother. Men and their mothers." She made an X with her flour-dusted fingers. "There's no good way to ask a dude if he thinks his mom might be involved in a murder. If you go there, you may be kissing your friendship with Daniel goodbye."

"Fair point," I conceded. "But we need to do something."

"*We* don't need to do anything. My advice is to let it play out."

"But I . . ."

She held up her finger to still my sputtering excuses. "I know, Dee. You're constitutionally incapable of sitting quietly on the sidelines, or of listening."

"What do you mean? I came in here explicitly to ask for your advice," I countered.

She patted me on the arm, leaving a floury handprint. "But did you come here to *listen* to it?"

"I mean . . ."

She held up her finger again. "You do you. You're a fixer, and I love that about you." Her eyes were full of pity as she added, "Just be prepared for the consequences."

As I walked out into the dining room, I told myself I was doing the right thing. Sure, Sonya had a point, but she didn't understand that it was my responsibility to fix this. If I didn't, people I cared about might get hurt. If I did just the right things, found just the right words, I could prevent harm from coming to them. Plus, I had a business to run. I was the boss, people's livelihoods depended on me, and that meant making tough decisions.

I found Daniel behind the bar, washing out the garnish bins. Melody was seated at a nearby table with her back to him, making cutlery roll-ups.

"Mel, can you go empty the dishwasher?" I asked.

She grunted sullenly, but obliged. With her dispatched, I sidled over to Daniel.

"What's up, *jefa*?" he asked.

When I'd walked into the dining room, my plan was to try my hand at a subtle approach, but as I took my seat at a bar stool in front of Daniel, I found myself blurting out, "What have you and Hadley been talking about?" So much for the right words.

He raised an eyebrow at my abruptness. "Puerto Rico. She was asking a lot of questions about my time living there, the place where I'm from, that kind of thing."

"That's all you talked about? Puerto Rico? It looked serious."

"At first, she was complaining about school, saying she didn't feel like she belongs at Palisades, that she was only there because her parents wanted her to go there. The usual college-girl problems. Then, she turned serious and started asking questions about me. I'm not sure why. She was grilling me, almost like a reporter. She said they visited PR a few times when she was younger."

"Did you ever cross paths with the Hoffmans?" I asked.

"Not that I know of. She said they mostly stayed in a resort. That's the typical *turista* move—sunbathe, hit the beach, go shopping in Old San Juan, rinse, repeat. I didn't think much of it." He'd continued to work as we were talking, but now he stopped, dropping his dishcloth onto the counter. He seemed to sense that I, too, had turned serious.

"You're sure you didn't know them before?" I asked.

"I was enlisted when she said they were there, on active duty a lot of the time. I was in Kuwait for almost a year. If I ever saw her or her parents, I don't remember them." His tone, always so playful, took on an unfamiliar flintiness. His posture was still open, his eye contact steady. But he seemed to be drawing himself inward, on guard.

"What else did Hadley ask you?" I pressed. So far, my mention of the Hoffmans hadn't made him flinch. Could it be that he somehow wasn't aware of his mother's conflict with Adrian? "Was she trying to find out something specific?"

He shrugged. "She asked about my family, why I came to Geneva Bay. If she was fishing, I don't know what she was fishing for."

He briefly recapped their conversation, which tracked with the elements of his backstory that I was already familiar with. I'd met Daniel when he was fresh out of the Army, slinging drinks at a beachfront dive tucked in among the Condado Beach mega-resorts. Most of those places catered to cruise ship day-trippers and served prefab Kool-Aid-tasting tourist swill. Daniel, by contrast, served me a piña colada so luscious and frosty I almost proposed to him on the spot. With his looks, his skills, and his palate, I knew he'd absolutely hoover up the tips if he ever worked in a place with upscale clientele and a cocktail program controlled entirely by him.

And my prediction had come true—here, he'd more than tripled his previous earnings and turned the bar into the restaurant's biggest revenue driver. When I offered him the job, he'd been especially keen to take it. His childhood home, where his mother still lived, had been walloped by Hurricane Maria. Then, to add insult to injury, one of the unscrupulous carpetbaggers who'd descended on the island in the storm's aftermath had taken advantage of the situation. Workers and building materials were in short supply for years after the storm, and many firms demanded huge upfront payments before beginning work. Daniel's mother had the misfortune to employ a contractor who ran off with the money—her life savings—and never showed up for a day's work.

"I don't know why I told her so much," he concluded. "I barely know her. It caught me off guard, I guess. Usually, I'm the one asking questions."

"Did you go skiing with her and Piper?" I asked. "Hadley said she invited you."

He shook his head. "No way. I water-ski, but you won't catch me freezing my *culo* off on some icy hill. I didn't think she was serious anyway. From everything I've seen, Hadley seems like the kind of girl who's only interested in fun. That's why I was surprised when she became so intense, asking all those personal questions."

"And that just came out of nowhere?"

"Yes," he said slowly. "Kind of like now. How you suddenly came out of the kitchen and started giving me the third degree." His tone still held amusement, but more and more wariness had crept in. "What's this about?"

"I just want to know if there's anything going on between you two that I need to worry about."

His jaw stiffened. "Why would you need to *worry* about anything that goes on between me and another consenting adult in my private life?"

"Are you sure there's no connection with your mother and the Hoffmans that you're not telling me about? I don't like being blindsided." He hadn't been there when his mother had gone off on Adrian, so it was possible that whatever that was about didn't involve him. If it did, though, I wanted to give him an opportunity to come clean.

"My mother?" He looked genuinely baffled.

I steeled myself, working up the courage to enter the danger zone. "For example, does your mother have some kind of relationship with Adrian Hoffman?"

"*Relationship? ¿Has perdido la cabeza?* Why are you bringing my mother into this?" He paused, a dark expression overtaking his face. "If we're going to talk about families, why don't you look to your own? How well do you know your sister's husband? Because Jonathan Savage is the man I saw on the road that night after the party, coming out of Daffi and Adrian's house. If anyone should be asking questions, it's me."

"Jonathan?!"

"I think you heard me."

I had indeed heard him, but my brain refused to believe what he was saying.

"That's why I haven't gone in to give my witness statement yet," he said. His dark eyes burned with intensity. "I realized pretty quickly that the police would want a description of the man I saw that night. I googled your brother-in-law, thinking I could at least rule him out. I didn't know the names of any of the other men at the party, but you'd mentioned his. Ever since I realized it was him, I've been dodging Capone's calls, hoping the investigation would focus on someone else so I wouldn't have to tell him about seeing your sister's husband acting suspicious at the crime scene."

"Jonathan must've realized tonight that you recognized him," I said, half to myself. "And what that would mean."

Daniel nodded. "Maybe. He didn't say anything to

me, but when we made eye contact, his face went white as a ghost."

"He got up from the table," I said, struggling to remember the scene. "Shea said something mean about his job and I assumed he was pissed about that. But he was looking straight ahead, not at her. Straight ahead, where you and Hadley were talking at the bar."

He nodded again, but his attitude toward me remained frosty. "He didn't seem too happy to see me again."

All this time, he'd been keeping mum to protect my family. Meanwhile, I was poking around in his private life, involving myself in some penny-ante romantic nonsense and casting aspersions. Even if he had been having an affair with Hadley, what business was it of mine? She was twenty-one, only five years younger than Daniel. He was my employee, not my child. Yes, I wanted to shield Melody, but maybe that was impossible. She, too, was a grown woman. And, from the fiery look Daniel was sending my way, bringing up the connection between Adrian and his mother had definitely been a mistake. Thank goodness Sonya wasn't the "I told you so" type.

The realization that Daniel had risked getting on the wrong side of the police in order to protect my family made me question my own motives. Had my prying really been about safeguarding Melody's feelings, keeping my staff out of trouble, or serving the best interests of the restaurant? Or had it come from a darker place—my constant impulse to control everyone and everything around me? An impulse, I realized with a painful flash of insight, that felt uncomfortably similar to Auntie Biz's obsession with enacting the perfect family Christmas.

Before we could discuss it any further, a sharp rap sounded on the glass of the locked front door. Capone's substantial physique was framed in the light that filtered out from inside. I exhaled a breath I hadn't even realized I'd been holding, as I rushed over to unlock the door. I'd gotten information from Daniel, all right. A little more than I'd bargained for.

I greeted Capone, trying to swat away the regret that was bubbling up inside of me. I hadn't had any interaction with him since our fight on the phone the previous day, when I'd laid into him about his harsh questioning of Jonathan. It now appeared that Capone's suspicions were far more justified than either of us realized. If there was an innocent explanation for Jonathan circling back to the Hoffman house, why had he freaked out when he clocked Daniel behind the bar? A fresh wave of regret washed over me. This was another way living here had begun to change me. I used to be a champion grudge holder, so convinced that I was always in the right. But now, living and working with people I cared about, I was starting to see that that particular championship podium was a lonely place to be. Still, my mouth couldn't quite find a way to form the words "I'm sorry."

Instead, I said, "This is a surprise. I figured you'd be burning the midnight oil on the La Cotti case."

He gave me the briefest kiss, then pulled away, his face grim. "I am. And the case keeps leading back to you."

I frowned in confusion. Was he referring to my in-laws? Or the dinner earlier that evening, which had included many of the people who'd attended that fateful party? Surely, he didn't think *I* had anything to do with Natasha's death.

Turning to Daniel, Capone said, "I need to speak with you. I have some questions."

Daniel, who had been wiping down the bar, threw up his cleaning cloth in exasperation. "Apparently everyone has questions for me tonight." Few people kept their cool as well as the former Army Reservist, but it seemed that even he had his limits. "Well," he let out his breath in an angry puff. "Shoot."

Capone looked from me to Daniel and back again. "It's been a rough night," I explained.

"I'm afraid I'm not going to make it any smoother," he said.

The door from the kitchen opened and Melody and Sonya peeked in. "Oh, it's you. We saw the car headlights," Sonya explained.

Capone greeted them, but didn't take his focus off of Daniel. "We should speak alone. Maybe upstairs?"

"I have work to finish up here, and my mother's coming soon," Daniel said. "We're going out for a nightcap."

"This conversation really would be better in private," Capone insisted.

The rest of us had been listening in silence, but at that moment, you could've heard a pin drop in the neighboring county.

Daniel seemed momentarily taken aback, but then shook his head emphatically. "I have nothing to hide." He shot a pointed look at me. "From anyone. Ask me whatever you want."

Capone gave him a "have it your way" shrug and said, "It's about your relationship with Natasha La Cotti."

"Why do you need to ask him about the dead woman?" Melody cut in. She took a protective step toward Daniel. "He didn't even know her. None of us did."

"I knew her." Daniel's voice was low.

"He already told us that," I said to Capone. "Remember? When the three of us were talking at the snow sculpting competition, I mentioned how her coat had been left behind. Daniel said he knew her. He wasn't hiding it."

"I remember." Capone turned back to Daniel. "I think you said something along the lines of 'I've seen her around.'"

"That's right," Daniel said.

"You didn't give a witness statement about the party," Capone observed. "You're the only one here who didn't."

"Nobody told me it was an ultimatum. I've been busy." Daniel shot another look at me. "My mother's in town visiting. I've been working. I didn't see any reason to rush over and make a formal statement. I have no information to offer that you haven't already gotten from dozens of other people."

"What about the man you said you saw that night?" Capone prompted. When Daniel didn't respond, Capone cocked his head. "Are you protecting him?"

My heart plummeted like an elevator whose cable snapped. Damn Capone's preternatural ability to read people's thoughts.

Sonya—daughter, niece, and cousin of lawyers— seemed to clock the seriousness of the situation. "Is he under arrest?"

Capone shook his head.

"Well, then he doesn't have to do anything he doesn't want to do," she said. "He doesn't even have to talk to you." She turned to Daniel. "This man may look like

Calvin Capone, but right now he's wearing his invisible cop hat. It transforms him into Cop Capone, who is not our friend." She took her phone from her pocket. "I'll call my uncle Avi."

Daniel once again shook his head. His expression had been tense, but now he smiled and held out his hands. It was hard to say if his shift in attitude was a show of trust or a provocation. "No need."

I noticed how Daniel dodged the question about the mystery man. Well, the no-longer-a-mystery man. No doubt Capone would circle back to it. He wouldn't have sought Daniel out at eleven o'clock at night if there wasn't something serious going on.

Capone took a seat at the bar. The rest of us busied ourselves with front-of-house tasks. With Jarka and Rabbit away and Daniel occupied, there was certainly no shortage of side work that needed to be done. But our primary task, of course, was to eavesdrop.

"Why didn't you come forward once you heard that Natasha La Cotti was dead?" Capone asked. "Surely someone told you the victim's identity by now? Word travels fast in Geneva Bay."

"Yes, I heard. But I told you. I had nothing to add. I have no idea how or why she died."

Capone opened his laptop and clicked open a web browser. "Why does a woman you *barely* knew have pictures of you on her social media?"

"I have no idea. I don't go on social media. We ran into each other a few times, enough that I knew her name. There aren't that many bars and clubs in Geneva Bay. You tend to run into the same people."

"It seems like you knew her *intimately*." Capone loaded the word with implication.

"So he was on her social media feed? What does

that prove?" Sonya demanded, giving up her pretense of sweeping the floors and stamping the broom against the ground. Since Daniel had refused a lawyer, she seemed to be taking up the legal-eagle mantle on behalf of the Dokter family. "He's a friendly guy. I bet he's in pictures with hundreds of people. Women ask to take a picture with him practically every night. You've seen it yourself. And he's not *intimate* with them . . ." She paused, realizing she wasn't on the most rock-solid of ground. "Well, he's not intimate with *most* of them. Probably."

Capone pulled up a social media feed on his laptop and signaled for Daniel to come out from behind the bar to look. The rest of us rushed over and peered over their shoulders. The account was clearly Natasha La Cotti's, with snaps of her looking glamorous in glamorous locations. The feed was a who's who of minor celebrity-dom—a retired baseball player here, a television actor there—a well-curated gallery of a certain kind of aspirational success. And scattered among the pics was Daniel. One shot showed Daniel and Natasha, surrounded by people, dancing next to the lake. Another was a close-up of her arms wrapping around him, her right hand worming its way under the front of his shirt. His face was only half in the frame; the picture focused in on his impressive pectorals. Yet another had Natasha, leaning close, whispering something into Daniel's ear, her lips mere millimeters from his face.

Someone let out a gasp. For all I knew, it could've been me. I caught a glimpse of Melody's face. She looked like she'd just been made to watch *The Texas Chainsaw Massacre* with her eyes taped open.

"Damn, Daniel," Sonya breathed.

Capone spun the laptop back toward himself. "It looks like you and Ms. La Cotti were close."

Daniel stood stock-still for several beats and then gave Capone a smile that would better be described as the baring of teeth. "You want to know what happened that night? There was an all-ages party at the yacht club. Lots of high rollers were in town for the regatta that weekend. Natasha came up to me during the party. She was all over me. Telling me how handsome I looked, how all the girls' eyes were on me. Then, she tried to pay me."

"For sex?" Capone asked.

Daniel shot a poison-tipped dagger of a look at Capone. "No, she wanted me to reel in some high school girls," he explained. "'Get to know them' is what she said."

There was another gasp. I glanced over at Melody, who seemed on the verge of hyperventilating.

"She wanted to pay you to hit on underage girls?" I was surprised I could even form coherent words, given that my lower jaw was on the floor.

The look on Daniel's face was as layered with complexity as one of his cocktails. A heavy measure of disgust. A shot of anger. And an unexpected ingredient: shame. He lowered both his voice and his gaze. "She wanted me to flirt with them, to find out who their parents were. Make sure they were rich."

"What the hell?" Sonya breathed.

"Then what?" Capone prodded.

"Then nothing. I told her to get lost. I left." He jerked his chin toward Capone's laptop. "She must've taken those pictures of me earlier in the night before that."

"You're sure that's all that happened?" Capone asked.

"Isn't that enough? Do you understand now why I

wasn't in a hurry to talk about her? What I said is true. I barely knew her. But I knew enough to know there was something wrong with that woman." He grabbed his coat and bag from behind the bar and slung them over his shoulder. "I'm clocking out. Goodnight, *queridos*."

I wondered if Capone might try to head Daniel off, but he'd apparently decided to leave the rest of his questions for another day. As we watched Daniel head toward the door, we were still grappling with his revelation. Yes, in one sense, he'd been telling the truth when he said he barely knew Natasha La Cotti. She'd hit on him one night and made a highly dubious proposition, which he'd instantly rebuffed. That wasn't a lengthy association. But clearly even that short interaction had made a profound impact on him. I'd never seen my happy-go-lucky bartender so off-kilter.

The sudden, painful awareness that I'd withheld from Capone the information about Daniel's mother being the person who threatened Adrian smacked me in the brain. I'd hoped to break it to him in a quiet moment. In a way that wouldn't make it look like Daniel or his mother were hiding anything shady. I'd justified the decision in so many ways, one of which was by telling myself that the connection from Daniel to his mother to Adrian to the dead woman was tenuous. Certainly too indirect to have bearing on the murder investigation. Now, it seemed that there were exactly zero degrees of separation between Daniel and Natasha La Cotti. Daniel had been protecting me by dodging questions about his suspiciously timed encounter with my brother-in-law. I'd been protecting Daniel by withholding information about his mother. And together, we'd created a big, hairy monster of a mess.

"Bye," I called out, as Daniel strode toward the door. He didn't look back. Instead, he waved his acknowledgment over his shoulder. It was a quick gesture, but I could've sworn his middle finger was aloft.

CHAPTER 18

I grimaced and turned back toward the dining room. When my eyes met Melody's, I saw that hers brimmed with tears. A trembling lip was the only warning sign before the dam burst. She heaved out a sob and buried her face against Sonya's chest.

Sonya rubbed her back. "Oh, Mel. What's the matter? Is it about Daniel?"

"No," Melody sniveled, her words muffled. She pulled out of Sonya's embrace and covered her face with her hands. "Okay, kind of. But it's not *just* about him. It's just, like, I'll never be the kind of person he wants to be with." She shook her hand toward Capone's laptop and wiped her face with the sleeves of her sweater before continuing. "Look at me!" she said, her voice rising in pitch. "I'm not glamorous. I'm not rich. I don't go to parties or have fancy friends."

"Do you even *want* friends like those?" I asked. "And what makes you think Daniel wants to be with someone glamorous? He seemed totally skeeved out by Natasha."

"What about Hadley?" she countered. "They're always talking. I bet she has interesting things to talk to him about, like skiing and college and stuff. What do I have to talk about? How I used to have to hook ninety heifers up to the milking machine at five a.m. every flipping day before school?"

"If he's not impressed by that, he doesn't deserve you," I said. "Real partnerships are based on respect and character." I made unintentional eye contact with Capone as I spoke, realizing my anger toward him had been replaced by remorse.

"I'm sorry." Melody rocked on her heels self-consciously. "I'm just really tired."

"No, *I'm* sorry, Mel," I said. "You're worth a thousand Hadleys. You do so much for the restaurant and for me and Biz that I never acknowledge. You work so hard. I'm sorry if I don't tell you often enough how grateful I am."

Sonya gasped. "Did Delilah O'Leary just say the words 'I'm sorry' twice in the same breath? Pretty sure that's a first."

A smile cracked Melody's frown. As she recovered from her outburst, she curled her hands into the sleeves of her sweater. "No, really. I'm sorry. I didn't mean to fall apart like that. I feel so dumb."

"I'm the dumb one for pushing you so hard," I said. "You've taken on a ton of extra work here and at home, too. I think both Biz and I have come to consider you part of our family."

She pressed her hands to her chest, her eyes welling up afresh. "You do? That means a lot to me."

"It's not necessarily a good thing," I cautioned. "We've been taking your help for granted. The O'Learys aren't very easy on each other."

Melody's mouth cocked into a half smile. "I've kinda noticed."

"Group hug!" Sonya called, sweeping us all into a collective embrace. "Well, my dears," she said, stepping back and clasping her hands together, "it has been a night."

"Mel, why don't you head home?" I said. "I can finish up here."

"I'll help," Capone said.

"Are you sure? There's still a lot to do." Now that Melody had stopped crying, she looked utterly exhausted. I kicked myself for not being more considerate in piling extra work on everyone. I'd been so focused on my own problems that I hadn't fully appreciated how hard it was for the others to pick up so much slack.

"We've got it, kiddo," Sonya assured her.

Thank you, I mouthed to her. If there was a Jewish version of sainthood, I vowed to nominate her for it.

Capone and I watched Melody depart as Sonya headed back into the kitchen. We were still standing near each other, and he slipped his arm around my waist. I leaned into him.

"I know I overreacted before with the Jonathan thing," I said. "You're just doing your job."

"It's okay. Sometimes I don't like my job very much. Like now, for example."

"You want to trade?" I asked. "I'll take over your murder case, and you manage my restaurant?"

"Tempting, but no thanks."

"Why would Natasha want to use Daniel as bait for teenage girls?" My voice was thick with disgust. "Is she a child trafficker or something?"

"I think we would've heard if there was a human trafficking ring involving well-connected families.

People tend to take notice when pretty, rich girls go missing." The statement was matter-of-fact, but betrayed a hint of world weariness.

We held each other for a moment longer, but then I pulled out of his embrace. I turned to face him, and, by extension, to face the music. I was already feeling low, and I knew it was about to get worse. My hamhanded attempt to talk to Daniel about Hadley had only succeeded in making him mad at me. That was bad enough under normal circumstances, but our falling out had come just before Capone gave him the third degree. Now, I had little chance of getting Daniel to trust me enough to tell me anything. Every single thing I'd done had backfired in spectacular faction.

I sighed. In for a penny, in for a pound.

"I have something to tell you. Some*things*, actually."

I launched into an explanation of how I'd run into Daniel and his mother at the resort, and how I'd realized that Angie Castillo was the woman who laid into Adrian Hoffman at the snow sculpting competition. "Then, there's Daniel's underwear . . ."

Capone's eyes widened. Part two of my tale came out sounding even more bizarre and incriminating than the run-in between Angie and Adrian. I'd thought I was walling Daniel off from danger. Instead, brick by misguided brick, I'd built a staircase that led my loyal friend right to the top of Capone's suspect list.

As I ended, I said, "There's no way Daniel killed Natasha La Cotti. He's a good guy. Better than good. I'd trust him with my life."

I braced myself, wondering if Capone was going to be upset with me for holding out on him. Instead, his voice grew quiet. "I want to believe that, too. I agree that Daniel is a good, trustworthy guy. But good guys can do bad things. Tell me, did you have eyes on Daniel after the party? At, say, nine thirteen p.m.?"

"No." I sighed.

I recognized the timestamp that had been on the surveillance video. The party had been scheduled to go from six to nine—on the early side because the first night of Hanukkah fell on a Sunday and many of the guests had to work the next morning. During that three-hour stretch, I could've accounted for almost every moment, since each aspect of the menu was precisely timed. Passed apps and cocktails starting at 6:15. Open the buffet at 6:45. Check and refresh every fifteen minutes. Desserts and champagne beginning at 8:15. After that, though, everything got scrambled. Like Alice in Wonderland, I'd followed a Rabbit and lost my bearings.

Mysterious footprints led me upstairs to witness the scene with Hadley. I'd bumped into Natasha, Adrian, and Jonathan. Jonathan led me to Piper. Then came the accident with the broken glasses. The party all but ended after that. I hadn't been paying close attention to the time, nor to everyone's exact whereabouts. Sonya, Melody, and I must've had the van fully loaded by nine forty since we'd arrived back at the restaurant just before ten. Working backward, Rabbit left before the end of the party, in time to get to his AA meeting, which meant he was gone before nine. Jonathan was gone shortly thereafter. The other guests had all left around then, too. After the scene Hadley made, no one wanted to linger.

I tried to drill down on Daniel's whereabouts. After he took Hadley upstairs, he was charged with packing up the bar, which stood at the base of the stairs. He'd popped into the kitchen a few times while we were packing up, but mostly he was alone in the main room. Then he drove Piper home toward the end of our clean-up time, probably just before nine thirty. That left a crucial, murky period in his alibi.

I walked across the room to rebolt the door. Then I began to examine the paper menus, separating the soiled ones from the clean ones that could be reused the following day. Capone took his cue from me, picked up a spray bottle and began to wipe down each of the check holders.

I cast my mind back. "I didn't actually see Daniel, but he did the work. And he was totally relaxed when he finished and drove my niece back to the hotel. I have a hard time believing Daniel or anyone else could violently push a woman to her death and then be so care-free, chatting to coworkers a few minutes later."

Capone set down his rag. He looked like he was weighing something in his mind. "What if I told you that your niece said, in her witness statement, that she saw someone in black clothes and shoes, the kind your crew wears, pass along the upstairs hallway right before Natasha died? That was at nine ten. She knew the exact time because she saw the person while she was on the phone, calling her father to try to get a ride back to the hotel. She showed me her call log."

I felt my stomach drop to somewhere in the subter-ranean layers of the Earth's crust. *My own niece had given damning evidence against Daniel?* Recovering my power of speech, I asked, "She's sure it was Daniel?"

"She's fairly sure it was a man, and you and every-one else have given statements saying that Rabbit was already gone. From the angle Piper was looking, downstairs up, she could only see legs. But she said Daniel wasn't at the bar. The only people we know for sure were up there were the Hoffmans, and that description doesn't match the clothes any of them were wearing. On the CCTV, we see Natasha La Cotti start talking to her killer at almost exactly that same time. They talk for a few minutes, and then the killer pushes her. It seems probable that whoever walked across the landing was going outside to meet Natasha."

How long would it take someone as fit as Daniel to mount a staircase and go out to the balcony where Natasha met her doom? A few minutes at most. I pushed the thought aside. "Or the killer came up the back stairs. Or hid out upstairs after the party. Or the killer was Hadley, Daffi, or Adrian, who were already up there. Those are all far more plausible scenarios than Daniel having something to do with Natasha's death."

"If he'd talk to me, *really* talk to me," Capone said, "then maybe we could clear this up. I don't want to have to compel him."

Usually, I was more than happy to play Pin the Tail on the Suspect with Capone. But I'd had enough. "Compel? As in arrest? You can't be serious." I pointed to Capone's laptop, my voice taking on a sharp edge. "Don't believe everything you see on social media. All you have there are pics of an older woman who's used to getting what she wants pawing at a hot younger guy."

"You could be right." His tone softened as he tried to de-escalate the situation. "I wish I could keep your family and friends out of this, but I have to do my job." He fell quiet, his eyes not meeting mine.

"What?" I demanded.

"I'm sorry, Delilah. But there's something else you should know. About your brother-in-law."

I braced myself.

"There are cameras on every entrance of the hotel," he explained. "We checked them all. Jonathan didn't come back until after nine thirty. Witnesses, including you, have him leaving around eight forty-five. It should be less than a ten-minute walk to the hotel. So where was he during that time?"

I opened my mouth to speak, but Capone held out a hand.

"Bear with me," he said. "Say he hung around after the party to talk to Natasha, instead of leaving like everyone thought. Things go south with the conversation. Maybe he gets angry and shoves her harder than he intended. When he realizes what he's done, maybe he panics, tries to hide her body. That forty-five-minute gap would give him the perfect amount of time to do all of that."

I remembered how Piper hadn't been able to get ahold of her father when her sleepover with Hadley fell through and she needed a ride home. "Wouldn't Piper have said something if she got back to the hotel and he wasn't there?"

"I had Rettberg double-check and then I checked the feeds myself just to be sure," he said. "For the better part of forty-five minutes, including the time Natasha was pushed, he was unaccounted for. When I interviewed your niece," Capone explained, "she said her father wasn't in the room when she got back. She texted him. He said he was in the bar. She said she'd come down and join him. He said he was already on his way back up. She showed me the texts. He appeared about twenty minutes later and she didn't think any more of it, other than that it took him longer than expected to get back. But there were no bar charges on his credit card or his room. The bartender who was on duty that night didn't recognize him."

I let out a shaky breath. I didn't like what Capone had to say, but I believed him when he said he wasn't doing any of this to hurt me. His duty, first and foremost, was to the truth—to getting justice for the victims of crime. And if one of my loved ones had been pushed off a balcony, I'd want him on the case.

And I'd want him to have all of the information. I sighed. Then, I spilled the last bit of intel I was holding onto—that Jonathan was the man Daniel saw coming from the house that night. "I know this doesn't look good," I concluded. "I'm only telling you because I *don't* think he did it."

"I'm sorry, Delilah. Believe me," he said. "I hate that I have to do this to you, to your friends, and your family. But I need to try to keep Jonathan here until I get to the bottom of this. I feel like the Grinch, stealing Christmas from everyone, or Hanukkah as the case may be."

I hefted a bin of used glasses from the bar onto my hip. "Well, Biz and I always wanted the whole family together at the holidays," I said bleakly. "But it never occurred to me that half the people around the holiday dinner table would be suspects in a murder."

CHAPTER 19

Christmas Eve dawned and I rolled over, taking a full minute to get my bearings. A shaft of sunlight cut through a gap in the curtains. I lay under a fleece blanket, curled up on the sofa, Butterball pressed up tight against my legs. *Where was I? Oh, yeah, the apartment over the restaurant.*

After the Daniel debacle and the revelations about Jonathan, Capone headed back to the station, looking to get a clearer sense of everyone's movements at the crucial moments just after nine o'clock on the night Natasha was pushed. Although he said he was taking a closer look at "everyone's" alibis, I suspected he'd be focusing particular attention on the whereabouts of a certain Puerto Rican mixologist and a certain Californian tennis coach. Sonya, despite her offer to stay behind and help me, had looked utterly worn-out. After all the extra effort she'd already put in, it didn't seem fair to make her stay late, so I sent her home. I'd finished clean-up and next-day prep alone.

I pushed myself to sitting as Butterball, too, stretched himself awake. As I rose, I came to remember that when I'd finally polished the last bit of stainless steel and labeled the last container of leftovers, midnight had come and gone. I'd been so exhausted, the thought of loading Butterball into his cat carrier to drive the eight minutes to my house seemed like an Everest expedition. Instead, I texted my family to say I was too tired to drive and camped on the couch in the upstairs apartment.

Had there been a tiny bit of inner rejoicing when I realized my work-related fatigue gave me a perfect excuse to stay away from my sister, and Biz, and whatever overblown holiday festivities were likely causing friction between them at that very moment? Maybe. Anyway, we were only open for lunch that day, so I could spend some time with them later.

I walked through the bedroom, past Daniel's kayak and Sonya's makeup table, past her racks of vibrant swing dresses and Mary Jane heels, past the shelf of Biz's thriving begonias. I threw open the curtain and opened the sliding door onto the apartment's lake-facing balcony. The morning was as clear and crisp as an ice cube. The blue of the sky penetrated all the way to the back of my sun-starved eyeballs. Below me, the frost-glazed lake grew more solid with each passing day. Although the temperature could hardly be considered moderate, it was at least tolerable. The arctic hellscape of the previous days had given way to one of those perfect Wisconsin winter days—a stunningly smooth Delftware landscape of blues and whites.

Butterball figure-eighted around my ankles. I leaned down to pick him up and tote him back inside. "What do you say, B-Man? Should we make some breakfast?"

He meowed his robust endorsement of that plan.

I scrounged in the cabinets and found one can of tuna and a tin each of anchovies and sardines. I emptied them all into a bowl. "Not exactly the feast of the seven fishes," I said, "but close." I gave him a gentle noogie and set him and the bowl on the floor to get better acquainted.

My phone pinged, and I saw that Rabbit had replied to my text from the previous day. My message to him had been matter-of-fact—he needed to explain his work-shirking pronto or, friendship be damned, he was fired. Definitely the kind of communication that fell more squarely in my wheelhouse than all of the sloppy, squishy mush I'd been dealing with the past few days. A few back-and-forth messages established that I'd meet up with Rabbit at the lakefront park.

I started to set the phone down, then picked it up again and searched through Natasha's social media feed. I felt like an intruder, pawing through the digital remnants of this dead woman's life. There were swaying palms at an art gala in Miami, a crab boil at sunset in New England. Natasha always the center of it all, her head, with its dramatic streak of white hair, thrown back in laughter. Pleasure. Success. Handsome men—arm candy like Daniel. The photos of him were posted over a single night in Geneva Bay the previous summer, which jived with his recounting of events.

A key clicked in the lock, and I turned to find Sonya letting herself in. "Oh, hey, Dee," she said. "I didn't realize anyone was here."

I put the phone down with a sigh. "Butterball and I slept here. I was so beat that I didn't trust myself to drive home," I said. "What brings you out at this early hour?"

"I wanted to make sure we have candles here," she said. "I thought I'd make brisket for family meal, after the lunch service. Then we can light the Hanukkah candles, and if anyone wants to, go hear them announce the winners of the snow sculpting competition. You don't have plans, do you?"

"Other than trying to solve this murder so I can clear my friends and family from suspicion, you mean?"

"Great," Sonya said, ignoring my sarcasm. She'd been carrying a tote bag and removed it from her shoulder. She reached inside, pulled out a brass menorah, and set it on the counter.

"I don't know if we have any candles that would fit that. Do regular-sized candles work?"

"No, but I think I left some here that do," she said. "They're in the Jew-mergency kit my mom made for me."

"Jew-mergency?"

"When I moved here she was worried because the stores don't always carry the things God's chosen people require." She used a footstool to reach the cabinet above the microwave and took down a cardboard box. As I watched, she unpacked two bottles of Concord grape Manischewitz wine. She held them up and explained, "These are for Passover, but honestly, it'd have to be a nuclear winter before I'd drink this. It tastes like melted cough drops." Next, she pulled out several jars of gefilte fish. At the bottom of her hoard was a box of thin tapers. She waved it triumphantly.

"Your mom knows that you work in a restaurant, right?" I said. "We can order any of this stuff from our suppliers and have it tomorrow."

She frowned. "I'm pretty sure my mom thinks me being an hour and a half outside the city is the equivalent of me working on the International Space Station."

"Well," I said. "I'm glad you're here, anyway. I've been thinking about killing a person."

"Anyone in particular?" she asked.

"Natasha La Cotti."

"I've got news for you, Dee. Someone beat you to it."

I opened the cannister of coffee beans, which, thankfully, was full. As I ground the beans and began making espressos for myself and Sonya, I explained. "What I mean is I've been thinking about how it was done. The list of likely suspects is short. Whoever it was must've known Natasha. On the CCTV footage, she was talking to them for several minutes before she was killed. Her body language didn't indicate that she was in distress. If it was an intruder, presumably she would've called for help or run away or tried to fight them off. And an outsider would need to come into the house unnoticed. They'd have to know the layout. Seems un-likely. The killer knew she was upstairs, which in itself tells us something."

"Exactly," Sonya agreed. Then, frowning in confu-sion, she added, "Which is what, exactly?'

"That she was likely meeting someone she knew. When you think about it, why was she still there? The party ended at nine. Yes, she was friends with Daffi and Adrian, but to hang out upstairs after everyone left? She must've had a good reason. Which makes it likely the killer was at the house that night and arranged to speak with her afterwards about something urgent."

"But doesn't that only narrow it down to everyone who was at the party?" Sonya asked. "That's fifty sus-pects."

"But almost everyone left around eight forty-five, after Rabbit dropped the glasses," I countered. "The only people who were still there were you, me, Melody, Daniel, Daffi, Adrian, Piper, and Hadley." I tapped my lips with my finger. "Although it's possible that one of the guests who left only *pretended* to leave and hid out upstairs or left and then circled back. Apparently, that's what my brother-in-law did."

"Say what?"

I filled her in on Daniel's ID of Jonathan as the man he saw leaving the Hoffman house, and Capone's revelations about the security camera footage.

She let out a long whistle. "Do you think he could've done it?"

"No," I said firmly. "He has bad knees. Whoever killed Natasha moved her body all the way from the backyard to the ski slope. How could he carry a body that far? He can barely walk up and down steps without pain. Even if he wasn't the father of my niece and nephew, I don't think he's our killer. But the timeline of his movements shows that it's possible for a person to have left and then return."

Sonya took a seat at the counter and grabbed the espresso I'd prepared for her. "Normally, this is where I'd tell you that catching the baddies is Capone's job, but after last night, I think the quicker we can take Daniel off the suspect list, the better. So, okay, let's do this."

"Agreed. There's a crucial thing I hadn't focused on until I started thinking about Jonathan. Which of the suspects are strong enough to move a body several hundred yards in that weather?"

"Of the people we know were still there?" Sonya enumerated on her fingers. "You, Daniel, Adrian, and Jonathan, if he didn't have bad knees."

"Besides the fact that I didn't do it, I also didn't have the motive or the opportunity," I said. "You and I were together the whole time. And I didn't know Natasha La Cotti."

I took a tentative sip of my espresso, then dispatched

it with a single swig. Immediate caffeine emergency averted, I began to root through the cabinets for breakfast ingredients. Even when I'd lived in the apartment full time, I'd never been particularly assiduous about keeping the pantry and fridge stocked. After all, we had an entire restaurant downstairs. Having just woken up, though, I wasn't quite ready to confront the bitter cold of the December morning, even for a brief sortie to gather supplies.

I sighed in relief when I found butter, sugar, flour, and milk. In the fruit bowl, there was a single orange—everything I needed to whip up a batch of crêpes Suzette. Like Auntie Biz said, all the ingredients were pantry staples. The thought sent a twang through my heartstrings. Biz was probably in the kitchen at that very moment, showing Piper and Caleb how to make them. And I was here. Had I really been too tired to drive, or had I, once again, let my work be an easy excuse for avoiding family entanglements? Which O'Leary sister was really the one who ran away?

I whisked together the mixture, poured a few tablespoons into a buttered skillet, and tilted the pan in a circular motion to distribute the batter. It only took a few seconds for the edges of the thin pancake to crisp and curl. I pushed thoughts of my family aside as I slid the finished crêpe onto a plate. No, I told myself. I wasn't hiding. I really did have pressing work right now. I needed to keep my restaurant going, and to do that, I had to clear my crew from suspicion. The only way to do *that* was to solve Natasha La Cotti's murder.

"We have to consider Daniel," I said. "See him the way Capone does. Objectively, Daniel had the opportunity, since he had at least a few unaccounted-for minutes just after the party ended. Piper told Capone that she saw someone in dark pants and shoes on the upstairs landing right around the time Natasha was killed. Daniel is athletic enough to get up and down the stairs quickly and strong enough that a shove from him could have sent Natasha tumbling. And more importantly, he's strong enough to carry a body the few hundred yards to where the snow was being made for the competition."

"Yeah, when you put it like that, it doesn't look good," she said. "But what would his motive be?"

"I can't see a clear one. He didn't like her, but to feel strongly enough to *kill* her? Besides, we *know* it wasn't Daniel. He just doesn't have it in him," I said.

"Well, the United States Army might beg to differ," she pointed out. "Soldiers are kind of known for violence. Sort of their brand. He never talks about his service. We have no idea what he was trained for, or what he's capable of."

I searched my mind for a rational counterargument, but all I could come up with was, "But it's Daniel."

We were both quiet, unwilling to let ourselves doubt his innocence. As I'd been speaking, I'd been heating butter and sugar together to create a thin caramel. Now I poured in the orange juice and zest. I folded the finished crêpes into quarters, layering the little pancake triangles into the orange-caramel sauce and letting them soak in the sticky-sweet citrus. If I were making these as a dessert, this was the point during the cooking process where I'd tip a little Grand Marnier into the pan and ignite it. I didn't have orange liqueur at hand. More to the point, I'd learned the hard way that handling a flaming pan before my second cup of coffee is a recipe for scorched eyebrows. We'd just have to do without the showmanship and the deeper flavor lent by the alcoholic combustion. I decanted my creation onto two plates.

"Well," Sonya said, accepting her plate, "if we eliminate Daniel and you, and assuming Jonathan is off the table because of his knees, that only leaves one person."

"Right. It *has* to be Adrian Hoffman," I said. "There was clearly something going on with him and Natasha. Whatever Hadley overheard between them seriously set her off."

"Maybe *she* went berserk and pushed Natasha in a fit of rage?" Sonya suggested.

"It would've been a delayed reaction, if so," I said, pointing out the lag time between the dish incident and the time Natasha was pushed. "Plus, she's too small to have moved the body. Who would've helped her?"

"Her dad? Parents do a lot of crazy stuff for their kids."

"I guess we should keep her in the mix," I said. "And her mom, I suppose, if we're keeping open the possibility of an accomplice. Daffi had a pretty big reaction to Angie Castillo threatening Adrian. I wouldn't put violence past her."

Sonya paused, chewing the bite she'd lifted to her lips. "Speaking of big reactions, just be aware that I may fall into some kind of orgasmic food trance. These crêpes are out of this world."

I bit into my portion. The pancakes were indeed cooked to spongy, silky perfection. And the tangy sauce, with a toffee-like richness, lit up every segment of my tongue. Never one to stop ninety-nine percent of the way toward impeccable, though, I had to admit that I missed the harmonious, boozy kick lent by the liqueur and its final, dramatic flambé. I chewed as I mulled over the possible scenarios.

"Hadley was *really* upset. She's overdramatic, but even she wouldn't throw a dish over nothing. But set that aside. Look at *her father's* personality. He's a bully. You've seen how he treats his wife and daughter. Plus, he's a big guy. Definitely big enough to carry a body a few hundred yards and dump it. Also, it was his house."

"That would make it easier for him to move around unnoticed," she agreed.

"Right, and if it was him, then a weird detail would make sense."

"Which is?"

I put down my fork and picked up Butterball. I paced back and forth, petting him rhythmically in the hope that the motion would get my brain juices flowing. "Why move the body at all? That's been nagging me. The killer probably had no idea there would be surveillance video of the murder. And if they did, they probably didn't know that there wouldn't *also* be surveillance video of the stretch of ground between the house and the ski slope. Why risk being seen? Pushing Natasha off the balcony took a matter of seconds, but hauling her frozen corpse across the distance of two football fields? There would be absolutely no way to play that off if someone saw you."

Sonya, always ready with dark humor, mimed heaving a body over her shoulder. Then, she gestured innocently to it, as if speaking to a third party. "What, her? She was like that when I got here."

"Not very plausible," I agreed. "So why not just leave her laying there and hope the cops would chalk it up to an accidental fall? If Adrian did it, it makes sense that he'd want to get the body away from his own house. Just on a psychological level, but also to muddy the connection to him and the place she died. Maybe he undressed her to make it look like she was attacked on her way back to the hotel."

"Well, I'm sold," Sonya said. "Let's shop this theory to Capone."

I shook my head. "We still don't have anything more than gut instinct to prove that Daniel *couldn't* have done it. Plus, I can practically hear Capone saying that we haven't covered all possible angles." I enumerated on my fingers. "Two people could've worked together. A party guest could've hidden out or circled back. It could've been an outsider who'd arranged a rendezvous with Natasha. I'm sure there are more possibilities that we're not even considering." I drummed my fingers on the top of Butterball's head.

Sonya's phone played "Rock Lobster" by the B-52's. She took it out of her pocket and answered a video call. "Hey, Mom! I'm here with Delilah and Butterball." She turned the phone around and I waved Butterball's paw.

If you looked closely, you could see that the face on the screen was, in many ways, similar to Sonya's. Pale skin, gray eyes, dark, pin-straight hair. But Sonya's mother's aesthetic was so different from her daughter's that anyone but the most careful observer would be hard-pressed to see that they were related. I'd never seen Fran Perlman-Doktor wear a lick of makeup or a stitch of clothing that wasn't rendered in grayscale. Sonya, by contrast, brought her usual retro pin-up girl panache even to this winter weekday morning with a tight, candy pink sweater tucked into cigarette pants and accessorized with a cyan blue silk scarf.

"Hello, Delilah, dear," Sonya's mother began. "It's so nice to see you! You look tired. Have you been sleeping? Sonya's been telling me about all the *crazy* things that've been happening. A dead body? In the snow? What is it with you girls and murders?" She let out a disgusted *pfft*. "When Sonya decided to go to *culinary school* instead of law school, I told myself that was going to be the one silver lining—she wouldn't have to bum around with *criminals* all day. And when she moved up there to the back of beyond, I thought, 'Well, at least a small town will be safer than Chicago.' But is it? Like hell it is. Every five minutes, I'm hearing about this dead body and that dead body." She took the briefest of pauses to breathe before continuing. "Then, I hear *you* finally have a nice boyfriend, and here I'm thinking that might set a good example and convince Sonya to find someone *nice* to settle down with, but then I come to find out the man is a Capone. An actual *Capone*, for goodness' sake!"

"Nice to see you, too, Fran," I said. "It's been too long."

Sonya mouthed *Sorry* to me.

"Sonya, honey, did you find the candles?" her mother asked.

Sonya turned the phone camera back on herself and tapped the box with her free hand. "Yep."

"Oh, good," her mother said. "I was just looking into how much it would cost to hire an Uber driver to bring some up there. A hundred-and-fifty-six dollars they wanted! Highway robbery. *Literally.* You know what? I'm going to overnight some anyway. I don't like the idea of you only having one box of candles."

"Mom, there are only four more nights of Hanukkah. There must be two hundred candles in here."

"One hundred and seventy-six," her mother corrected. "They come in packs of forty-four." I heard a series of high-pitched barks through the phone's speaker. Sonya's mother said, "Oh, look, here's little Miranda, back from her walk with your father. Miranda, come and say hello to your cousin, Sonya."

"Isn't that your uncle Avi's dog?" I asked, coming around to look at the little white poofball of a creature that had appeared on the screen. I'd never met Miranda, but I remembered Sonya's uncle telling me about her. You don't soon forget a pet who's named after a constitutional procedure.

"Yeah," Sonya confirmed. Turning back to her mother, she asked, "What's Miranda still doing there? I thought Uncle Avi and Aunt Ruthie were supposed to pick her up when they got back from Palm Springs last night."

Her mother flapped her hands in aggravation. "Oh, you wouldn't *believe*. They've been stuck at the airport in Denver for almost two days. There was a blizzard—over a foot of snow, they got—and their connection got cancelled. There hasn't been a *single flight* in or out since Tuesday night. Tuesday! They're staying at some godforsaken Ramada and Ruthie said they were lucky to get even that. Can you imagine? What a nightmare. Anyway, they're rebooked on a redeye tonight, so they'll pick Miranda up tomorrow. Isn't that right, snookie? You get another day with your Auntie Fran . . ."

Sonya's eyes flew to mine, her brow a mass of confused wrinkles. The sound of Fran Perlman-Dokter's continued patter was overwhelmed by the *whoosh-whoosh* of my own heartbeat in my ears. I felt like my blood had been replaced by frigid air.

No flights out of Denver since Tuesday night. That couldn't be right. Shea said she and Caleb had flown through Denver yesterday. I remembered it distinctly, and by the look on Sonya's face, it was clear that she did, too.

I took out my phone and searched "Denver airport closure." The first hit confirmed what Sonya's mother said—not a single flight had gone out the previous day. I'd wondered how Shea managed to book a last-minute flight in the run-up to Christmas when they seemed so difficult to come by. I'd chalked it up to my sister's doggedness. But now I had the real answer—there *was* no flight yesterday. Why had my sister lied?

CHAPTER 20

I was still pondering Shea's strange fiction about her flight as I walked toward the lakefront park, where the snow sculpting competition was in its final day. Sonya and I had speculated six ways to Sunday, but hadn't managed to come up with a plausible reason for my sister to lie. The best I could figure was that she'd somehow misremembered their connecting airport. But a slip like that was so out of character for my sister that I could hardly credit it. Another person flying across the country with a toddler might be frazzled enough to make a mistake like that. Not Shea. I set that conundrum aside, trying to focus on my immediate task. I was meeting Rabbit. After all we'd been through, I hated to even think about letting him go, but I needed to be ready for the possibility. I was a businesswoman and an O'Leary. Fool me once, shame on you. Fool me twice, and get ready to be out on your ass.

The weather was the best we'd had in weeks—blue skies, next to no wind, and a clean blanket of white powder on the ground. All of the snow the sculptors were using had been replaced, reset, and repacked. I guess nobody wanted to chance coming across another unpleasant surprise. Despite the fresh start the day offered, the atmosphere was somber as the teams of sculptors went about their work. The ribbing and easy camaraderie I'd witnessed when the contest opened had morphed into tension. The sculptors had been up most of the night racing to finish their creations and were probably running on fumes.

When I demanded a meeting, Rabbit said he'd be at the park with Everleigh and, no doubt reluctantly, invited me to join them. He was definitely on his guard—meeting me in a neutral location and bringing along his daughter. For all my toughness, he knew I had a soft spot for kids.

The park bustled with visitors, and I scanned their faces, looking for Rabbit's familiar careworn expression. It was hard to take in the whole vista at once, since the area was punctuated with food stalls and gigantic snow mounds, which in turn were surrounded by scaffolding to allow the sculptors to reach the higher elevations of their creations. I cut between the churro van and the cocoa kiosk, wondering if Rabbit had taken Everleigh to the ice rink on the far side of the park. As I emerged at the edge of the rink, the sound of voices caught my attention. I flashed back to the last time I'd been here, when I'd seen Daniel's mother giving Adrian Hoffman what-for. Again this time, the speakers were familiar. Instead of walking forward to greet them, I instinctively pressed myself against the side of the churro van. That was Rabbit, *my* Rabbit, talking to Daffi Hoffman. No, not talking, *arguing*.

Daffi's words carried through the still air. "I need your assurance—"

Rabbit cut her off. "This ain't the time or place. Can't you see I've got my daughter here?" He gestured to the rink, where dozens of skaters orbited the ice. "Besides,

I already gave you my word. Don't know what else you want from me."

"The promise of a convicted criminal isn't going to cut it," Daffi said. "If it's a question of more money . . ."

Their voices dropped and I edged closer, straining to hear over the rumble of the cocoa kiosk's generator. Why would Daffi Hoffman be talking about money with Rabbit? It seemed that she wanted something he had . . . but what? My thoughts flashed back to the phone call Rabbit's mother overheard. Even though Maureen Blakemore couldn't hear the other end of the conversation, her instincts told her he was talking to a woman. And she'd heard him mention money. Could Rabbit's "mystery woman" be Daffi Hoffman? This conversation betrayed no sign of intimacy. If there was a connection between them, it wasn't romantic.

"Delilah? I thought that was you!"

A hand on my arm made me jump. I spun around to find Harold Heyer next to me, holding Jarka by the hand.

"You're back," I sputtered. "How was the trip?"

"Best trip ever," Harold gushed. "Bulgaria is an amazing country. Such rich history. Amazing food. And the people . . ." He clapped his hands together. "Each one just as warm and friendly as Jarka."

I bit my tongue at that last observation. "Warm" and "friendly" weren't words often associated Jarka Gagamova. Clearly Harold's rose-colored glasses were still Coke-bottle thick. I took stock of the incongruous couple. Harold's chubby-cheeked face was fuchsia from the cold. In thick-soled winter boots, he stood five-and-a-half feet tall. He seemed be sporting an ill-advised mustache, which perched below his button nose like an underfed caterpillar. He wore a lime green Sherpa hat festooned with an enormous pompom.

While Harold was comprised entirely of gentle undulations, Jarka was drawn in severe angles. Her jawline and cheekbones looked like they could double as sharpening steel. Her hair, dyed red as a maraschino cherry, was adorned by a pair of enormous, fuzzy earmuffs. Where Harold was credulous, she was shrewd. In Harold, optimism abounded, while Jarka saw the world in bleaker terms.

But in that moment, they were united, both by their lack of fashion sense and their matching ear-to-ear grins. I could count on one hand the number of times I'd seen Delilah & Son's austere Bulgarian server smile. And I'd certainly never seen her so giddy with happiness. I wondered if whatever came over Auntie Biz this time of year had gotten to Jarka as well.

I'd barely formed the thought before Harold revealed the reason for their joy. "We're getting married!"

"Is true," Jarka said, her eyes twinkling. "I tell Harold Heyer we should be married and he consents. But I did not know that my sweet Harold has also a plan to ask me for marrying him."

"I'd brought a ring to Bulgaria! I was just waiting for the right time to ask, but she beat me to it!" Harold gushed. He held up Jarka's hand, which was encased in a leather glove, but presumably sported the ring. He shook it like a terrier with a squeaky toy. Harold, always effusive, practically vibrated with energy. That was normal. What happened next, though, caused me to question whether there'd been a glitch in the space-time continuum.

Jarka let out a giggle and batted her new fiancé

playfully away. The laugh was . . . girlish. The feeble slaps on his chest were . . . coquettish?

Turning to me, she said, "Yes, Harold Heyer and I have true love. He is so supporting of me and such a sweet, sweet man." She removed his hat and stroked his egg-bald head. "He also has many skills that facilitate sexual climax. So we will be married even though it is institution designed for selling things of no use and for benefitting men. Together, my little strawberry, Harold Heyer, and I will smash this . . . what is called?" She kissed his head and replaced his hat.

"Do you mean the capitalist patriarchy, my dumpling?" he offered.

"Yes." She gave a brisk shake of the head, the counterintuitive Bulgarian way of indicating agreement. "We will smash this capitalist patriarchy."

That was the Jarka I knew.

A smile broke across my face. The first smile in days that arose from a place of pure joy. "I'm so happy for you both."

"What a stroke of luck running into you," Harold said. "We've been counting the minutes until we could tell you, but we thought nobody would be at the restaurant yet, with it being so early still."

"Sonya's there," I said. "If you need any help wedding planning, she'll be more than happy to lend a hand."

My bestie was a sucker for romance. Although she'd accused her parents of wanting to rush her down the aisle, she was usually miles ahead of them. After a date or two, she'd be picking out centerpieces and selecting invitation fonts. No doubt she'd jump at the chance to put all that pent-up know-how to work assisting the happy couple.

Jarka took Harold's hand and they rushed off toward Delilah & Son. He turned to throw a dopey wave at me before she yanked him away. I wished I could go with them. Instead, I turned back to where Rabbit and Daffi had been, only to find they'd been replaced by a young couple trying to wrestle a snow-suited baby into a stroller.

Dammit. Had he vamoosed without facing me? I scanned the ice-skaters as they passed and found little Everleigh among them. She pumped her arms back and forth, showing surprising grace for such a young child. Even if Rabbit had been willing to evade me, there's no way he would've left her out there alone. I looked around again, this time following the whole circumference of the waist-high barrier that had been constructed at the edges of the rink. There, on the far side, stood my quarry. I glanced again at Everleigh as she skated past, trying not to let the bounce of her Shirley Temple curls soften my resolve. *Actions have consequences.* I put on my game face and repeated those words to myself like a mantra.

Rabbit clocked me as I approached him, but didn't move toward me. Instead, he pulled a cigarette away from his lips, blowing out a cloud of smoke in one dejected exhalation.

He tipped his chin in acknowledgment. "Hey, chef."

"Hey." I crossed my arms over my chest and put on a stony face.

He stubbed out his cigarette with the toe of his boot and gripped the edge of the barrier that surrounded the rink. Everleigh skated past and gave her father a mittened wave. He waved back as his large, green eyes lit up. "She loves ice skating. She could stay out there all day." He beamed with pride, but as soon as she passed, his face crumpled. "I guess you're here to fire me," he said. Not a question, but a statement.

"Probably," I conceded. "You know I don't tolerate slackers, and you've never been one. You always work hard and your standards are almost as high as mine. I appreciate that. But something I hate more than slacking is lying. There's just no place for it in my restaurant. So out with it. I want the truth. Why did you call off work?"

"I needed the time off."

"We have a system for requesting time off. Why did you need to take off so suddenly?"

He exhaled in a deep, ponderous hiss, the sound of a just-discovered tomb being crowbarred open. "To look for a place to live. I've been staying with my mom since I got out of Oakhill. Her lease is up at the end of this month, and she's moving down to Texas. The landlord wants to sell the house, so I can't renew the lease."

"Your mother said you had a new place lined up."

"I did." He sighed. "But it fell through when the criminal conviction check came back. I put my record on the application forms, like you're supposed to— arrests, time served, all of it. I wasn't hiding nothing. The guy who showed me the place said it'd be okay, but his manager nixed it. Said it was a nice complex and they couldn't have riffraff living there. I've been trying every place in town. Some won't even let me pass Go. Some got a company policy not to rent to felons. I finally thought I had something, but then that fell through, same day as the Chrismukkah party. I only got one more week to find a place."

"I'm sorry," I said.

"I don't even got any friends I can crash with," he

said. "Most've them have places that are too small or else they've done time, and it's a condition of my parole not to be around other convicted felons."

I thought back to his friend Travis Staggs, Mr. Mystery Meat Mobile, whose rap sheet I'd seen in Capone's office. If those were the social circles Rabbit moved in, I wasn't surprised that the pool of potential roommates was so shallow.

"So in a week's time," he continued, "I'm looking at living outta my car."

"Why didn't you say anything?" I asked. "I'll be damned if you're going to live in your car while I live in a six-bedroom house."

He flashed a sad smile. "That's real generous of you, chef. I guess I was ashamed. I ain't even told my mom. I put her through enough over the years. No way I'm gonna make this her problem, just when she's finally getting on with her own life. I ain't told Everleigh's mom, neither. Until I got a place of my own, I can't keep Everleigh for overnights. That's part of the custody arrangement. I gotta have my own place if I'm gonna share custody. If I don't, I'm in violation of the agreement, and the whole thing might get tanked."

Everleigh glided around the rink again. This time she noticed me and cut her way across the ice toward us. "Daddy, do you want to see my twirl?" She didn't wait for an answer before executing a passable pirouette. "I'm going to be in the 'Lympics when I'm a grown-up!" she announced, before rejoining the revolving pack of skaters.

Watching her go, Rabbit's eyes brimmed with emotion, his face heavy with the weight of letting down the ones he loved.

"I ain't gonna ask you to go easy on me," he said.

"I lied to you. It's a hard habit to break. The Twelve Steps help, but sometimes telling the truth is almost as hard as laying off the bottle."

"I thought you were drinking again," I admitted. "When you were so skittish at the party and then went AWOL."

He put his hand over his heart. "Haven't touched a drop, chef. Hope I never do."

As we'd been speaking, my wheels were turning. If he needed his own place, there was a perfectly serviceable apartment over the restaurant. Sonya could get a storage unit for her surplus clothes and accessories. And she certainly didn't *need* an on-site makeup studio. We could reconfigure the employee locker room and office space downstairs to add a shower for Daniel. Although I would have to make it crystal clear that semi-nude strolls around the downstairs space were *not* on Delilah & Son's menu. I'd have to speak with my ex, of course, as he was the building's owner. The covenant that had come with me gaining custody of Butterball specified that neither me nor Biz could stay in that apartment—Sam's way of ensuring that I actually lived in the mansion he'd essentially gifted me. But the document said nothing about Rabbit.

My mouth was half-open to put the offer into words when I recalled the scene I'd witnessed moments earlier. Daffi's words echoed in my head: *The promise of a convicted criminal isn't going to cut it . . . What had Rabbit and Daffi Hoffman been talking about?* After what he'd pulled, did I really want to further entangle my life with his by letting him live in the apartment? I needed to be sure I could trust him.

"Were you meeting someone here? Besides me, I mean?" I asked.

He paused a minute before shaking his head.

I hesitated. Should I admit that I'd been eavesdropping on their conversation? And that their back-and-forth *definitely* didn't sound like the kind of casual chat you might have if you ran into a hired waiter you'd only met once. I decided to press on. He said he was committed to telling the truth. It was time to put him to the test.

"So I *didn't* see you talking with Daffi Hoffman just now?" I prodded. I understood why he hadn't told me the real reason he'd bunked off work, but if I was going to go to bat for him with Sam, I needed total honesty.

"Yeah, but I wasn't meeting her. She came here, looking for me." His eyes were no longer on Everleigh. Instead, he gazed evasively into the middle distance.

"Why was she looking for you?"

He clamped his lips shut, his green eyes boring into mine. "Chef, you better think twice about how bad you want to know the details. Because if I tell you, then you're gonna have to carry this weight." He touched his chest. "I don't want to do that to you."

Once again, my mind flew back to something Rabbit's mother said. *One of these days, he's gonna pull somebody down with him.* Here I stood, on the shore of what seemed to be a deep and murky ocean of trouble. And there was Rabbit, offering to show me what lay beneath the waves.

"It's easier to carry something heavy if you share the weight," I said. "I can take it."

He sighed. "Well, let 'er rip, then. What do you wanna know?"

"Did you meet with Daffi on the night of the party, too?" I asked. "Because I went outside that night to look for you. Instead, I found your footprints, and another set of footprints. High heels. It looked like you followed them into the house. If you're into something bad with Daffi Hoffman, tell me. Maybe I can help."

He mulled it over, pulling a pack of cigarettes from his pocket before thinking better of it and replacing them. "Those were her shoe prints, all right. Me and Daffi recognized each other straight off, even though it'd been years since we'd seen each other. I never even knew her real name before that night. Me and my buddy Travis met her years ago, outside a pawn shop."

The name rang an immediate bell. "Travis Staggs?"

His eyebrows shot up. "You know him?"

"Let's just say I know of him," I replied. "What did she want from you and Travis?"

"She was looking for somebody who needed some quick cash and wouldn't ask too many questions. She paid us five grand to help her set up some bank accounts. She had some money that she needed to squirrel away where nobody would find it. She just needed our IDs and for us to sign some papers. Easiest money I ever made."

"But you knew it wasn't on the up-and-up?"

He let out a bitter laugh. "I did a lot worse back in those days."

"And Daffi recognized you at her party?" I asked.

"Yeah," he said. "She must've saw me go outside, so she came out to talk to me. She wanted me to come with her upstairs."

"Why?"

Before he could answer, a pained cry rose from the ice.

"Daaaadddy!"

My eyes flew to the rink, where Everleigh sat on the ice about ten feet in front of us, clutching her elbow.

Tears burst from her eyes. In a flash, Rabbit vaulted over the barrier, slipping and sliding his way to his daughter. I looked for a way to follow him, but I lacked the agility to hurdle over the barrier or traverse the slippery surface.

A teenage couple stood next to Everleigh. The boy squatted down. "I'm so sorry! Are you okay?"

"Sorry!" his girlfriend echoed, turning to Rabbit. She nudged her boyfriend in the midsection. "He's such a klutz on the ice. He lost his balance and bumped into her pretty hard."

Everleigh winced, cradling her injured arm. Between shuddering breaths, she said, "My elbow." She wiped her streaming face with the mitten of her uninjured arm. "It hurts."

By now, Rabbit had moved the couple aside. He knelt next to his girl, cradling her, stroking her hair, and shushing her cries. "Come on, baby. Let's get you to the Urgent Care. Make sure nothing's busted." Gently, he helped her up, and together they made their way off the ice, away from me. Away from my lingering questions.

CHAPTER 21

My steps were heavy as I trudged through the packed snow on the shore path back to Delilah & Son. Not only had I *not* resolved my dilemma about Rabbit, but now I had a host of new worries. Last week, if someone had asked me whether I trusted my staff, my answer would've been an unwavering yes. But the events of the past few days had embedded a splinter of doubt in my brain. Had it been a mistake to allow my crew into my heart so completely? And what about my *actual* family? Jonathan was clearly hiding something, and Shea had lied to me.

With these questions swirling in my head, the last thing I expected to see was Capone's service vehicle, a black Dodge Charger, pulling into the restaurant's parking lot. His car door flew open just as I reached him. The expression on his face was grave.

"What's up?" I asked.

He closed the door and leaned against the vehicle, looking as weighed down as I felt. His amber eyes were undergirded with dark half-moons of fatigue. "You're not going to like it," he said.

"I haven't liked most of what you've had to say lately."

"Have you seen Rabbit? He wasn't at his house. I hoped he'd be here."

My brow wrinkled in confusion. *Why is he asking about Rabbit?* "I just left him. Everleigh got hurt at the ice rink. He was taking her to get checked out by a doctor."

He was silent, pondering something.

"Is this about him and Daffi Hoffman?"

He did a double take. "What *about* him and Daffi Hoffman?"

"Um, never mind."

"Delilah." His voice was very "disappointed dad."

I let out a groan. After what happened with Daniel, I didn't want to chance trying to perfectly time my disclosures. But there was a danger that if I revealed the connection between Daffi and Rabbit, Capone might uncover the whole, ugly truth—the full scope of which I myself still didn't know. I groaned again and stomped my feet in the snow. I looked hard at Capone. His warm amber eyes were full of concern. He was dogged in his pursuit of justice, but he used a chisel much more often than he used a wrecking ball. I'd have to trust him.

"I overheard Daffi and Rabbit talking. Arguing. About money." I quickly recapped what Rabbit had told me about their sordid history. "And he was with her on the night of the party. The footprints I saw, the ones he followed inside, they were hers."

"That might be important. Did he say what the bank accounts he and Staggs opened were for? Or why, if that happened years ago, it's coming back up now?"

"We didn't get that far," I said.

"Well, none of that is on Rabbit's rap sheet or

Staggs'," he said, half to himself. "And he didn't explain why she wanted to talk to him that night?"

"Nope. Everleigh fell, and he had to go to her." I paused. "If that's not what you came here to talk about, what is?"

"I've had Rettberg combing through surveillance footage for the past couple of days. Every angle of every camera on the Grand Bay property for the entire night of the party, then cross-referencing the footage. For those staying at the resort's main hotel, she used the lobby cameras to determine when they came back."

"You told me that already," I said impatiently. "That's how you knew Jonathan didn't come back to the hotel right away."

"Well, for those staying or living in town, she also matched license plates to the vehicles of known party guests and tracked when they drove out the main gate."

"Must See TV," I deadpanned.

"She wants to make detective someday, and unfortunately that's how you pay your dues. Can't tell you how many credit card statements and phone records I poured over when I was coming up the ranks."

As Capone was speaking, my internal alarms began triggering, one by one. His voice was even. His body was almost motionless. The only signs of life were the frosty, little puffs that formed with each of his exhalations. To a casual observer, he was the picture of tranquility. But I knew by now that when, in others, emotions would be rising to a fever pitch, Capone became unreadable as a stone wall. The stronger the emotion, or the worse the news, the less you'd see it reflected on Capone's face.

"What does this have to do with Rabbit?" I asked, trying to tamp down the worry in my voice.

"Rabbit's car left the resort property at eight thirty-eight p.m."

"That sounds right," I said. "He left early. I told Stanhope all of this in my witness statement. I'm sure other people confirmed that, too. Hadley collided with him and he smashed some glasses. She got a cut on her leg, and that really shook him up. That was just after eight thirty. He wanted to get over to Saint Benedict's for the AA meeting they have there. He's done it a few times before when he's having a hard night. I've told him he has a free pass to get himself to a meeting any time he feels himself slipping."

Capone's eyes met mine. I braced myself. "Only problem is," he said, "at nine oh five p.m., Rabbit's car came back to the Grand Bay." He paused for a moment, waiting for the news to land. "We don't have footage of anything beyond him coming through the entrance gate. There are no cameras along that road until you get closer to the hotel. But it was definitely his car, and he was definitely driving. The video shows his face clear as day."

"But," I sputtered, "the AA meeting." My face and hands were numb, whether from being out in the cold for so long or from shock, I didn't know.

"I checked with the woman who runs the Saint Benedict's meeting. Rabbit didn't go that night."

I recalled with sickening clarity what Rabbit's mother had said—privacy was for suckers when it came to addiction. So, it seemed, was trust. When Rabbit referred to the weight he was carrying, did he mean the weight of whatever crooked financial dealings Daffi had roped him and Staggs into all those years ago? Or something much more recent, and much, much worse?

I looked toward the restaurant, with its hip Art Deco–inspired Delilah & Son logo. Melody had designed it. Rabbit and Daniel had helped me hang it. I'd come to Geneva Bay as a card-carrying cynic, but this place, my team, had gradually lulled me into letting down my guard.

"Nine oh five." I latched onto the detail. "He came back at nine oh five? As in eight minutes before Natasha was pushed?"

Capone nodded. "It's not a lot of time, but I clocked it. Two minutes' drive from the gate to arrive at the house. Three minutes to get around the back and let yourself inside, if you hurry and you know where you're going. Like, say, if you'd been up there earlier in the night with Daffi Hoffman, and gone in that same way, knowing the door was unlocked."

I swallowed hard. I'd trusted Capone by revealing the content of my conversation with Rabbit. And now, moments later, he was throwing it back in my face as evidence that my dependable coworker could be a killer. Could this be the life-wrecking secret that Rabbit alluded to? He was supposed to have been at an AA meeting miles away. He was a smaller guy, sure, but he was surprisingly strong. I'd seen him hoist fifty-pound sacks of flour off the back of a delivery truck like they were filled with cotton balls. Could he have used that wiry strength to carry a freezing corpse? *Oh, god. What had he gotten himself into?*

When I spoke, my voice came out as a croak. "You said Piper saw someone, someone with black pants and shoes like my crew wears, on the upper floor at nine ten. That would fit the timeline."

He gave a single, grave nod of his head. "Natasha La Cotti appears on the CCTV video on the balcony at nine ten," he continued. "Her back is to the railing. She's talking to someone. That's exactly when Rabbit would've arrived if that's where he was headed. They talk for a few minutes. At nine thirteen, she's pushed."

I wrapped my arms around myself and rubbed my hands up and down for warmth. My numbness had morphed into a bone-chilling cold. "It looks bad, but that's all circumstantial, right?"

"It's enough for an arrest," Capone said. "Especially with his priors."

"Rabbit killing Natasha La Cotti makes no sense. None of his previous arrests were for violent crimes. Besides, what did he have to gain? What was the connection between the two of them?"

"I didn't have a good theory about that, but with what you overheard, I'm thinking he could be connected to Natasha La Cotti the same way he's connected to Daffi Hoffman—money," he said. "If he's involved in shady business dealings with Daffi, why not with one of her friends? And that shady business doesn't even need to be something especially terrible to provide a strong motive for him to commit murder. Hell, he could be selling them dime bags of weed. Rabbit just laid out for you how strict his parole conditions are. He's only one setback, one minor infraction, away from his entire life being derailed. Back to prison. Losing custody of his daughter, probably forever. Who's going to bring her to visit him when his mom moves to Texas? The stakes of him getting caught doing *anything* illegal are extremely high."

I couldn't meet Capone's eyes. Anger welled up inside me at the unfairness of it all. Capone was only doing his job, but why did every piece of evidence he uncovered have to lead back to someone I cared about?

I knew he was only the messenger, but damn, the instinct to shoot was strong. My fury extended to Rabbit, too. How dare he lie to me about an AA meeting? I'd vouched for him to a judge and his parole officer. Given my feelings, I was surprised by the next words out of my mouth.

"Please don't bring him in today," I said. "Let him be with his daughter. It's Christmas Eve."

"Okay," he said.

"Okay?" I repeated, shocked that I'd gotten my way so easily.

"I could use the time to strengthen the case. What you overheard hints at a motive, but I'm not going to destroy a man's life on a hint. If he doesn't start telling the truth—the whole truth, though . . ." He trailed off, noticing my head-to-toe shivers. "It's cold. Let's go inside." He took me gently under the arm and steered me toward the restaurant.

I dug my heels in. "I can't. Jarka's in there with Harold. They're telling Sonya about their engagement. I can't ruin their moment."

"Okay." I didn't resist as he unzipped his coat and pulled me to him. The warmth of his body and the clean, pine-forest fragrance of his skin filled my senses. I threaded my arms around his back and laid my cold cheek against his warm one.

"Please keep looking. I know it looks bad, more than bad, for Rabbit. But it's not him. If you could see how hard he works, even when he thinks no one's looking. If you could see him with his daughter . . ." I leaned into him. "Please."

He spoke quietly, his words ruffling the hair around my ears. "I won't stop until I find the truth. I promise. But at this point we're focusing on a fairly small list of suspects." He proceeded to lay out a process of elimination very similar to the one Sonya and I had followed. Only his was backed by hard evidence—the video footage and license plate details that Officer Rettberg's diligent policework had afforded. The list he came up with was almost identical to ours, i.e., people who were known to Natasha La Cotti and who remained in the house at the end of the party—the three Hoffmans, Piper, Daniel, me, Sonya, and Melody. Based on the CCTV footage, he added Rabbit's and Jonathan's names.

Cozy as I was, I pushed out of his embrace. "I hate all of those possibilities. Well, except Adrian Hoffman. I'd arrest that dude myself if I could, for being an asshole in the first degree."

He cracked a smile.

"But you need to look harder, a lot harder, before you decide it was Rabbit. Last night, you had Daniel in your crosshairs because of some social media photos. And now, a few hours later, you're telling me . . . Actually, what are you telling me? That Rabbit's a killer because he ditched an AA meeting? Or my brother-in-law did it because he didn't beeline it back to the hotel? Or maybe we're all in it together? Maybe I'm the don of a crime family and I put a hit on Natasha myself? There are just too many loose ends for me to accept that any of them are involved in her murder."

He sighed and zipped his coat. "Joke if you want, but you hate lying as much as I do. Each one of them lied, or at the very least omitted important information. Daniel minimized his connection to Natasha La Cotti. And he hid his mother's vendetta against Adrian."

"He may not know anything about that," I cut in. "Neither of us have been able to fully quiz him about it."

"True," he conceded. "But your brother-in-law lied to his own daughter and to me about his whereabouts during the crucial period of time when Natasha was killed."

"He's got bad knees, though. He couldn't have carried her body."

"He could be faking," Capone pointed out.

"And Rabbit . . ." I crossed my arms again, this time more in petulance than because I was chilly. "Fine. I admit that I'm baffled. But I want more proof. They might each have perfectly good reasons for not telling the truth."

"Well, you potentially gave me at least three reasons Rabbit would lie." He counted on his gloved fingers. "Fear that he'll end up back behind bars, fear that he'll lose his job, and fear that he'll destroy his relationship with his daughter."

I regarded him closely. "Why are you even telling me any of this?" Capone was notoriously tight-lipped about sharing details of a case, yet here he was, tipping his hand about sensitive evidence. "Why do you want me to know all of this?"

"Because I care about you, and I trust you, and I need you with me on this. I need you to understand why I'm doing what I'm doing. I know your instincts are to protect your nearest and dearest, but I can't have you fighting me on this."

He seemed to be holding something back. "And?" I demanded.

"And because I want your help. You need to convince Rabbit to come clean with me. Let him know that if he's covering up some bush league, misdemeanor crap, he needs to tell me. If it's within my power to give him cover on some petty nonsense in order to get to the truth about a murder, I will."

"What about Jonathan and Daniel? You want my help with them, too, I take it?" My voice was as cold and brittle as the icicles that hung off the restaurant's roof. I wasn't angry with Capone, not really. But I hated the position dating him had put me in. I thought being questioned by him was bad, but now that I was on the "inside," what he was asking me to do was straight-up black-ops torture. How could I help him find the truth without feeling like I was betraying people who trusted me?

He nodded. "Daniel needs to come in and make a statement. If he's protecting his mother, he needs to stop. I don't want to have to *make* him come down to the station, but I will." He didn't try to disguise the threat. It was ugly, but it was reality. He would stop at nothing to find the truth.

"What about Jonathan?" I asked.

"You've told me a bit about your sister and her family. Jonathan's a tennis coach. Shea's an engineer on a government contract at JPL. Neither of them come from family money. Her salary is publicly searchable, and it's not crazy high, especially not by Pasadena standards. I asked around about tennis coaches' salaries. The pro at the Grand Bay Resort makes less than fifty K with no benefits, and apparently that's considered pretty good. Unless you're coaching Novak Djokovic at Wimbledon, you're not making bank. Yet your brother-in-law was staying in one of the most expensive suites at the hotel. Piper mentioned that they flew out here first class. His clothes, the rental car, his haircut—it all smells like dead presidents to me. I want you to find out where the money is coming from."

"About Shea . . ." I said. While we were on the subject of lies, I realized I had another one to drag out into the brutal light of day. "We can't completely rule out that she was there that night. She didn't arrive when she said she did." I explained to him about the flights.

"That sounds an awful lot like you're shopping your sister as a potential suspect," Capone observed. "I thought I was supposed to lay off your friends and family?"

"It would serve her right. For like six months when I was eight, she made me believe I was dying of Dutch Elm disease. I really don't know what she might be capable of."

He chuckled and shook his head. "And people have concerns about *my* family background."

"So I guess I'm your confidential informant, or whatever you call it? Someone who narcs on their own friends and family?" I couldn't keep my words from holding the tang of acid.

"Delilah, please." His voice was soft. "We both want the same thing."

"Oh? *You* want to punch you, too?" I snapped, only half kidding.

"We both want to find the truth. To see that justice is done."

I was quiet for a moment. I knew what he meant. If a cook on my line owned up to burning a hundred dollars' worth of pine nuts or using cayenne instead of paprika in a rub, I could let it go. I could forgive half a dozen major screw-ups if the person admitted what they did. What got somebody fired on the spot, though, was covering up a mistake and then lying to me about it.

Capone was the same. If he wanted to, he'd be fully justified in arresting Rabbit. He could do it right in front of Everleigh. He could haul Jonathan down to the station in the middle of dinner and demand an explanation. He could question Daniel *and* his mother, make sure their mother-son Christmas was one they'd never forget.

But he was taking a softer approach, hoping I could ferret out the truth. I trusted Capone, and I had to admit that I could see the wisdom of his plan. Whatever Rabbit was into, his best chance of getting out of it was to cooperate. But was he likely to be able to muster the courage to do that on his own? Doubtful. Daniel could be completely innocent. In fact, I believed he was. But he wouldn't be free of suspicion until he spilled what he knew. As for Jonathan, I, too, had questions. There was something rotten at the core of my sister's marriage. I'd sensed it, and I wanted to know the truth.

I closed my eyes and took in a deep lungful of the frosty air. When I opened my eyes, I met Capone's gaze with a new resolve. "I'll try."

CHAPTER 22

As I watched Capone's car turn on to the main road, I found myself staring across the ice-and-salt-crusted asphalt of the parking lot, toward the restaurant. December 24 was almost always a dead day for restaurants, with most potential patrons choosing to spend time with visiting family or flop on the couch with some takeout. We had enough lunch tables booked to justify opening, but I was expecting a relatively easy shift. I was glad we'd decided to close after lunch and stay closed until December 27. My crew had worked so hard over the past few weeks, and the break would do us all good. Even though I'd finished most of the prep in the wee hours last night, there was a lot to be done to catalogue and store all the food that could be saved until we reopened. I'd intended to get that underway this morning.

Picturing the scene inside, though, kept me rooted in place. Jarka and Harold would've found Sonya and shared their good news. Her pent-up romanticism would be bursting forth in a volcanic explosion of questions and plans—"How did the proposal happen? Show me the ring! Have you set a date?" and on and on and on. I could see the lights on in the dining room and kitchen.

Knowing Sonya, she'd already be whipping up a variety of sample wedding cake flavors for them to try. After what Capone had just told me, I'd be a black cloud in their blue sky. I climbed the back stairs, retrieved Butterball, and texted Sonya to let her know that I'd be back in time for opening. Then, I hopped into my Jeep and headed home.

A single car stood in the driveway, a nondescript sedan with Florida plates, Shea's rental. I called a hello as I walked into the house. Stooping down, I unlatched the cat carrier, freeing Butterball from his prison. After a brief pause to give me the evil eye for being the agent of his confinement, he beelined it for his favorite spot, the sunny bay window in the kitchen.

I called out again. Hearing no reply, I climbed the stairs. I wasn't sure who or what I hoped to find. I wanted to check in on Melody, to see if she'd recovered from the emotional upheaval of the previous night. I'd promised Capone that I'd try to rattle the truth from my brother-in-law about the unexplained gap in his timeline for the night of the murder and uncover the mystery of his recent cash infusion. I *needed* to talk to my sister, to try to get to the bottom of her odd lie about her whereabouts. In that moment, I very much didn't want to see Auntie Biz, my niece, or my nephew. They all seemed caught up in the magic of the holidays, and here I was, blowing in like an ill wind, with tidings of murder, emotional entanglements, and lies.

The bedroom doors gaped open, the east-facing doorways spilling sharply demarcated rectangles of winter sunlight into the hall. Specks of dust danced in the shafts of yellow light, creating an uncanny snow globe effect. Finding no one upstairs, I circled the downstairs rooms. The kitchen, usually the home's hub, was empty; a stack of clean pans in the drying rack was the only evidence of that morning's breakfast. I was about to conclude that they'd all gone out when a mew from Butterball drew me to the kitchen door. I opened it, intending to let him outside. Instead, he stopped at the foot of a wicker chair on the sunporch, where my sister sat, statue-still, facing the frozen lake.

The room was glazed in, and on sunny days like this, the afternoon would bring a fleeting hour or two of greenhouse-effect warmth. At this hour, though, the morning air was still chilly enough to create white billows of vapor from my breath. Shea barely stirred when Butterball and I entered the room. She wore a hip-length black puffer coat, hat, and mirrored sunglasses. She hunched in the wicker chair, her long legs drawn up into the cradle of her arms. An untouched mug of coffee sat on the table next to her, the cream congealed, not a wisp of steam rising from it.

"Shea?"

"They went to the resort." She answered my unasked question. "Snow tubing."

"Are you sick?"

She uncoiled her legs and straightened up in the chair. "Jetlag," she replied crisply, turning her face away.

I pulled a chair directly opposite her, so close our knees almost touched. Her complexion was ashen, her bare hands red with the cold. I reached out and whipped off her sunglasses. Her eyes were bloodshot, their rims bright pink. I hadn't seen my sister cry since we were children. She barely shed a tear when each of our parents died, but now the tears threatened to spill forth. I took hold of her icy hands.

"Please, Shea. Stop this. Tell me what's wrong."

She stiffened and pulled her hands away.

"Oh forget it!" I yelled, throwing my own hands up in frustration. "I'm trying to be what's-her-name, the woodland creature princess, but this is hopeless." I stood up and collected Butterball in my arms. "Enjoy your misery."

As I stomped toward the kitchen door, she heaved a sigh. An exhalation so long suppressed it felt like the vacuum releasing on a submarine. "Mom died on a day like today. Do you remember? It had snowed for days, but that day was clear. The sun was so bright. They told us they thought the glare kept her from seeing the patch of ice she spun out on. In January, it'll be twenty-three years."

I stopped in my tracks, holding my breath. Shea and I never talked about that day. "I remember," I said.

"I hate the snow. I hate this time of year. I hate being this close to where she died. When I'm here, and the weather is like this, I feel like *she's* here. And she'd be so disappointed in me."

Shea's voice was as flat and icy as the surface of the lake, her words so unexpected that I walked back toward her and sat in my chair.

"How can you say that? Mom waitressed at Zorba's for fifteen years. She never finished high school. I can't even count how many times she told us she wanted more for us, and your life is everything she could've dreamed of. You're so successful."

She let out a bitter laugh.

"I don't understand," I said. "You're the one who went to college, like she always wanted us to. You're a literal rocket scientist, for Christ's sake. She wanted us to have happy marriages and kids. You and Jonathan have that. He worships you."

Emotion lit up her eyes. "None of it is real! I work on contract at JPL, and my project is ending soon. I don't think they'll renew it. The program manager absolutely flayed my work in our last review."

"You can find another job," I said. "You have your family to pull you through."

"The kids? They *love* Jonathan. They tolerate me. Jonathan makes them laugh. I make them eat their vegetables. He plays with them. I make them floss. Piper always preferred spending time at her mom's, even though I tried so hard with her, and since she started at Palisades, I hardly see her. Caleb is such a daddy's boy that when Jonathan"—she took a steeling breath—"when Jonathan leaves me, Caleb's not going to want to have anything to do with me."

"What?! Jonathan's leaving you?"

Instead of answering, Shea put her sunglasses back on. She rose and walked over to the back door. The sunlight was streaming in now, but her tall, black-coated form blocked it like a storm cloud. Seeing her framed there, against the backdrop of the snow-covered lawn, I gasped. A realization hit me with such force, it stole the air from my lungs. The figure lurking in the bushes. I'd felt that there was something familiar about the way the person moved. The lithe grace. And now I realized that I'd seen it a thousand times on the high school basketball court and in the backyard games of our childhood. How had I not recognized that it was Shea?

"Oh my god. It was you. Running through the yard during the snowstorm."

She didn't try to deny it. "I was tailing Jonathan. I thought he was here, but he and Auntie Biz and Piper had already gone out."

"So you *weren't* on the flight yesterday. You were already here."

"What tipped you off?" she asked, her voice betraying surprise.

I pulled Butterball back into my lap, cuddling him for warmth. "You couldn't have connected through Denver. The airport was closed on the day you were supposed to fly. And Caleb mentioned you staying in a hotel. That didn't fit with what you'd told me. I don't understand. Why were you following Jonathan? How long have you and Caleb been here?"

"Since Sunday," she admitted. "As for Jonathan, I was following him because I thought he was lying about where he was going and who he was with. I needed to see for myself."

"I still don't understand. Why didn't you tell us?"

She leveled an "are you serious?" look at me. "Tell you that I dragged my toddler halfway across the country so I could follow my husband around like a crazy stalker and try to catch him in a lie?" She let out a rueful, mirthless guffaw. "That my life's falling apart and I'm one boiled bunny away from the psych ward?"

I shook my head, more in disbelief than in disagreement. My hyperrational sister was admitting that she'd done a giant swan dive off the deep end. I had so many questions, I barely knew where to start. "If you were hiding out in my bushes, where was Caleb?" I sputtered.

"I booked a room for us at a hotel in Janesville," she explained. "My friend Carly lives there. She babysat while I was tailing Jonathan."

"I remember her," I said. "You used to hang out when we'd visit Auntie Biz."

"Yeah. We've stayed in touch. I didn't fill her in, either, in case you're wondering. No one knows. I told her Jonathan and I had some social engagements to attend. She loves kids and was happy to help."

"I wondered why you didn't say anything to me or Auntie Biz about Jonathan and Piper being in town," I said. "Even for you, that seemed pretty cold." She didn't even blink, accepting the harsh assessment without trying to defend herself. "Now that makes more sense. You were worried we'd mess up your spying."

"And you almost did," she shot back. "I nearly ran into Biz at the supermarket in Janesville. Luckily, I clocked her before she could get a good look. Southern Wisconsin is too small. It's impossible to be incognito."

So my aunt's sighting of the Shea look-alike had been the real deal.

"I still don't understand. Why did you think Jonathan was lying about coming here?"

"Because he's lied before." She sank deeper into the wicker chair. Her posture, usually charm-school perfect, slumped into a C-curve. There was no anger, no tears, no big show of emotion. But when she spoke, her voice was laden with bitterness and pain.

"Last summer," she began, "he had to work on our anniversary. Running a tennis clinic at the Yacht Club in Boca Raton, or so he said. I lined Piper up to sit for Caleb and flew out over the weekend to surprise him. He wasn't in his room, so I left my bag at the desk and went to grab some food. I walked right past Jonathan having dinner at one of the hotel restaurants. Sitting under the palm trees with an ocean view, eating lobster with some woman I'd never seen before. I assumed it was a client of his, something like that. My first instinct was to walk right in and introduce myself. That's how sure I was that he'd never cheat."

She took off her sunglasses and rubbed her eyes. The winter sunlight was harsh and unforgiving, painting each line on her weary face in stark relief. Butterball, sensing her distress, sprang from my lap into hers. She regarded him with a sad smile. "Something kept me from going in. The two of them seemed so intimate. He'd never behave that way with someone he was coaching. I hid behind a potted palm and called him on my cell. When his phone rang, he stepped away from the table to take the call. He told me he was in the middle of watching a match and couldn't talk."

"Oh, Shea, I'm so sorry." I, too, had a hard time casting Jonathan as a cheater. His devotion to my sister seemed so genuine. But try as I might, I couldn't think of another reason my brother-in-law would lie.

"There's more," Shea said. "While I was there, I checked at the club's tennis facility, where he was allegedly coaching. There was no tennis clinic. They'd never even heard of Jonathan Savage. I went back to the front desk, picked up my bag, and flew home."

"Didn't Piper wonder why you came back early?" I asked.

"I told her I missed my connection." She shook her head. "I should've known something was up with him. About two years ago, out of nowhere, his coaching career took off. He was being flown all over the country to coach—Boca, Miami, Montauk, Martha's Vineyard. I didn't understand how he was getting so many new clients. I'd always been the one with the steady paycheck, and I'd been panicked because the project I've been working on wasn't going well and was up for renewal. I'd encouraged Piper to apply to Palisades. She and I worked like crazy on that application. We really bonded over it, but the whole time, I didn't know how we were going to afford it if she got in. Then like a miracle, Jonathan started bringing home these huge checks. He started paying for things. Buying things for the kids. And not just clothes and toys. I'm talking about trips to Disneyland. A car for Piper. Her tuition at Palisades paid in full, with money to spare."

"Did you ask him where all the money was coming from?"

"Of course. He'd tell me he got a tip from a grateful client or a consulting fee or that he'd been hired to run a private clinic. And I believed it. I forced myself to believe. Even though I know what tennis coaches make." She swallowed hard, as if the words had jagged edges. "He's not *that* good. He's had two knee surgeries. Some days he can barely walk. I've seen him with his students. He's sitting on the sidelines with his leg propped up and iced, on his phone, barely even watching them play."

"You've said this to him?"

"Of course not. It would kill him." Her voice cracked as she added, "It's killing me. How bad I wanted it to be true. He's always been insecure about his career. I know he was proud of me for having a good job, but he hated that he couldn't provide and that I had to shoulder the stress of supporting us. I wanted to believe that he'd finally struck it big. And I was so sure that he'd never betray me that I somehow made myself believe people were flying him across the country and paying him ten thousand dollars to lead a five-day tennis clinic."

She'd resumed her customary ballerina posture and measured tone. No histrionics or hysteria for Shea. Still, watching her was like watching fissures form in a wall of solid rock. The cracks crept up the façade, little by little, until I was practically holding my breath, fearing the entirety of her life might crumble to dust before my eyes.

"So you think he's having an affair? That the woman you saw him with in Florida is his sugar mama? Or what, he's a gigolo?"

"As far as I can tell, there's only one woman. He's doing something for her, and it sure as hell's not coaching." She shifted suddenly and Butterball hopped down from her lap. "I bet you think this serves me right."

I opened my mouth to protest, but there was no point in trying to pretend. "Yeah, part of me does."

"I know I haven't been a good sister to you. Not after mom died, not on this trip, not ever."

I didn't know what to say. Hearing her admit it should've made me feel better. The truth of what I'd felt all these years was laid bare. But it didn't. Not at all. I thought she'd ignored me because her life was busy. I thought she'd belittled me unintentionally, just by virtue of being so damn good at everything. But now it seemed like she was telling me that she'd known all along how poorly she'd treated me, and she just hadn't cared enough to do anything about it.

"I was jealous, I guess," she said. "After mom died, you had Auntie Biz. You two had so much in common. I had nobody. Dad just disappeared into himself and stayed gone for years. I tried so hard with Jonathan to build the family I wanted, and for a while, I thought I had it. But when it started to fall apart, I realized how alone I was. I had no one to talk to. I was too . . ." She waved her hand. "I don't know. Embarrassed? Ashamed? Maybe angry that this is what my life had become. Stalking my own husband. Begging my kids to love me."

"They do love you."

"Piper appreciates me, I think. Maybe even loves me. But what's a stepmother next to a father? And Caleb prefers Jonathan, too. Always has. Daddy's fun. Do I look like fun to you?"

I sidestepped the question. Fun for a roomful of Advanced Psychology students, maybe. She seemed to think that if she didn't keep all the plates spinning in perfect synchronicity—career, kids, marriage—her life was an abject failure. I'd connected the dots a long time ago between my mom's death and my own rabid perfectionism. Since that awful day, a four-alarm fire burned inside me, making me feel that if I didn't dot every *i* and cross every *t*, another terrible thing would happen. My response to that unpredictable, stupid, random patch of ice was to become gripped by the compulsion to overprepare to the nth degree. But now I saw that I'd gotten off easy. While I'd always held the firm conviction that our mom's love for us was unconditional, and that it stretched beyond the grave, Shea seemed haunted by the mistaken belief that she'd turned out to be unlovable, a disappointment.

"Look, you don't have anything to be embarrassed about," I said. "*He's* the liar." I was quiet for moment, thinking. There was no question that Jonathan had betrayed her. He'd lied about where his money was coming from and who he was spending time with. But there were still so many unanswered questions. "Have you outright confronted him? Given him a chance to confess?"

She shook her head. "I needed to be sure first. That's why I came here. I thought I could find out what he was up to, once and for all. I hung around the hotel, and I saw the same woman again. I found out her name."

She pulled out her phone and handed to it me. It was open to a social media app, to Natasha La Cotti's profile. I saw again the procession of ritzy restaurants and hotels, only this time a pattern rose up with face-smacking obviousness. The dates. *"I've been running some tennis clinics in Boca and Montauk. I alternate about every six weeks,"* Jonathan had said, describing his jet-setting lifestyle. And here was Natasha in Montauk, then six weeks later in Florida, Miami, Martha's Vineyard. All the places Jonathan said he'd gone to coach. I clicked on the date of my sister and Jonathan's anniversary. Natasha's photo was tagged "The Yacht Club, Boca Raton."

As my wide, horror-stricken eyes met Shea's, she nodded. "She's the woman I saw him with. I saw them together the night of the Hoffmans' party. They took the shuttle together, with Piper." Her expression was grim. "I hadn't seen the news. I didn't know that she was the one who died until I 'arrived'"—she flashed a pained smile as she bracketed the word with air quotes—"yesterday and met everyone at the restaurant."

"Oh my god. So you found out that she was killed right before you came to see me and Biz in the kitchen?! No wonder you were such a b"—I bit my lip and swapped out an alternative B word—"bundle of nerves. That must've been awful."

"What could I do? I was so deep into my game of psycho wife cloak-and-dagger. I couldn't admit that I'd been here the whole time, or that I already knew who Natasha La Cotti was. Or that I'd followed Jonathan." She clutched her midsection, drawing breath in short, shaky gasps. "Dee, he went back to the Hoffmans' house that night. After the party. I saw him go inside, and I know he lied to Piper about it. He's been leading a double life with that woman for almost two years. What else is he capable of?"

CHAPTER 23

Hard as it was to break away from my sister in her hour of need, I had to get to work. Butterball again seemed to sense that Shea needed him, and he settled in alongside her on the porch rather than clamoring for the treats that usually accompanied his journeys to and from the restaurant. I left my sister with the promise that we'd meet up at the snow sculpting competition that evening to see the winners announced.

I was the last of the restaurant's staff to arrive as I screeched into the parking lot at 11:25, with only five minutes to spare before the doors opened. Once again, we'd be short-staffed. Piper had offered to work again, but I figured we could manage, now that Jarka was back. I texted Rabbit to check on Everleigh, and he sent a brief reply telling me her arm was fractured and they'd have to go to the hospital to get the bone set. Biz wouldn't be helping out that day, having chosen to spend time with the Savages. I felt an impulse to call and warn her about Jonathan. But what would I say? I settled for a data dump text to Capone. I was done protecting my brother-in-law.

Miraculously, despite the bumpy start to the day, I found lunch preparations in full swing. Jarka and

Harold's happiness seemed to have buoyed the collective spirit. Jarka was not only doing her part, but she'd roped Harold into helping out as well. He was practically skipping as he ferried clean glassware from the kitchen to the dining room, gazing across at Jarka with moony eyes. A besotted Harold Heyer plus glassware didn't seem like a safe combination, so I made a mental note to put him in charge of the host station, where his exuberance would be an asset rather than a liability.

Given how bleak everything had looked after closing the previous night, I hadn't even been sure if Daniel or Melody would show up that day. But there they both were, bustling around and getting things done. Daniel was behind the bar, blending up a batch of that day's featured cocktail—a Puerto Rican eggnog-like drink called *coquito*. His expression was uncharacteristically solemn, but there was no sign of the anger that had been on show the previous evening.

Melody, too, was slightly subdued, but composed. She came over as I stamped the caked-on snow from my boots. "Everything okay, chef?" she asked. "Sonya said you had some urgent stuff to deal with."

"Yeah, it's still kind of ongoing," I said. I could already see the first customer of the day pulling into the parking lot, and there was no way I had time to summarize the morning's events in anything under an hour. "*You* okay?" I asked.

She glanced at Daniel and nodded. "I will be, once we figure out who killed that lady and clear our friends' names. That's what's important."

I squeezed her arm then cruised back to the kitchen to find Sonya ticking the last item off the prep list.

"We good?" I asked.

"Great. I proposed a pink-and-white color scheme for the wedding. Jarka wants gray, but I think I can talk her around. We'll host the whole thing here. A ceremony on the patio so the lake will be in the background of the photos. Although the weather is always a factor with outdoor ceremonies . . ." She caught sight of my face. "Oh, you mean with prep. Yeah, all good. How'd it go with Rabbit?"

I filled her in on the latest, as I tied my apron on and washed my hands. The first orders came across the ticket printer just as I finished telling her about the video evidence from the resort. "It's weird," I said, starting to pull out the ingredients to make a Curried Cauliflower Calzone and a small eggplant and sausage pie. "But as the evidence gets more and more damning for Rabbit, the more convinced I am that it wasn't him."

"Well, it sounds like he's into *something*," Sonya said.

"Whatever it is, it can't be murder." I laid overlapping rings of low-moisture mozzarella onto a dough base. "He's stressed, but if he'd killed someone, he'd be distraught." Because I was making deep-dish, my next step after cheese was toppings—a thick layer of baked eggplant and spicy nduja sausage. "Honestly, I don't think he'd go anywhere near Everleigh if he'd done it. He's too protective of her, to the point that I think he'd protect her from himself if necessary." I finished the pie with rich, chunky marinara sauce, using a ladle to spread a saucy spiral that covered the entire top. As I spoke, I realized that the doubt I'd previously harbored about Rabbit's innocence had evaporated. There had to be a good explanation for his mysterious interactions with Daffi Hoffman and for his return to

her house on the night of the party. I was determined
to find out what it was. I was also determined to make
sure he had a roof over his head come next week. I took
out my phone and fired off a text to Sam, my former
fiancé.

Sonya nodded to my phone. "Your text earlier said
you talked to Shea, too?"

I frowned, pocketing my cell. "Yeah, that's a train
wreck." I quickly ran through the main points—Shea's
ham-handed game of transcontinental cloak-and-
dagger, Jonathan's probable infidelity, and the worrying gap in his whereabouts at the time of the murder.

Her eyes had grown wider as I revealed each detail. Eventually, she gave up the pretense of working
and stood staring at me, slack-jawed. "That's beyond
a train wreck, Dee. That's a jumbo jet crashing into a
helicopter, and then the flaming wreckage of *that* falls
from the sky and causes a train wreck."

We said goodbye to our last patrons just before three
o'clock and spent the next hour and a half getting the
restaurant squared away for its brief Christmas hiatus.
While the rest of us finished accounting, packaging, la-
beling, and cleaning, Sonya, Harold, and Jarka busied
themselves setting a seven-top to serve a Hanukkah-
themed family meal. Since it was also Christmas Eve,
Daniel had invited his mother to join us. Just as our activity petered out, the bell over the door rang.

"Yoo-hoo!" Angie Castillo called out. "Hope I'm not
late."

"You're just on time, *Mamá*," Daniel said, coming
from behind the bar to introduce her around.

She embraced each of us in turn, bathing us in com-
pliments, cheek kisses, nasally vowels, and clouds of

hairspray and baby powder scent. She seemed especially taken with Melody. Taking Melody's face in her hands, she said, "You're a positive doll, *mija*, like the angel on top of a Christmas tree."

We were just past the winter solstice, so darkness was already falling a few minutes later as everyone gravitated to the table, where the meal was set. Usually, family meal was a simple affair—maybe a quick pasta with roasted veggies or an unpretentious stew that made use of leftover ingredients. Today, though, Sonya had gone all out. Since the morning, she'd been braising her legendary brisket, a marbled, succulent cut of beef. She'd slow-cooked it with caramelized onions, garlic, herbs, and red wine until everything married with the meat juices to form a rich glaze. The end result was luscious, mouthwatering meat bathed in velvety sauce, the whole thing tender enough to fall off your fork. Next to the brisket, a golden, braided loaf of challah was still steaming from the oven. On the far side of that, a heaping plate of leek and potato latkes stood next to a bowl of bitter greens salad doused with a mustard vinaigrette. For dessert, she'd baked both an apple-and-honey cake and a raspberry rugelach.

Sonya placed the center candle in the menorah, plus five more—one for each day that had passed since the inauspicious first night of the holiday. Once the stage was set, she peered out the window. Deep shadows had gathered over the lake. She watched intently until the last rays of sun were swallowed up by the tree-lined western shore. "Aaaaand . . . sunset," she said, striking a match to light the center servant candle from which all the other candles were lit.

As she lit the tapers, she sang a blessing in Hebrew. Out of nowhere, an angelic falsetto voice joined her.

"*Barukh ata Adonai.*" The voice emanated from Harold Heyer, who sang in earnest and word-perfect Hebrew, the bald dome of his head shining as brightly as the baubles dangling overhead. Sonya, who'd been momentarily thrown off by his singing, pulled herself and the rendition together. When they finished, we turned to him in surprise.

"You're Jewish?" Sonya asked.

"Lutheran. We had an Israeli au pair when I was little," he explained.

Jarka clutched her fiancé's arm, beaming. "My Harold is full of surprises."

We sat down to eat, and my grumbling stomach reminded me that I'd had nothing since my early-morning crêpes Suzette and coffee with Sonya. The troubles of the past few days were temporarily set aside as we gorged ourselves on the delicious food. Conversation flowed, and despite Rabbit's notable absence, it felt like the old days, before the specter of suspicion had taken up residence among us. It wasn't until we finished the meal that the looming investigation pushed itself back to the forefront of my mind. As the second round of desserts was passed, I found myself alone in the kitchen loading the dishwasher. Angie came in with a bus tub full of dishes.

"Thank you for inviting me," she said. "I can see why Junior likes it here. It's like one big, happy family."

My smile was pained. "Not so happy the past few days."

"Oh, yes," she said lightly. "Junior mentioned that there had been some trouble at a party you catered."

I almost dropped the wineglasses I was loading into the glass rack. Did she truly not understand the magnitude of what we were dealing with? Or was she being deliberately obtuse? "*Some trouble?*" I repeated.

"Something about a lady falling? He didn't go into details." She set the bus tub down and waved her hand, a red-lipped smile still fixed on her face.

I hadn't intended to grill her, not here, with the holiday glow all around us. But I couldn't let this stand. Her son could end up in serious trouble, and she was talking like it was a small inconvenience. With my usual go-for-broke interrogation style, I slid the glass rack into the dishwasher, pulled the lever down to start the machine, and repainted her rosy picture of events. "A woman named Natasha La Cotti was pushed to her death. Murdered. Daniel is under suspicion, in part because he knew her. But also because of you."

"What?" Now it was her turn to look aghast. "He said there'd been a death at the party. He didn't say it was murder. What does this have to do with me?"

Daniel chose that very moment to come into the kitchen. "I need a lemon for Harold's tea . . ." Taking the temperature of the room, he looked dead at me. "What's going on?"

His accusatory glare didn't faze me. It was time to get everything out in the open, once and for all. "You didn't tell your mother about the murder? Or that Capone questioned you?"

He put his hands on his hips. "She's on vacation. I didn't want to upset her."

Angie rushed to her son's side. "What's this about, *mijo*? Capone, the detective, the one you told me was related to Al Capone, he suspects you?" She crossed herself. "*¡Ay, Dios mío!*"

"So you also didn't tell her that the murder happened

at *Adrian Hoffman's* house?" I enunciated the name and watched as the color faded from her face. "I saw you. That day at the snow sculpting competition."

She turned to her son, her brow crinkling. A rapid exchange of words in Spanish ensued. While I was technically conversant in the language from my many years in restaurant kitchens, I struggled to keep up with a warp-speed dialogue that carried the emotion of a telenovela on steroids. It seemed that Daniel had been keeping the details of the murder from his mother, not wanting to worry her. Now, he filled her in about his nauseating encounter with Natasha La Cotti—the social media post, the high school girls, all of it. Likewise, she'd told her son nothing of her run-in with Adrian. She, too, was hoping to keep him from getting upset.

The pace of the words finally began to slow. Angie looked wobbly and I rushed over with Auntie Biz's stool so she could sit down.

"Thank you, Delilah." She clutched her chest and took in a deep breath, as if she'd just run a long distance.

"Am I right that '*contratista*' means 'contractor'?" I asked.

She nodded.

"So Adrian Hoffman is the contractor who was supposed to fix your house after the hurricane? The one who ran off with all your money but did none of the work?" I leaned on the counter, feeling a little breathless myself. I'd followed enough of the conversation to finally understand the reason for her vendetta against Adrian. And it was a doozy.

"That *man*"—she practically spat the word—"almost ruined us. I only met him once, but I recognized him as soon as I saw him at the competition."

"I remember Daffi saying he was in real estate. I didn't realize he was a contractor."

"*Contractor.*" She mimed spitting on the floor. "He's a criminal. After the hurricane, his company started to fix a neighbor's place, and seemed to be doing good work. None of us had been able to get anyone even to come out to give an estimate, but here was this company who seemed to be able to find building materials and laborers. *We* sought *him* out, believe it or not. Didn't even ask for references. That's how desperate we were. A bunch of us, practically the whole street, signed on with his company. He asked for fifty percent up front to secure our spots. Then two weeks after the last check cleared, he was gone. Left our neighbor with half a roof. My insurance company told me later that it's a common scam after a disaster. Not that they covered any of the losses, mind you. That sort of thing happened all over the island."

Daniel turned to me, his palms out. "I didn't know Adrian, *jefa*. I was deployed that year. When I came back, I tried to help get the money back, but I only ever knew the name of the company. We sued, but the company had declared bankruptcy. Nobody got a cent."

"Ritzy vacation home, fancy car, and probably paying a mint in private school tuition," I said. "He doesn't seem bankrupt to me."

"No," Daniel agreed, his lips pressed into a tight line. "Our lawyer figured that he probably rolled all of our money into another company or an offshore account. We had to drop the suit at a certain point. There seemed to be no hope of getting our money, and we couldn't keep paying the legal fees."

"Daniel and his sisters tried to get me to forget about

it," Angie said. "I ended up in the hospital from the stress."

Her son looked at her tenderly. "We didn't want to lose another parent to a heart attack. It seemed easier to work and help her get the money to fix the house that way. That's why I didn't tell you about the murder, *Mamá*. I didn't want to upset you."

She placed her hand on her son's cheek. "And that's why *I* didn't tell *you* about seeing that horrible man. I was afraid you'd worry. Or try to confront him yourself."

It seemed that my family wasn't the only one that sometimes kept secrets to its detriment.

"You should tell Capone about Adrian," I said.

"Capone? The detective?" Angie pursed her lips.

"You can trust him. He's a friend."

"Really?" Daniel said. "The way he rode up on me the other night didn't feel too friendly."

"Well, *mijo*," Angie said, "it's probably better to tell him than have him find out on his own."

"Speaking of telling people things . . ." My face formed a sheepish grimace. "The other night, I, um, knocked over Hadley's purse. Your boxers were in it."

"My *boxers*?" Daniel's face was a mask of confusion.

"I take it you don't know how they got there?"

"No idea. I've only talked to her a few times. I have no clue how she'd get hold of them."

There was no hesitation in his voice, no evasion in his gaze. Still, I had questions. "I've been wondering," I said. "I understand why you dodged Capone's questioning initially. You'd recognized Jonathan as the man who came back to the house and were trying to protect my family. I'm grateful. But why didn't you tell Capone right away about Natasha trying to get you to flirt with underage girls? It sounds like she was into something dodgy. Why'd you let him suspect *you* of something when you were holding on to a possible reason someone else might want her dead?"

He firmed up his jaw. "I didn't want to talk about it. The way that woman treated me . . ." He shook his head and clamped his teeth shut.

"What is it, Junior?" his mother asked.

He shook his head again, but this time he answered. "Look, I'm not trying to compare my experience to what women go through. If someone gets handsy with me, I don't have to fear for my safety. I can protect myself. But sometimes, it feels like people like Natasha La Cotti think they own me. I'm the hired help, there to smile pretty, flirt with them, and serve them drinks. I understand the bargain—I do my thing and they give me good tips. But some people take it too far. Grabbing me and trying to slip me their room keys. Usually, I can laugh it off, but that night with Natasha, what she was asking me to do . . ." He swallowed hard. "She seemed so sure that I'd do it if she just paid me enough. That's what bothers me the most."

The door to the dining room burst open, and Melody, Sonya, and Jarka streamed in, all bundled up in their winter coats.

"What's taking so long?" Sonya asked.

"Yes," Jarka said. "My Harold already has left for announcing who wins the snow competition."

"We've got to hustle," Melody said, glancing at her watch. "We're supposed to meet Biz and your family."

Sonya cocked her head. "Everything okay?"

Daniel, Angie, and I exchanged glances. We'd experienced several years' worth of revelations in the past ten minutes.

I pasted a smile on my face. "Peachy."

CHAPTER 24

As we stepped out into the dark, quiet evening, my emotions were in tumult. The air was sharp with cold, but my crew seemed buoyant, chatting about Jarka and Harold's romance, the holidays, the soon-to-be-revealed outcome of the contest. Christmas lights festooned the shore path and guided our steps from the restaurant to the park. All around us were the sounds of excited voices and squelching footfalls on the snow-covered path. The docks had been removed for the winter and the lake, usually filled with the gentle lapping of waves, was frozen into silence.

Daniel and his mother walked arm in arm, their disclosures having brought them closer together. I, too, had experienced a moment of relief, almost catharsis, as Daniel and Angie cleared up some of the swirling questions. I now understood why Angie hated Adrian so passionately—the man had stolen her life savings during a desperate time and gotten off scot-free. Daniel's motivations, too, had become clearer—he'd been dodging Capone in part to avoid telling him what he knew about my brother-in-law's whereabouts. But he'd also wanted to spare his mother from learning the details of the investigation and spare himself from dredging up the deeply uncomfortable experience he'd had with Natasha.

Any relief I felt was more than tempered by the implications of new information that the Castillos had brought to light. I was now more convinced than ever that Daniel and his mother had nothing to do with Natasha's death. But two new possible motives had crystalized—both strong enough to kill for. Natasha was a consultant, and she seemed to have a professional connection to Adrian. Could she have been involved with his dubious business practices?

And then there was the matter of the underage girls. I'd been mulling it over since Daniel's initial admission about his encounter with Natasha. I trusted Capone's instinct that a human trafficking operation in Geneva Bay was unlikely to have gone unnoticed. So why else would Natasha seek out young, rich girls? To sell drugs? To somehow fleece their parents? Natasha's behavior had made my preternaturally self-assured bartender feel abused and ashamed. I'd seen the same complex emotions pass over my brother-in-law's face when her name was mentioned. What was she capable of? What would happen to someone who actually *did* become involved in whatever scheme she was running?

Before I knew it, our little group had reached the park. The whole place was crisscrossed with lights, and a small stage had been erected next to the food vendors. Harold, the head of the Chamber of Commerce, was there now, conversing with the other organizers. All around us, fantastical effigies rose high off the ground. Here was a Kraken, reaching out with its tentacles to pull a ship into its gaping maw. Next to that was a toy chest, spilling over with dolls, trucks, and games. Beside that stood a formidable-looking blindfolded Lady Justice sculpture. The carving of the scales she held aloft had been cleverly done: even though they were supported from beneath by snow, they looked like they were suspended in midair. Under the glittering lights, the statue looked more like marble than snow.

"Aunt Dee!" a voice called out.

I turned to find Piper jogging in my direction. "Everyone else is still looking at the sculptures," she said. "I told them I'd find you and stake out a spot near the stage. They'll come over when it's time to announce the winners."

My crew, too, had fanned out to take a final look at the snow carvings before the judgment was announced. Only Jarka had stayed near the stage. She stood next to me and Piper, gazing up at her beloved as he made final preparations. I introduced Piper to Jarka and the two greeted each other.

"How was snow tubing?" I asked my niece.

"Good. Caleb loved it. We were out most of the day. I lost a glove at one point when we were on the hill, though, and I think I got a little frostbitten. I bought new mittens at the ski shop, but my fingers are still numb." Piper took off her mitten and held up her hand. The tips of her index and middle fingers were red and swollen, like she'd touched a hot stove.

Jarka's forehead creased in concern. She shined her phone flashlight on Piper's hand. "In Bulgaria, I am a doctor," she explained, moving closer to examine the skin. She handed me her phone so I could continue shining the light as she turned my niece's hand gently over with her own. "Yes, this is frostbite. Mild, but you must be careful to not make it worse. You should not be out in cold. You must warm your hand in water

that is not hot, only warm. Then keep it up like this."
She moved her own hand to demonstrate that the ap-
pendage should be elevated. "Once the fingers are not
numb no more, it will be very full of pain, I am sorry
to tell."

Piper frowned. "Dang. I guess I'll have to tell Hadley I can't ski tonight."

"To ski would not be wise," Jarka said. "You should
go inside as soon as possible."

"I'll go back to the house after this. I'm glad I ran
into you. I was going to power through because it
doesn't really hurt, it's more like pins and needles."
Piper examined her hand as she put her mitten back on.
"It's weird how much frostbite looks like a burn."

"The pain, when it comes, will feel also like a burn,"
Jarka confirmed. She took her phone back and slipped
it into her pocket. "Burning and freezing are similar in
this way. I have always found this interesting. When a
body becomes hypothermic, sometimes the person has
a strange feeling like they are becoming too hot. Even
they take off their clothes. Paradoxical undressing, is
called. I saw this sometimes in my hospital, if a person
has been drinking very much of alcohol and then he
falls asleep out of doors. Usually, if a person takes off
his own clothes, this is the body's last attempt to survive. It maybe is too late to save this person."

"Yeesh, sounds like an awful way to go," Piper said,
tucking her frostbitten hand into her armpit. "Freezing
to death but feeling like you're burning up."

While they were talking, Hadley had come up to join
us. "What are you talking about?" she asked.

"No skiing for me tonight," Piper said, shooting a
pouty frown at her friend. She pointed to her mittened
hand. "Frostbite. I'm bummed because the light show

at the end of the session is supposed to be extra cool tonight. They're doing red and green for Christmas. Maybe we can watch it from your house?" She tilted her head toward me and Jarka and explained. "If the weather is clear, you can see the show from Hadley's place. When the slope is all lit up, you feel like you're right there."

Hadley appeared not to be listening. Her eyebrows drew together and she gave a series of rapid blinks. "What were you saying before? About people freezing to death?"

"Jarka is a doctor," Piper explained. "She was telling us about frostbite and hypothermia. How your body goes so haywire right before you die that you actually think you're overheating and start stripping. Isn't that an awful way to die?"

I stared at my niece. For days, jumbled flashcards had been piling up in my brain. Clues, suspects, motives, alibis. Who had pushed Natasha La Cotti? How and why had the killer moved her body from the back of the house to the ski slope? As the girls and Jarka were talking, that unordered mess of thoughts had been reshuffled. Now, card by card, the deck was being laid out flat. On the night of the party, I'd had the disquieting vision of Natasha wandering coatless in the snow. I'd never imagined it would prove prophetic. But now, I watched as the images in my mind organized themselves into coherent rows.

Natasha's body plummeted to the earth into the mounded snow below the balcony.

Her limp form slid out of the camera's range.

Someone took off her clothes.

Someone moved her body.

She had frostbite.

I practically pounced on Jarka. "Frostbite only happens when you're alive, right? Can a dead person get frostbite?"

She drew back slightly, reacting to the sudden force of my emotion. "Frostbite can only happen to living tissue, yes. Dead tissue does not do this."

"Would a hypothermic person, say someone who'd fallen into the snow, be disoriented? How would they act?" I asked.

"The person would seem almost like drunk. Clumsy. Confused."

"If it was dark, might they walk toward bright lights?" I asked.

"Yes, probably. This would be instinct."

"Natasha fell on to packed snow," I explained. "If she was knocked out by the fall but not killed, she might've woken up a short time later, having slid down the hill away from the house. She didn't have her coat on and she'd been drinking. It was freezing that night. She would've been hypothermic. She would've been turned around. Maybe she had a concussion. And then at ten o'clock the LED show on the ski slope would suddenly light up the night. The slope looks closer than it is." I turned to Hadley and Piper. "You said it can feel like you're right there, right?"

They nodded, both wide-eyed.

"Maybe she thought she could reach it and get help," I continued, "or maybe she was so out of it that she just followed the light. She would've gotten colder and colder as she walked toward it."

"Natasha is the dead woman who everyone is telling about?" Jarka asked. "While we were in Bulgaria, my Harold has much distressing calls from coworkers about having to change the plans for the snow sculpture contest."

I realized that, having just gotten back from abroad, Jarka was nowhere near up to speed on the case. It sounded like she'd heard the basics from Harold. With his job at the Chamber of Commerce, he would've been told the reason for the contest's delay. There was no time to fill her in, but with her quick mind, she seemed to have caught the implications of my line of questioning.

"Was this woman found without her clothes?" she asked.

I nodded. "She was partially undressed, but didn't seem to have been assaulted."

The bones of her jaw locked into a somber expression. "As hypothermia became worser, this woman maybe feels like she was overhot, as I tell you. Takes off clothes."

"Geez, do you really think that's what happened?" Piper asked. "How terrible."

"That can't be right," Hadley said, shaking her head in disbelief and horror. "She couldn't have survived a fall like that, could she? Besides, if she took her own clothes off, where are they?"

"It was incredibly windy the next day. Plus, it snowed," I said. "They're probably out on the golf course somewhere, blown around by the wind and buried under the snow. It's a huge, open area. They might not be found until spring."

"How her body was found?" Jarka asked.

"She was buried under the snow the machines made at the resort," I explained. "The workers who moved the snow used heavy machinery. They didn't see her, and dumped her body into a truck along with the snow that was bound for the contest." I gestured toward the huge sculptures that surrounded us.

Jarka shook her head solemnly, as if that confirmed her suspicions. "Hypothermic cause of death may explain this, also. In final stages, as death becomes near, the rational brain stops to work and instinct, like animal, takes over the mind. The person seeks shelter and digs in the ground—how is this called? *Burrows*, like a forest creature, trying to find warmth."

I struggled to swallow down the acid that rose up in my stomach as the picture of Natasha's final minutes became clearer. The cold had reduced a beautiful woman, so glamorous and in control, to an animal, ripping her own clothing from her body as she stumbled toward the dazzling ski slope lights, clawing into the ground in a primitive bid for survival.

Feedback from a microphone cut through the air. "Thanks so much for coming, ladies and gentlemen," Harold said. "We've tallied the votes, and we'll be announcing the winners of Geneva Bay's twentieth annual snow sculpting competition in just about five minutes."

Hadley seemed insensible to Harold's voice, still picturing the same horrific scene I was. She swallowed hard and squeaked out a few words. "I didn't know any of that. About how she was found. The police just told us that she died after she fell off our balcony. I thought she died instantly."

"Yeah, I can see why they didn't tell us the whole story," Piper said, laying a hand on her friend's back. "The details are pretty gruesome."

As the color faded from Hadley's face, her freckles stood out like spilled ink. Despite her queasy appearance, I couldn't halt the torrent of realizations that were gushing out of me. I slapped my forehead as another one hit.

"She walked *by herself*!" I said. "She wasn't carried. That's why there was only one set of footprints. The police have been trying to figure out who buried her in the snow the machines made. She buried *herself*!"

"Yes, this would be the animal instinct," Jarka confirmed.

"Capone needs to broaden his search," I said, pulling my phone from my pocket. "He's been focusing on people who were strong enough to move a body. But if what I think is true, the body moved itself. If she lived long enough to walk a few hundred yards and burrow into the snow, then everything makes sense. The frostbite. Her being undressed. How her body ended up so far from where she fell. Why the workers didn't see her. She buried herself deep in the snow by the ski slopes, trying to survive."

"God, how awful," Piper said. "If she'd only turned around and walked back to Hadley's house instead of toward the ski slope. It was right behind her."

"Sometimes, people have freezed to death just on their own front yard," Jarka said. "So confused do they become."

"Plus, if she still had her wits about her, she might've been too scared to go back to the house," I said. "Maybe she was trying to get away from the person who pushed her." I pulled one of my gloves off with my teeth and dialed Capone's number.

Piper covered her face with her mittened hands. "It sounds like just *the most awful* way to die," she murmured. "I wouldn't wish that on my worst enemy."

My phone was still ringing when a sound rose from Hadley's throat, a resonance between a sob and a scream. Instead of trailing off, her cries continued to escalate. A tremor began in her hands, and little by little took hold of her entire body. Her expression grew wild, eyes darting from face to face, looking for solace, but finding none.

CHAPTER 25

Everyone within hearing distance turned to see the cause of the commotion. Hadley's parents, Auntie Biz, and the Savages rushed over, followed by Sonya, Melody, Daniel, and his mother.

"Stay back and give space to her," Jarka cautioned as the crowd surged around the panicking girl.

"Who the hell are you?" Adrian Hoffman barked. He elbowed past us, knocking into me and sending Jarka stumbling to the ground.

Showing surprising agility, Harold vaulted down from the stage to Jarka's side, helping her to her feet. My phone flew out of my hands with the force of the blow, but I was barely aware of it. Instead, my eyes were locked on Hadley, who was in a state of acute distress. Her eyes bulged and her shrieks had been replaced by an even more disturbing sound, a series of low, whimpering moans, the cries of an animal caught in a steel trap.

Daffi took hold of her daughter's shoulders. "My god, Hadley, what's wrong?"

The sounds Hadley was making formed into words, barely coherent, but still intelligible. "I didn't know what to do. I didn't know what to do!"

"What are you talking about?" Adrian demanded. "Pull yourself together."

Hadley wheeled on her father. "I'm sick of trying to keep it together!"

"You're being a baby!" he snapped.

"Well, *you're* a criminal!"

Daffi's mouth fell open. "Hadley! Don't talk to your father that way."

"You're just as bad," Hadley shot back. "You knew what he was doing and you did nothing to stop him! You just drank until you didn't care anymore. You didn't want to think about what he was doing."

"What do you mean, Hads?" Piper asked.

"He was stealing money from people whose houses got wrecked by hurricanes and floods and stuff." Hadley turned to her father again. "I know you think I'm dumb, but I figured it out. All the different companies you had." She turned back to Piper. "Whenever there was a big natural disaster, he'd set up a new company to fleece people. I always suspected his business wasn't legit, and then when I was talking to Daniel about what happened to his family, I finally figured out how it all worked."

Adrian turned to Daniel, and noticed Angie standing there, too. "What did you tell her?" he demanded.

"My son told your daughter the truth," Angie said, stepping in front of Daniel protectively. "That you stole my life savings and all my neighbors', too. And now your daughter knows that her father is a monster."

Now it was Daffi's turn to face off. She stepped between Angie and her husband. "So file a complaint with the Better Business Bureau." She spat the scorn-laced words toward the Castillos. There was nothing but contempt in her eyes for the people her husband had hurt.

"You were in on it, weren't you?" I demanded. "That's why you tried to pay Rabbit off. Because for all these years, you've been helping your husband launder the money he stole from people like the Castillos. You assumed Rabbit and Travis Staggs were lowlifes you'd never see again. But then you ran into him."

"Maybe if you'd hire a better class of people, we wouldn't have problems like this," she said, casting a disgusted glance at my crew.

My blood boiled as I continued. "That's how you worked it, isn't it? Adrian stole the money, and you helped him hide it. That's why there wasn't any money for them to go after in a lawsuit."

"Daffi, don't say another word," Adrian hissed. Turning to me, he said, "Look all you want. You'll find I have zero liability in any of this. Everything *I* did was aboveboard."

"Are you kidding?" Hadley said. "Mom, you're going to take the fall for all of this crap? We both know he's the one who pulls the strings."

Daffi spun back toward Hadley. "Your father just did what he thought was best for our family."

"Leave it to you to protect him." Hadley's mouth curved into a bitter sneer. "You always do. You're his henchwoman. That's how you can stand to buy stuff with money he stole from good people like them." She leveled a finger at Daniel and his mother. "Or maybe you drink because you *can't* stand it—how you married a crook and raised an idiot daughter all so you could use stolen money to pay for me to get into a school *I shouldn't even be at*!" The end of her sentence rose in pitch, the words practically ablaze with fury.

"What are you talking about?" Piper interjected.

"Honey, it's none of our business," Jonathan said. In

all the tumult, I'd barely noticed that he and my sister were standing just behind me. Biz, thankfully, had taken Caleb over to the hot cocoa stand, away from the unfolding drama. "Come on," Jonathan said, putting an arm around his daughter's shoulder. "Let's give them some space."

Hadley's rage burned out like flash paper as she turned to face her friend. "They paid to get me into Palisades. They *paid a bribe*. I heard them. Talking. That night. At the party." Her breaths came in a rapid-fire staccato. For a moment, I thought she might pass out, but she took in a deep gasp and continued. "The night of the party, I came upstairs to get something from my room and I saw my dad go into his room with Natasha. They shut the door. It seemed super sketch, so I listened in. They were talking about my grades. Whether Natasha knew someone who'd take a bribe to help me pass my classes. They started talking about how she'd taken money from my dad to get me accepted to Palisades in the first place. Apparently, that's how she got to know my parents. Through her business."

"I don't understand. Does she work for the school?" Piper asked.

"No," Hadley said. "She's some kind of college consultant. She works with parents like mine to get kids like me into schools like Palisades, through backdoor channels. That's how I got in—she had someone with a connection to a coach at Palisades who was willing to say I was an athletic recruit"—her gaze dropped—"for tennis."

"But you don't play tennis." Piper's tone was confused, but even as she spoke, the expression on her face morphed from incredulity to painful understanding. The change was as quick as the stab of a knife. "Oh my god." She looked like she might throw up.

Sonya and I made eye contact as we simultaneously mouthed the same four-letter word.

"What did you do, Jonathan?" My sister stepped forward, her voice strangled with anger. "You used to play doubles with Jimmy Hannigan, the coach at Palisades. *You're* the connection!" She shook her head. "That woman! I thought you were having an affair with her!"

"What? No!" Jonathan protested. "I would never cheat. I love you. Everything I did was for our family."

He tried to reach for Shea, but she recoiled from his touch. "Well, I wish you *were* having an affair," she said, "because this is worse. All that money you said was from coaching clinics. You were funneling bribes."

Jonathan turned to his daughter, pleading. "I had to. My knees are shot. I wasn't getting any new clients. And then Natasha approached me. It didn't seem like a big deal. I just had to write a few letters of recommendation for kids, saying I'd coached them in high school and that they seemed like good prospects, set up a couple meetings, and be the conduit to Jim and the other college coaches I know. That was all. She took care of everything else."

Now it was my turn to feel queasy. "When I saw you upstairs on the night of the party, you said that there was a problem with Hadley. You knew you were busted, didn't you?"

Jonathan hung his head. "I didn't know exactly how much she'd heard, but when I met her coming down the stairs, she said that her parents were liars, and that she was at Palisades based on a lie. She was really drunk. I knew we needed to find out how much she knew, and stop her before she started blabbing."

So many things that had happened over the previous few days now made sense. I remembered the painful awkwardness of the dinner I'd hosted at the restaurant. How both my sister and Hadley had made snide remarks about Jonathan's tennis coaching career. My sister had dug the knife in because she thought her husband was using his coaching as a cover for an affair with Natasha La Cotti. Hadley had been venting her disgust at the entire charade. Jonathan knew that Daniel most likely recognized him as the man he'd seen on the road that night, so he was probably already on edge. And when both Hadley and Shea made comments about his tennis coaching, he must've wondered if the jig was up. He and Adrian had abruptly left the table to "get fresh air"—that was them doing damage control, trying to figure out how to keep the whole thing from blowing wide open.

Shea took an angry step toward her husband. "Did you kill Natasha? When you went back over there that night? Were you trying to shut her up before Hadley exposed her and she could link you to the scam?"

"Oh, god, Shea," he said. "How could you think that? Of course I didn't kill her. I went back over there to talk to Hadley. Tell them, Daffi."

"That's right," Daffi said. "I called him to come back and talk Hadley out of doing anything rash. She was so angry, threatening to tell everyone."

I turned to Hadley. "But you didn't tell anyone. Talking to Jonathan changed your mind?"

She looked from her mother to her father to Jonathan. "They all came at me. Them and Natasha. Right after the party ended. You and your people were still downstairs," she said to me. "They said that if I told, it would mess things up for"—she cast a pained look at Piper—"everyone."

Piper gaped at her father. "Dad, did you cheat to get me in, too?"

"I didn't. I swear. You got in fair and square."

"How can I believe anything you say?!" she demanded. She stepped alongside Shea, and they faced him like a two-woman firing squad. "*You're* the one who had the most to lose if Hadley blew up your little scheme. And Natasha was the link to you. If you got rid of her, they'd have a hard time connecting it back to you."

"Please." His voice cracked. "Please. I love you both so much. I would never kill anyone. I didn't kill Natasha."

Part of me knew that the crowd who'd congregated around the stage was still there, right behind me. The cocoa kiosk was off to my right. The ice rink, too. It would now be a few minutes past six. Spectators would be anxious, wondering what was delaying the announcement of the contest winners. Time hadn't stopped. But to me, in that moment, everything seemed frozen in place. Because, finally, I knew the truth.

When I spoke, my voice was clear and steady. "No. You didn't."

Everyone wheeled toward me, stunned. I was a little stunned myself. As my sister and Piper zeroed in on Jonathan, my attention had been elsewhere, as a ghastly realization dawned. This whole time, we'd been focusing on the suspects with the strength to move a body, trying to uncover the possible motivations for doing so. But now that we knew that Natasha had most likely moved herself, it became clear that the crime was the work of a single, impulsive moment. An act of rage and desperation. Of all the suspects, there was one person who'd been pushed far enough that night to push back.

"How can you be sure it wasn't Jonathan?" Shea asked.

"Because it was Hadley." I lowered my voice to address the young woman. "Wasn't it?"

Hadley looked around the wall of people in front of her—me, Melody, Sonya, the Castillos, the Savages, Jarka, Harold, her parents. We formed a protective half-moon between her and the crowd of spectators who'd come to find out who won the contest. As she faced us, little by little, her body seemed to deflate. "Yes."

"It's not true," came a pained whisper from Daffi. "I don't believe it."

"I saw the video," I explained. "Of Natasha being pushed off the balcony. The killer was talking to her and then suddenly flew into a rage and shoved her. Only Hadley had a reason to be that furious. Maybe other people wanted Natasha dead, but any of you would've planned it out. You were using your heads, strategizing, trying to figure out what to do about your 'problem.' But Hadley had discovered that she'd been betrayed in the worst possible way." I recalled the look on her face when I'd first seen her—almost blind with fury, smashing a plate against the wall.

"Oh, Hads," Piper said, her voice heavy with pity.

"You set her up to fail at that school," I continued,

eyeing Daffi and Adrian, "and then made her feel stupid when she did. Her own parents deceived her and manipulated her. That anger needed to be vented." I turned to Hadley. "You were pushed too far, so you pushed back."

A tear threatened to trickle down her cheek, but her expression remained eerily serene as she addressed her parents, her voice filled with venom. "I came back out of my room after you had your little 'pep talk' with me. Natasha was out on the balcony. Alone. I went out there to talk to her, to yell at her, I guess. But she wouldn't let me talk. She was saying all this BS about how *lucky* I am to have the opportunity to go to Palisades. Like I should be thanking her for making me go to a school where I feel like a complete moron most of the time. I lost it. I shoved her. But I didn't know she'd fall over the railing like that. She was there with me one second and the next thing I knew, she was on the ground, sliding down the hill. I thought she was dead. She wasn't moving. I didn't know what to do!"

Everyone gaped at Hadley for what must've been a solid minute. It seemed we, too, didn't know what to do.

Adrian finally broke the silence. "You never could handle pressure. You're just like your mother."

He fixed his daughter with a reptilian gaze, empty of guilt or compassion. Hadley might be a killer, but Adrian Hoffman was a true villain. Not that his aim had been to hurt people like the Castillos or sully people like Rabbit with the fallout from his dirty deeds. He simply didn't care about the consequences of his actions as long as he got what he wanted—status,

influence, bragging rights, wealth. No one else mat-
tered, not his wife, not even Hadley. Daffi seemed to
have lost herself completely, no longer able to tell right
from wrong. But Hadley still had a soul. And that was
almost worse.

I thought back to the pictures on Natasha's social media feed. She'd surrounded herself with B-list celebri-
ties, washed-up athletes like Jonathan, and nouveau
riche social climbers like Anthony and Daffi. People
who'd tasted just enough money and status to make
them hungry for more. What lengths would those parents go to to make sure their kids got a leg up? How
many more Hadley Hoffmans were out there, unaware
that their worlds were about to come crashing down?

"You're going to hang your own daughter out to
dry?" Angie Castillo sputtered in disbelief. "As if none
of this is your fault?"

"Back off before I have you put in jail for harass-
ment." He grabbed his wife and daughter by the arms
and took a few steps, seemingly intending to pull them
away. Having none of it, Daniel squared up to him.
Adrian dropped his grip on the women and faced Daniel. "What are you going to do, big man?"

Daniel cocked his arm, making it crystal clear what
he intended to do. Sonya and Jarka both leapt to take
hold of him.

"Don't take his bait," Sonya cautioned. "He'll have
witnesses if he wants to bring an assault case," she
added, gesturing to the crowd around us, which, I noticed, now included Biz and Caleb.

"Son's right." Furious as I was, I had to concede that
Daniel didn't need an assault charge leveled against
him when he was only just in the clear for Natasha's
murder.

A sneer curled Adrian's lips. "Yeah, *amigo*, listen to the boss lady."

"Okay, that's it." Unbeknownst to my brain, my own fist had curled into a ball and was halfway to Adrian's face before Shea caught it midair.

"Dee, no," she said. "Caleb's watching."

"Listen to your sister, Delilah," Biz said. She'd been holding my wide-eyed nephew in her arms, but now she handed him off. "Melody, please take Caleb to go watch the skaters." My great-aunt followed them with her eyes until they walked out of range. Then, with a swiftness that astonished me, she let fly a winter-booted kick, aimed squarely at Adrian Hoffman's nether regions. The man cried out as he folded like a discount futon, hitting the snow with a dull thump. Daffi knelt next to him, while Hadley stood with her arms crossed, regarding both of her parents with disdain.

Biz turned back to the rest of us, who were watching her with reactions ranging from horrified to starstruck. She lifted her shoulders to her ears. "What? Somebody needed to do it. They're not going to press charges against a feeble old lady."

As we stood staring, a young man jogged up, his eyes fixed on the stage. His face was bright and expectant, and he seemed not to have noticed Adrian writhing on the ground behind us. He nudged Harold with his elbow. "Hey, buddy, did I miss it? Who won the contest?"

Under normal circumstances, Harold's face bore a smile so constant I'd often wondered if it was tattooed on. Just then, though, his expression was a total blank. Harold looked at the stage, then at Hadley, a young woman who'd just admitted to killing another person.

A young woman who'd been horribly deceived by her own parents, who'd just pressed the detonate button on the life they'd tried to buy for her.

Harold pulled an envelope from his pocket and ripped it open. "Lady Justice," he read. "Justice won."

The guy nodded, pleased with the outcome. "Cool."

CHAPTER 26

"Where are we on the beef tenderloin?" Biz looked toward the kitchen island of our shared house, where Sonya was placing a burgundy-and-mushroom-stuffed roulade of beef, piping hot from the oven.

"It needs to rest for about ten minutes before I slice it," Sonya said.

"And the scalloped potatoes?" Biz asked.

"Daniel already took them to the table," I said. "They'll stay hot."

"The glazed carrots and minted peas shouldn't go out until the last minute, but you can start taking everything else," Biz said.

"The *pitka* is ready," Jarka said, gliding past with a loaf of traditional Bulgarian Christmas bread. She'd already explained that Biz, as the eldest guest, would break the loaf into pieces and share it out as part of the meal. A coin was baked inside, and whoever got it would be lucky in the coming year. As she made her way to the dining room, I thought of just how much we'd need that luck.

Hadley's Christmas Eve confession had set off a frantic twenty-four hours of activity. My call to Capone had connected before Adrian knocked the phone from

my hand, and he'd heard enough to motivate him to
burn rubber to the lakefront park. He and two squad
cars arrived just in time to take the poor girl to the station for booking and her parents in for questioning.
Daffi and her husband had been released, pending further investigation of their role in the college bribery
scheme and the swindling of vulnerable disaster victims. Hadley was currently cooling her heels in jail,
waiting for her post-holiday arraignment.

Everyone's plans had been scrambled, and the small
crowd Biz and I had been expecting to host had bal-
looned to include Jarka and Harold, Melody, Daniel
and his mother, and Sonya. I'd reached out to Rabbit,
to reassure him that he'd still have a job when we reopened, if he wanted it. Little Everleigh had suffered a
hairline fracture in her elbow, resulting in a cast. Their
dinner plans, too, had been thrown for a loop. After
I'd filled him in on Hadley's confession, Rabbit had resolved to tell his whole story to Capone, even though
he knew the consequences to himself could be dire.
He said it didn't seem right that the girl would suffer
while her parents, who'd set her on her path, walked
free. He'd gotten away with being a part of Daffi and
Adrian's money-laundering scheme all those years ago,
but would he escape consequences if he revealed it all
now? It had been a horrible week for my friend. Thus,
Rabbit, his mother, and Everleigh were all invited to
join our dinner. My sister and her kids would be there
as well, while Jonathan, for his part, was occupying a
cell adjacent to Hadley's at the police station in town.

I shifted a few pies out of the way to make space
for the side dishes that were emerging, bubbling hot,
from the oven. The smell of the savory roast beef, with
its crisp, fatty outer crust and soft, juicy interior, was

intoxicating, as it melded with the earthy aromas of vegetables and bread. Herbs and spices added further complexity to the scent, making me giddy almost to the point of dizziness. Days of intense stress, erratic eating, and iffy sleep probably compounded my light-headedness.

"Anyone want a top-up of *coquito*?" Daniel's mother breezed into the kitchen hefting a pitcher. The indulgent drink, which married coconut milk, sweetened condensed milk, and a hint of vanilla with a not-so-subtle kick of Puerto Rican rum, had been in heavy rotation during dinner prep.

I held up my glass. "Hit me."

Piper came in, with her baby brother perched on her hip. "Is Butterball in here? Caleb and I set up a little obstacle course for him in the living room." She turned to her younger sibling. "Caleb, tell Aunt Dee the name you came up with for Butterball."

My nephew broke into a fit of giggles and then yelled out, "Potato tiger!"

"It's because he has stripes like a tiger, but when he curls up, he's shaped like a potato," Piper explained, smiling.

Harsh. But accurate.

"No, I haven't seen him," I said. "Which is weird because usually he'd be lurking around the kitchen, hoping we'd leave something unguarded."

"Hot meat coming through," Sonya called out as she slid past me with a sizzling pan.

"That reminds me," I said, winking at her, "I better go and tell Capone that we're almost ready to eat." I headed down the hallway and up the stairs to my bedroom. The door to the en suite bathroom was ajar, allowing billows of steam to escape.

I sidled up to the opening and peeked through the steam. A well-muscled male form was toweling off in front of the sink. Capone had come straight to my house from the station, where he'd been hard at work trying to tie up the loose ends of the murder case, and passing details of the college bribery and disaster embezzlement cases on to the Feds.

"Dinner's ready," I said, stepping into the steam.

He finished wrapping his waist in a towel, pulled me close, and eyed me seductively. "How long do we have?" he asked.

"Not long enough," I said, pressing myself into the warm, damp skin of his bare chest.

He gave me a lingering kiss, then pulled away with a reluctant sigh. "Let me put on some clean clothes. I'll come down with you."

I tore myself away and waited in the bedroom. Capone appeared a moment later, dressed in black slacks and a green sweater that hugged the contours of his torso. The look on his face was perplexed.

"Everything okay?" I asked.

"I know I brought a full change of clothes, but my boxers are missing," he said.

"Did you have your bag with you when you questioned Hadley?" I asked, thinking of how Daniel's underwear had inexplicably ended up in the girl's purse.

He shook his head. "I never take personal items into an interrogation room." He shrugged. "Commando Christmas, I guess."

"You *are* spending the night tonight, right?" I ran my fingers over his chest.

Capone smiled, his lips slightly parted, and pulled me into another kiss.

He'd already filled me in on the basics of the investigation. Since yesterday evening's drama, he'd managed to put together a more complete picture of the raft of wrongdoing that surrounded the Hoffmans. First, there was the matter of Adrian's duplicitous business practices. Daffi, it seemed, had been in on her husband's schemes. Capone had only had time to scrape the snow from the tip of the iceberg, but what he'd learned so far seemed to indicate a pattern. Hadley was right to call her mother a henchwoman. It appeared that Adrian led the legitimate side of the business and left Daffi holding the bag for all the dirty work. An image was emerging of a wife who'd fused her wants and needs with her husband's. I'd seen for myself how he controlled her and undermined her, and it wasn't hard to imagine how, little by little, she'd become an extension of him.

Unable to completely protect her daughter from Adrian's malign influence, Daffi had blurred the line between mothering Hadley and enabling her. It wasn't clear whose idea it had been to send Hadley to Palisades, but it suited both their purposes. Daffi was perhaps trying in her own way to help her daughter, but there was little doubt that she needed to justify her misdeeds by ensuring that Hadley was successful. And Adrian had wanted an accessory more than a child, something he could show off to his friends. Having a daughter at a prestigious school amplified *his* prestige. He'd probably given little thought to the consequences for Hadley.

While Daffi and her husband had lawyered up and clammed up almost immediately, Hadley had been singing like a full gospel choir. She signed a confession, reaffirming that Natasha's murder had been an accident. Whether that would reduce her culpability would be a matter for a judge and jury.

Capone sent his investigative team back out to the golf course, where they'd fanned out and, following the direction the wind had been blowing on the night of the infamous party, were able to locate Natasha's missing clothes, embedded in a snowdrift. The partial shoe prints that Jankowski found proved to be a perfect match for the shoes the dead woman wore when she stumbled to her doom.

"Rabbit should be here any minute with his mother and Everleigh," I said. "You and he were going to talk this afternoon, right? I hope you found out what you needed to know because I have a strict 'no interrogating people at the Christmas dinner table' policy."

"Yeah, we talked, and he filled in a few holes for me," Capone said. "You already knew that he followed Daffi upstairs on the night of the party."

I nodded. "Yep, he told me she was the wearer of the mystery high heels."

"She knew he'd recognized her and wanted to talk to her husband about paying him off to continue to keep silent. They gave him a check for five hundred bucks. But Rabbit got halfway to the AA meeting and had second thoughts. He drove back and returned the check, told them to keep the money. Daffi, apparently, thought he was trying to play hard ball. She called him later that night, offering more money."

"That's the call Rabbit's mother overheard," I said.

"Exactly. Daffi didn't trust him. She thought if she could get him to take the money, then he wouldn't dare talk. He'd be tying his fate to theirs, and if they went down, he'd go down with them."

"So she approached him again when she saw him at

the park, when Everleigh was ice skating?" I guessed. "The money argument I overheard was a continuation of her effort to bribe him?"

"That's right."

"So what happens to Rabbit now? If Daffi and Adrian aren't talking, I guess the prosecutors will need him as a witness to help bring them down. That could really mess things up for him with his parole, couldn't it?"

"Well, it turns out that Travis Staggs and his stolen meat van are something of a Christmas miracle for Rabbit. Staggs has already agreed to testify against them in exchange for going easy on him for the meat thing. We won't need Rabbit to get involved. I've already talked to the DA about the money laundering and convinced him not to pursue either Staggs or Rabbit for it."

"Oh, thank god." I held my hand to my heart. "I'm so relieved for him, and it also means that my crew's efforts haven't gone to waste."

"What efforts?" he asked.

"I hatched a plan when I found out that Rabbit is losing his housing as of next week," I explained. "I reached out to Sam about letting him live above the restaurant for the time being, and he was all for it. While Biz and I were cooking today, Melody, Sonya, Jarka, Harold, Daniel, and Daniel's mom gave the place the full *Extreme Makeover* treatment. They cleared out all their junk and redecorated. Best of all, they sectioned off part of the bedroom and installed a built-in purple sparkly Batman unicorn bed for Everleigh, complete with curtains and a slide, so she'll have a place to stay when it's Rabbit's turn to have her. I happen to know that was high on her Christmas list."

"Whoa," Capone said. "They did all that today?"

I nodded. "I popped over this afternoon with Shea

and the kids to take a look. It's incredible. Melody is great at stuff like that. The curtains around the bed are two-sided. On Rabbit's side, they're navy blue, very manly. And on Everleigh's side, it looks like a glitter bomb exploded." Noting his raised eyebrows, I added, "In a cute way. We're going to take Rabbit and Everleigh over there after dinner to surprise them."

The two of us headed downstairs, where we found everyone gathering around the dining table. Rabbit, his mother, and Everleigh had arrived and were already in their seats. The girl had collected at least a dozen signatures on her bright purple cast. Rabbit gently stroked her blond head as Melody squatted in front of her, drawing an elaborate picture on her cast of Batman riding a unicorn. I couldn't wait to see Everleigh's face when she realized a mural of the same design appeared on the side of her new bed.

"I love purple," Everleigh said. "That's why I picked it for my cast."

"I have a feeling Santa knows that," Melody said.

"I got lots of presents this year, because I was super-duper good. Did you get what you asked for?" Everleigh asked her.

Melody's glance fluttered to Daniel. "Not yet."

Everleigh gave her a comforting pat on the arm. "Maybe next year, if you're super-duper good. Daddy says Santa knows what's best."

Melody smiled. "Well, your daddy's very smart."

Jarka and Harold sat at one end of the table, their heads tipped close together, lost in a dreamy world of their own. At the other end, Sonya, Daniel, and Angie raised glasses of *coquito* in a toast. Probably a bawdy one, judging by how hard they were all laughing. In the center, Piper and my sister feigned amazement as

Caleb hid under his napkin, pretending to be invisible. Biz, who was carrying in a bowl of red cabbage slaw, stopped to watch them. Her eyes brimmed with happiness. I knew that we had, at most, another week of Holiday Biz before the spell would be broken and Grumpelstiltskin Biz would return. But I knew with equal certainty that this Biz would emerge again next year, with all her joy and frenzy and crazy expectations and *extra*-ness. This holiday season had been as imperfect as it possibly could have been, and yet it felt like the beginning of something new and hopeful. Like just maybe we could take off our costumes, turn down the stage lights, and be our messy selves.

The gathering was impromptu. The collection of guests a surprise. But we'd somehow managed to pull off our own version of a perfect holiday. The lights were soft, with candlelight reflected in the glasses and silverware. The sounds of chatter and laughter and clinking dishes filled the air. No one had noticed me and Capone. I paused in the archway that led into the room, stilling him with a touch of my hand. Like Biz, I found myself on the edge of tears, a lump catching in my throat. We'd had to extend the dining space with a folding table to accommodate everyone and still it overflowed—with people; with dishes of colorful, appetizing food; with love. Here, finally, was the big, family Christmas I'd been dreaming about my whole life.

Capone squeezed my hand and looked at me for the all-clear to go in. I nodded and took my place next to my sister.

"You doing okay?" I asked her.

She smiled ruefully. "As okay as I can be, I suppose. I took the kids to see Jonathan this morning. That was hard."

"How's he holding up?"

"Surprisingly okay, once we got there. He was so terrified that we all hated him. But we don't."

My mouth fell open. "You're going to forgive and forget? After what he did?" This was the woman who, as a girl, had held a stone-cold grudge against me for months when I accidentally dropped her library book in the bathtub.

She let out an incredulous puff of air. "No. Not remotely. Neither is Piper." Her hard expression softened as she continued. "But she and I talked about it. We're his family, and he's all alone in jail. He needs us." She shook her head. "Honestly, I don't know if I can ever trust him again. I don't know if I'll stay with him, but I'll see him through this and at least make sure he makes bail and gets a good lawyer. I talked to Sonya's uncle earlier. He said that if Jonathan is willing to flip and name names, he thinks he could get off with little to no prison time. He's a comparatively small fish. Natasha was running this scam a few different places." She took a sip of wine. "I guess *she'll* be spared a trial at least. Cold comfort."

I grimaced as I speared a slice of beef tenderloin. "Literally."

Shea took the platter from me and continued. "Jonathan cheated other people out of an education. Someone like me—a smart kid who worked their tail off and got good grades—didn't get into Palisades because he supplied someone like Hadley with phony tennis credentials."

"And it's not like he did Hadley any favors," I observed. "This ruined her life. Her confidence was already shot because that school was too hard for her. How will she ever trust anyone again after her own parents betrayed her like this? They all set her up to fail—Natasha, Jonathan, her parents. And instead of admitting what they did when they could see that she was struggling, they just doubled down."

Shea spooned brown-sugar-glazed carrots on to her plate as the dish came past. "I don't understand why he felt like he had to do this. If he'd done it to provide more financial security for the kids, maybe I'd get it. Misplaced paternal instinct, or something. But he told me today he did it because he thought it would make *me* happy. Where would he get that idea?"

I was still trying to channel woodland princess vibes, but I decided to mix in some home truths. "Do you want my guess?" I asked. "He's madly in love with you, but he's intimidated by you. He was trying to make you proud. You seemed so far beyond him. You're so far beyond all of us. How many families have their very own rocket scientist?"

She looked stricken. "I don't want to be beyond anybody, especially not my family. Sure, I'm driven, but so are you."

"I'm a workhorse, but you're a frigging Pegasus."

"I beg to differ," she said. "Look at this meal. Look at you. You're this successful businesswoman, surrounded by people who'd do anything for you. And you even referenced Greek mythology. I thought you never read anything except cookbooks."

"Greek mythology?"

"Pegasus."

"That was a *My Little Pony* reference," I clarified. "Don't you remember Flitter, the purple one with wings? Auntie Biz gave her to me for Christmas when I was seven. I think I still have her in a box somewhere. I should give her to Everleigh to go with her new decor."

"I was eleven that Christmas," Shea said. "I got clothes."

"You still played with me, though. You were Princess Primrose. She had a—"

"Butterfly on her butt. I remember." She spooned some mashed sweet potatoes from the passing bowl onto my plate. The recipe was simple—oven-roasted potatoes whipped with butter and cream into a burnt orange mousse. The secret was to spike them with the merest hint of vanilla. We both looked down at the autumnal mound of fluffy spuds and then at one another. "These were always your favorite," Shea said. "The one thing mom could cook."

"She also boiled a mean hot dog," I said.

"And her Kraft mac and cheese was . . ." Shea kissed the tips of her fingers.

Just then, Biz, who'd been futzing with the centerpieces, came up behind us and put a hand on each of our shoulders. Her eyes were soft and luminous. "I wish your parents could see the two of you. They'd be so proud."

Shea stiffened, and I braced myself for the usual barbed reply. Instead, my sister looked at her own children. Piper was cutting up her brother's meat as he said something that made her laugh. Shea's eyes, too, grew soft. "Yeah," was all she said, but for now, it was enough.

I hadn't been wrong to think that her perfect façade was on the verge of cracking open. What I hadn't realized, though, was that those cracks might allow a little light to get in and a touch of tenderness to seep out. For Biz, the holidays allowed her to channel her control freak tendencies into something a little kinder. For me, helping my friends did the same. None of the O'Leary women would ever be good at the touchy-feely stuff, but maybe Biz, in her own weird, dysfunctional way, had the right idea. Maybe we could, every once in a while, choose to play against type.

A commotion broke out at the end of the table—an alarmed exclamation, followed by the clatter of dishware and scraping chairs. I looked up to find Capone dashing toward the living room. The rest of the assembled guests rose in a mad scramble and followed him. In the chaotic jostling of bodies, it took me a second to understand that we were all chasing Capone, who was chasing Butterball, who was gunning it toward his cat bed with a large object in his mouth. The cat reached his bed and nestled down, heedless of the crowd that surged in from the dining room.

"What's going on?" Biz demanded. "Why did you get up so suddenly?"

Capone pressed his lips together, the color rising in his cheeks. "Nothing. Sorry. I didn't mean to startle everyone. I caught a glimpse of Butterball out of the corner of my eye and . . ."

He seemed unwilling to continue, but he didn't need to. I'd already bent down to investigate the mysterious object that Butterball was using to make a nest of sorts within his cat bed. Some sort of paisley cloth. I extracted it and held the item aloft.

"Are those . . ." Sonya began.

"Potato Tiger stole some undies!" Caleb said, cackling.

Capone exhaled deeply, his chin falling to his chest. He held out his hand for the garment, which he took hold of and stuffed into his pocket.

"I've heard of cats doing that," Melody said. "Stealing socks and"—she looked at Daniel and blushed crimson—"*things*, and hiding them in weird places."

I looked again at Butterball's bed. It was upholstered in a soft, knobbly material, almost identical to the furry texture of Hadley's designer purse.

"Well," Sonya said, "I, for one, am glad we got to the *bottom* of this."

Daniel picked up Butterball and gave him a gentle scratch. "I guess I'm not this cat burglar's only victim."

I shook my head. "In the future, let's try to remember that some mysteries are better left *un*solved."

RECIPES FOR SLEEP IN HEAVENLY PIZZA

TEAR-AND-SHARE CHRISTMAS TREE PIZZA BREAD

Sonya here. Not everyone celebrates Christmas, but no matter your background or religious affiliation, the people of the world are united by a common love of melted cheese. Hence, we developed a crowd-pleasing holiday recipe that's essentially pizza, but in a festive guise. At Delilah & Son, we always have extra pizza dough knocking around, but if you're making this at home, you can use any brand of good-quality pre-made dough.

It may seem strange that I'm recommending using mozzarella sticks for this—the kind you put in a kid's lunchbox—instead of some fancy artisanal cheese. But for this recipe, you want to keep the moisture level low so the dough balls stay crispy.

Servings: 8
Prep Time: 20 mins
Cook Time: 20 mins
Total Time: 40 mins

Ingredients

- 7 mozzarella sticks
- 1 pound refrigerated pizza dough
- Egg wash (1 egg whisked with 1 tbsp water)
- 1/4 cup melted butter
- 1/4 cup grated Parmesan
- 1/2 teaspoon garlic powder
- 1/2 teaspoon Italian seasoning
- 1 tablespoon fresh basil, cut into a thin chiffonade
- Marinara, warmed (for serving)

Instructions

Step 1

Preheat oven to 450°. Line a large baking sheet with parchment paper. Cut mozzarella sticks into 1-inch pieces and set aside. If you're me, you'll need one extra mozzarella stick so that you can peel off some cheese strands, drape them over your top lip, and walk around the kitchen pretending you have a cheese mustache until Delilah notices and tells you to get back to work.

Step 2

On a floured surface, divide pizza dough into two equal pieces. Stretch and roll each piece of dough into a long rectangle, then cut the dough into 2-inch squares (you'll need 30–35 squares).

Step 3

Wrap a dough square around each piece of mozzarella, forming a tightly sealed ball. Arrange the balls seam-side down in the shape of a Christmas tree on the baking sheet. You can, of course, make other shapes if you prefer. What you do with your balls in the privacy of your kitchen is your own business and don't let anyone tell you otherwise. Brush egg wash on those doughy little balls and bake them until golden, 15 to 20 minutes.

Step 4

Meanwhile, whisk together the melted butter, Parmesan, garlic powder, and Italian seasoning. Brush your balls again! This time with the butter mixture. Sprinkle the basil on top. It's important to serve this warm so that the cheese will have maximum gooeyness. Add a side of marinara for dipping.

SONYA'S SUFGANIYOT (HANUKKAH JELLY DONUTS)

These Jewish donuts, which are a cross between beignets and jelly donuts, are a traditional Hanukkah food. During the eight nights of Hanukkah, Jews eat fried foods, like latkes and donuts, to symbolize the miracle of the oil. What's the miracle of the oil, you ask? Well, thousands of years ago, the Seleucid Empire ruled a big chunk of the Middle East. If you haven't heard of the Seleucids, that's fine. For the purposes of this story, they are the bad guys. The Seleucids wanted to Hellenize the Jews. I know that sounds like something delicious involving mayo—which I would be very much in favor of—but it actually means they wanted Jews to give up their faith and culture. A little ragtag bunch of Jews said a resounding "No siree Bob!" and fought back *and* won! After that, they wanted to rededicate their temple, which had been destroyed during the fighting. They had a jar of consecrated oil lying around, as you did back then, apparently. That oil should've only lasted for one day, but instead it burned in their lamps for eight.

I admit, as miracles go, it's a little underwhelming. Like, "Wow! I thought I was out of cream cheese, but there was enough left to schmear *both* sides of my bagel!" What can I say? People used to be more easily impressed.

Anyway, the word "sufganiyot" (pronounced soof-gahn-eeyot) is based on a Hebrew word meaning "spongy dough." The singular form is sufganiyah, but there's no need to know the singular form, because no one eats just one of these. Those factoids, plus the Torah portion I learned for my bat mitzvah, are the extent of my Hebrew, so I hope you enjoyed that little language and culture lesson.

Sufganiyot are traditionally filled with jelly or jam, but if your crowd doesn't care for jelly donuts, explore the vast universe of filling options: custard, cream, Nutella, or dulce de leche. The sky's the limit!

Servings: 24
Prep Time: 30 mins
Cook Time: 15 mins
Total Time: 45 mins, plus 1 to 2 hours for the
    dough to rise

Ingredients
- 1 cup warm water, heated to about 110°F*
- 1 tablespoon instant/rapid-rise or active dry yeast (Note that this is a little more than one packet.)
- 3 cups all-purpose flour

- 1/3 cup confectioners' sugar, plus extra for dusting
- 1/4 teaspoon salt
- 1 large egg, plus 1 egg yolk
- 2 tablespoons vegetable oil, plus about 2 quarts more for frying
- 1 teaspoon vanilla extract
- About 1 cup jam or jelly (or another filling of your choice)

*Note: Warm water helps activate the yeast. The temperature doesn't need to be exact. Try to get it about the temperature of a warm bath. If you place your hand under the stream of water in the faucet, it should feel hot but not so hot that it feels like it's going to melt off the top layer of your skin.

Instructions

Make the dough

Combine the water and yeast in a small bowl and let sit until foamy, about 5 minutes.

Meanwhile, in a large bowl, combine the flour, confectioners' sugar, and salt. Whisk the dry ingredients and set aside.

In a medium bowl, add the egg and egg yolk, 2 tablespoons of oil, and vanilla. Now whisk it! Whisk it good! Then add the water/yeast mixture and whisk until combined.

Add the liquid mixture to the flour mixture and stir with rubber spatula until the dough comes together. It should be a bit sticky. If the dough is too dry, add warm water, a teaspoon at a time, until the dough comes together. Cover the bowl with plastic wrap and let it rise on the countertop until it doubles in size, 1 to 2 hours.

Fashion your donuts

Set yourself up for success by getting organized. I know it seems like a hassle, but believe me, once the chaos of frying begins, you'll be glad you spent the time to get everything where it needs to be.

Line a baking sheet with a few layers of paper towels. Line another baking sheet with parchment paper, and dust heavily with flour. Generously dust a clean countertop and your hands with flour. Basically just coat yourself and your entire kitchen in flour.

Scrape the dough out of the bowl onto the counter and dust the dough with — you guessed it! — more flour. Pat the dough into ¼-in-thick rectangle (it should measure about 10 x 12 inches in size), making sure the bottom doesn't stick. Add more flour to the counter and your hands as needed. Using a pizza wheel or very sharp knife, cut the dough into twenty-four 2-inch squares and transfer the squares to the floured baking sheet, leaving a little space between them. Sprinkle the squares lightly with flour.

Fry those bad boys

If you have access to a deep fryer, that will improve your life considerably in every way, but especially when it comes to batch-frying donuts. Assuming you are *not* fortunate enough to be blessed with a deep fryer, you can add about 2 inches' worth of oil to a large, heavy pot and heat over medium to 350°F. Measure the temperature with a candy/deep-fry thermometer, or if you don't have one, drop a 1-inch cube of bread in the oil. When it takes about a minute to get golden brown, the oil is at the right temperature.

Place a few dough pieces at a time in the oil and fry

until golden brown, about 3 minutes, flipping halfway through frying. Adjust the heat if your donuts seem to be browning too quickly or too slowly. Using a metal slotted spoon, transfer the donuts to the paper towel–lined baking sheet. You might want to cut the first one open, to double check that it's cooked all the way through. If so, repeat with the remaining donuts. If not, adjust the frying temperature and time to ensure your donuts cook on the inside without burning on the outside.

Fill those suckers

When the donuts are cool enough to handle, use a paring knife or the tip of a squeeze bottle or piping bag to puncture the side of each to form a pocket in the center. Place the tip of the squeeze bottle or piping bag into the pocket and squeeze 1 to 2 teaspoons of jam or jelly inside. Alternatively, if you don't have the right tools or just can't be bothered futzing with these, you can serve the filling on the side as a dipping sauce.

Using a fine sieve, dust the donuts generously with confectioners' sugar. Serve immediately.

SONYA'S BUBBE ILENE'S IMPERFECTLY PERFECT LATKES

No Hanukkah celebration would be complete without latkes, aka potato pancakes. Like a lot of grandmas, my bubbe Ilene never measures, unless you count "handfuls" and "pinches" and "schmears" as measurements.

The most important part in this recipe isn't getting the quantities perfect, it's eating and enjoying the latkes with your friends and family.

Step 1

Take a lot of potatoes and some onions; shred them in the food processor. Mix them with a couple of eggs, some flour, some salt, in no particular order.

Step 2

Drain it all in a colander and squeeze out excess liquid before frying them in oil. A lot of oil.

Step 3

Blot on paper towels to get rid of extra oil.

Step 4

Serve with sour cream or applesauce (or both). Eat. Enjoy.

Step 5

Call your mother. She wants to know how you're doing.

THE CASTILLO FAMILY'S *COQUITO* (PUERTO RICAN EGGNOG)

This is Angela Castillo, Junior's mother. This was my Daniel Senior's recipe, God rest his soul. During the holidays, our family always has plenty of *coquito* in the fridge. In small-town Puerto Rico at Christmastime, beware, because friends and family can show up at any time of the day or night. Especially at night, because that's when the *parrandas* happen. These used to happen all over the island, but sadly they're less frequent now.

Here's how a *parranda* goes: Your friends or family

members show up on your porch late in the evening, after you're in bed. The ringleader signals everyone to start belting out Christmas carols at the top of their lungs and playing whatever instruments they brought. You jump up out of bed and go downstairs to be serenaded. Here's where your stockpile of *coquito* comes in handy! You invite the *parranderos* into your house, where everyone eats and drinks and sings for maybe an hour or two. Once everyone has had enough, you become part of the *parranda* and move on to the next house with the whole group. And so on and so on until the whole neighborhood is up and partying. Another word for *parranda* is "*asalto*," or "assault." You can see why! This is a sneak-attack party.

Prep Time: 10 min
Resting time: 4 hours to infuse and chill the
    coquito

Ingredients

- 1/8–1 cup white rum, such as Don Q (depending on how strong you want your *coquito*)
- 1/2 cup coconut rum, such as Malibu (optional)
- 1 (5 oz) can evaporated milk
- 1 (14 oz) can sweetened condensed milk
- 1 (14 oz) can coconut milk
- 1 (14 oz) can cream of coconut, such as Coco Lopez*
- 1/4 teaspoon cinnamon
- 1/8 teaspoon nutmeg
- 1 teaspoon vanilla
- 2 cinnamon sticks, plus more for garnishing

*If you can't find cream of coconut, you can use coconut cream.

Instructions

Mix all ingredients except for the cinnamon sticks in a blender. Place the 2 cinnamon sticks into the mixture and chill in the refrigerator in glass bottles for a minimum of 1 hour, preferably overnight. Remove the cinnamon sticks. Shake well before serving. Serve cold in a small glass, garnished with a dusting of fresh nutmeg and a cinnamon stick.

Note: *Coquito* makes a great gift! Pour some into a pretty bottle and bring it as a hostess gift to a holiday party. What party wouldn't be improved by the addition of rum and sugar?